Magus to the Hermetic Order  Master of Dimac, poet, adve... pianist; big game hunter, ... mountaineer, lone yachtsm... topless go-go dancer; Robert R... smoking, communicating with the dead and lying about his achievements. He lives in Sussex with his wife and family.

Robert Rankin is the author of *Web Site Story*, *Waiting for Godalming*, *Sex and Drugs and Sausage Rolls*, *Snuff Fiction*, *Apocalypso*, *The Dance of the Voodoo Handbag*, *Sprout Mask Replica*, *Nostradamus Ate My Hamster*, *A Dog Called Demolition*, *The Garden of Unearthly Delights*, *The Most Amazing Man Who Ever Lived*, *The Greatest Show Off Earth*, *Raiders of the Lost Car Park*, *The Book of Ultimate Truths*, the *Armageddon* quartet (three books), and the *Brentford* trilogy (five books), which are all published by Corgi books. Robert Rankin's latest novel, *The Fandom of the Operator*, is now available as a Doubleday hardback.

For more information on Robert Rankin and his books, see his website at: *www.lostcarpark.com/sproutlore*

ARMAGEDDON
THE MUSICAL

Robert Rankin

CORGI BOOKS

ARMAGEDDON THE MUSICAL
A CORGI BOOK : 0 552 13681 6

Originally published in Great Britain by
Bloomsbury Publishing Ltd

PRINTING HISTORY
Bloomsbury edition published 1990
Corgi edition published 1991

11 13 15 19 20 18 16 14 12

Set in 10/12pt Palatino by
Kestrel Data, Exeter, Devon.

Corgi Books are published by Transworld Publishers,
61–63 Uxbridge Road, London W5 5SA,
a division of The Random House Group Ltd,
in Australia by Random House Australia (Pty) Ltd,
20 Alfred Street, Milsons Point, Sydney, NSW 2061, Australia,
in New Zealand by Random House New Zealand Ltd,
18 Poland Road, Glenfield, Auckland 10, New Zealand
and in South Africa by Random House (Pty) Ltd,
Endulini, 5a Jubilee Road, Parktown 2193, South Africa.

Printed and bound in Great Britain by
Cox & Wyman Ltd, Reading, Berkshire.

For Alison

VIEW WHAT THOU WILT SHALL BE THE WHOLE OF THE LAW

Planet Earth rolled on in ever decreasing circles around the sun. As it had been carrying on in this fashion for more years than anyone cared to remember, there seemed no cause for immediate alarm. Not that things were exactly a bundle of laughs down on old terra firma at the present time, oh dear me, no. Things had never been quite the same since, in a moment of gay abandonment, outgoing US president Wayne L. Wormwood had chosen to press the nuclear button just as the New Year bells were gaily chiming in the arrival of the twenty-first century.

This generally unwelcome turn in events had caught many with their trousers well and truly down and had definitely taken the edge off much of the auld lang syning. But it did, at least, offer followers of the late great Nostradamus the dubious satisfaction of spending their final four minutes saying 'I told you so' to anyone who seemed inclined to listen.

The Nuclear Holocaust Event, as the media later dubbed it, was a somewhat noisy and unsettling affair, and was considered by the naturally pessimistic to be 'the end of civilisation as we know it'. Of course it was nothing of the kind and a surprising number of folk did come out of it relatively unscathed, if not altogether uncomplaining. The governments of the day rose to the occasion with such remarkable aplomb that one might have been forgiven for thinking that they were expecting it all along. Although the water was a bit iffy and lamb looked like being off the menu for some time to come, the TV was back on within the week, which can't be bad by any reckoning. And it was encouraging to note that not only had unemployment been cut at a stroke, as had long been promised, but racial intolerance ceased virtually overnight, mankind now being united beneath the banner of a single colour. A rather unpleasant shade of mould green.

But, as someone almost said, you can't please all of the people all of the time. And, even now, fifty years on, with the smoke beginning to clear, radiation on its way down and that nebulous something, oft referred to as normal service, restored, there were still no outward signs of euphoria evident upon the faces of Mr and Mrs Joe Public. Not that anyone was actually heard to complain, and why should they? Today's nuclear family had very much to be grateful for. Three square meals a week, unlimited cable television, a constant room temperature, low overheads and free waste disposal. And leisure time had really come into its own.

Of course, the prospect of spending your brief span banged up in a bomb-proof bunker, watching TV and awaiting further developments, was not everyone's cup of enzo-protein synthatea. But you did, at least, have the satisfaction of knowing that, even here, you could play your part in the glorious rebuilding scheme.

Active Viewing was now the name of the game, down below. The console of the TV terminal put everything that was left of the world at the finger stumps of the bunker-bound. And there was a great deal to see. The re-education programmes, the devotional exercises, the food operas, the game shows, not to mention the public service broadcasts. It was all there, and the choice of what you watched, and when, was all yours. A constitutional right. All the government asked was that you did watch. So, as an incentive and to ensure just reward, they had instituted a system which was, in its way, every bit as fundamentally brilliant and divinely inspired as had been the wheel clamp in twentieth-century London.

Every TV terminal now had an inbuilt Electronic Eye Scanning Point Indicator, or EYESPI for short. This marvel of modern technology was capable of recognising the viewer by the individual patterns of their irises, iris 'signatures' having, of course, been registered at birth with the mother computer. Once recognition had been established, this ingenious little doodad totted up the number of weekly viewing hours being put in by the active viewer in question. Once these were logged, food, medical supplies and rehousing credits then could be allocated accordingly.

It was a wonderful system: unbiased, democratic, free for all to take advantage of and with an obvious appeal to mankind's naturally competitive spirit. So wonderful was it in fact, that the TV stations felt impelled to extol its virtues every hour upon the hour. Its simple majesty being summed up, rather succinctly (and not a little poignantly) in the famous hymn jingle, 'The more you view the more you do, the more we vet the more you get.' (No. 4302, New World TV Hymnal.)

But, as has previously been stated, pleasing all the people all of the time is an incomplete science. And so this system, as near to perfect as any that can be imagined, had its dissenters. Not that any of them actually came out into the open to complain about it, of course. No chance of that. They were far too busy glued to their TV screens in a desperate attempt to clock up sufficient rehousing credits.

1

There are only five great men and three of them are hamburgers.
Don Van Vliet

Back in those carefree days of the 1980s it was very much the vogue amongst the well-to-dos to seek out dilapidated character properties for conversion. Medieval timber-framed barns, oast houses, clapped out windmills, all were considered dead chic. And you really weren't anybody if you didn't possess, at the very least, a Wesleyan chapel with all its bits and bobs intact, that you had painstakingly tortured into a design studio, complete with en suite bathrooms, fitted kitchen and solarium.

Few there were with sufficient foresight to consider what the twentieth century itself might offer in the way of character property. In fact, it wasn't until well into the 1990s that the potential of such derelict period pieces as supermarkets, Habitat stores, fast breeder reactors and battery chicken houses was fully exploited. By the year 2050, however, there was hardly a building standing above ground that hadn't been commandeered and converted.

Rex Mundi occupied an apartment built high in the north-west corner of Odeon Towers. The building was of the pre-NHE persuasion and had long ago been a cinema.

Rex shared his living room with a weighty section of mock Rococo ceiling cornice and an enormous gilded cherub. This grinning monstrosity had once bestowed its distant smile upon several generations of cinema-going heads. Now it stared with equal cheer, if somewhat foreshortened vision, into the ragged length of sacking which served Rex as carpet. But it was a small price to pay for overground accommodation. Six floors beneath Mrs Maycroft shared her rooms with several rows of cinema seats, and the young woman who lived in the tobacco kiosk never complained. As for the old couple who had been allocated the gents' toilet, well that didn't bear thinking about. All in all Rex had done quite well for himself.

On this particular morning, Rex sat in his homemade armchair, facing the flickering TV screen. His was the classic seated posture of the Active Viewer. Relaxed yet attentive, right thumb and forefinger about the remote controller, expression alert, eyes wide. But here all similarities ended. Rex Mundi was fast asleep.

His old Uncle Tony had taught him the technique when he was but a leprous lad, and there was no doubt that it did pay big dividends. It had already earned Rex sufficient rehousing credits to get him overground and he actually possessed a surplus of food and medico rations. His generosity with these made him quite popular and respected locally. But the greatest benefit to Rex was that it left him plenty of time to indulge in his own personal studies. These centred upon a book his Uncle Tony had bequeathed to him, a curious volume entitled *The Suburban Book of the Dead*. Uncle Tony had pressed the crumbling tome upon Rex with the simple statement, 'Knowledge is power'.

Shortly after this, he had spontaneously combusted

while watching his favourite game show. 'The way he would have wanted to go,' Aunty Norma put it.

Rex set to work to unravel the inner mysteries of the old book. But it was no easy matter. The language was archaic, penned somewhere during the middle years of the previous century, and much of it left Rex completely baffled. Yet he felt that he owed it to the old boy, who had, after all, passed on to Rex a most efficient method for beating the system, whilst leaving little else behind as a testament to his existence but for a pair of smoking boots and a charred remote controller.

Of Rex's rooms, there was little that could be argued in their favour. They were above ground, dry for part of the year and sufficient to his needs. The bedroom housed a mouldy bunk, the living room an armchair and a TV terminal. But for the gilded cherub, the only anomaly that would have drawn the visitor's eye, should Rex have ever had a visitor, which he never did, was a mural which occupied an entire wall of the living room. This was indeed the proverbial thing of beauty, so real as to be virtually photographic. Beneath a sky of the deepest blue, white crested waves broke upon a beach of golden sand, where tall palms bent under the weight of ripening coconuts; upon the horizon a liner cruised, a single plume of white smoke rising from a funnel.

Although Rex enjoyed looking at the mural, he didn't pretend to understand it. He had never seen the sea and the liner puzzled him greatly. Why, he asked himself, should anyone build a factory so far from the nearest subway terminus?

The masterpiece had been painted for him, in exchange for food, by a young man who had taken up temporary lodgings on the sixth-floor landing. Rex never knew the young man's name and once the painting had been completed, he had left without a word. The painting was an enigma, but it touched some distant chord in Rex and brought a considerable brightness into the otherwise gloomy surroundings.

As the day's first newscast began, a tiny doodad, concealed in the chair's back, sang happy awakenings into Rex's cerebral cortex and drew the lad awake. Rex yawned and thumbed the remote controller. The smiling face of the lady newscaster diminished and was gone. Rex stumbled blindly towards the bathroom, which, along with the kitchen, was too unspeakable to merit a mention. Here he bathed his eyes and scratched at the stubble on his chin. As sight slowly returned, he glimpsed his cloudy image in the shaving mirror.

'Damnably handsome,' he assured himself.

And indeed Rex wasn't a bad-looking specimen by any account. A trifle grey-green about the jowls, but nothing a quick spray of Healthiglo Pallorgone couldn't deal with. And he did bear an uncanny resemblance to a certain Harrison Ford of ancient days. This might just have been the product of happy coincidence, but the fact that his mother had been allowed access to the state sperm banks, whose stocks had been cryogenically laid down in the 1990s, probably played some part in it.

Rex attended to his daily toilet, picking off any flaky bits and doing what little he could to make himself look presentable. From the three he possessed, he chose the shirt which was the least crisp beneath the armpits and gave it a dusting with Bugoff Personal Livestock Exterminator. Once clad in his most dashing apparel, he opened a tin of synthafood and took breakfast. Unfortunately, the label had come off and Rex was unable to identify the contents. His morning repast completed, he fought off the feelings of nausea which inevitably followed mealtimes. Today they were somewhat more acute than usual, Rex having just consumed a tin of paint.

Rex belched mightily and zipped himself into his radiation suit. Screwing on the weatherdome, he stepped through the airlock, primed the anti-theft devices on his front door and set off down the stairs to face the new day.

And it wasn't a bad one by any account. Although the clouds hung but a few hundred feet above the rooftops and the crackles of the early electrical storm offered uncertain illumination, at least it wasn't raining. Rex switched on his chestlights and pressed on through the murk towards the nearby subway terminus. Today was to be the first day of his first-ever job and he had no wish to be late.

'Morning Rex, phew what a scorcher, eh?' The voice on the open channel belonged to Thaddeus Decor, who lived in the Coca Cola machine on the street corner.

Rex offered him a cheery wave. 'Morning Thaddeus, how's the wife?'

'Her knee's a lot better, thanks to that gangrene jelly you let me have.'

'Glad to hear it.'

'Young Kevin is down with the mange again.'

'I'll drop you something in later.' Rex continued upon his way. Thaddeus grinned toothlessly through his weather-dome.

'Thanks mate,' said he. 'You're a real toff.'

The passage leading into the subway was brightly lit by the techniglow of a hundred holographic advertising images. Rex plodded through the smiling ghosts ignoring their jolly banter. Once through decontamination he removed his weatherdome and queued for travel clearance. When his turn came, he pressed his face to the EYESPI. 'Destination?' the automaton enquired.

'The Nemesis Bunker,' Rex replied, proudly.

Circuits purred, information exchanged, the electrical voice said, 'Thank you, Mr Mundi, you are cleared for travel. Have another day.'

The morning train lurched painfully into the station and shuddered to a halt. It was not unduly crowded and Rex chose a vacant corner of the seatless carriage to squat in. The journey took a little over an hour, but it did at least offer Rex the opportunity to catch the morning newscast on the carriage TV, learn what was considered right with the world and clock up a few legitimate food and medico credits.

The newscast was much the same as ever. Things were looking up. The economy had never been healthier. Production had reached a record level. There had been several more authenticated sightings of blue sky. The road cones were expected to come off the M25 at any time now. Rex raised his eyes to the last one, but anything was possible.

The broadcast ended with a little bit of station propaganda, dressed in the guise of human interest story and comical tailpiece. Today it concerned an old lady who had clocked up an unprecedented number of credits, watching a rival station. So many, in fact, that the station's controller saw fit to visit her in person to offer his congratulations. Eliciting no response at her bunker door, his associates had cut their way in. And there was the old dear propped up before the screen, staring on oblivious. She had been dead for three weeks.

'Predictable,' muttered Rex, who was sure that he had heard the tale before. Happily, his stop came just as the station songsters were launching into an excruciating

16

new ditty 'Every Mushroom Cloud has a Silver Lining'. The train rattled into Nemesis Terminus, deftly sweeping aside any fallen objects. Today only two antisocial types chose to make the morning leap to oblivion. The driver considered this about average for the time of year and tuned the cab TV to his favourite foodie.

When the closing credits of her favourite show had finally rolled off the screen, the fashionable young woman behind the reception desk lowered the volume on her terminal. With mock surprise, she stared at the young man who had been standing there for the last twenty minutes, patiently flicking dandruff from the interior of his weatherdome.

'What do you want?' she asked, without charm.

'Rex Mundi.' The lad smiled encouragingly towards the stone-faced harpy.

'So what?' There was something in the woman's tone that suggested to Rex that casual sex was probably out of the question.

'I'm expected, or was anyway.'

'You're late.'

Rex opened his mouth to speak, but thought better of it. If the receptionist could carry on in this fashion, it was more than likely that she held considerable sway with some high muckamuck on the Nemesis board of directors, possibly even the Dalai Lama himself. No doubt in a horizontal capacity, Rex concluded, in-accurately.

'I have an appointment to see Ms Vrillium.'

The receptionist gave her terminal console a desultory tap or two.

'Ah yes, you're . . .'

'Late?' Rex said. 'Perhaps if you would be so kind as

to direct me to the office of the lady in question, I might make up a few lost minutes.'

'You'd never find it,' said the receptionist, sighing hopelessly. 'Others have tried. Men, what good are they, eh? One brain between the lot of them.' Rex examined his finger nails. They didn't bear examination.

'Possibly someone might be kind enough to show me the way then.'

The receptionist peered about the otherwise deserted entrance hall.

'It would seem,' said she, at length, 'that all are engaged in their various business pursuits. Perhaps you'd better come back some other time.'

Rex stared into the smiling face. He could always make it look like an accident. Say she just fell and broke her neck. But then, what if he was discovered? It could very easily spoil his chances of early promotion. 'Is my sister Gloria about?' he asked casually.

'Gloria?' The name took a moment or two to sink in, but when it finally did, the effect was nothing less than magical. 'Gloria Mundi?' said the receptionist in a still, small voice. 'Station controller?'

'Got her in one,' said Rex brightly. 'My sister, if you could just give her a buzz, I'm sure she wouldn't mind showing me the way. It was she who arranged the interview, you see.'

The receptionist who personally conveyed Rex to the door of Ms Vrillium's office appeared to have undergone a miraculous transfiguration. Having provocatively wiggled down the corridors before him, she now took her leave with a comely wink and a husky, 'See you later, big boy.'

Rex watched her depart. What a charming woman, he thought, I know I'm just going to love working here.

It's surprising just how utterly wrong it's possible to be, when you really put your mind to it. For whilst Rex stood in that corridor, regarding the receptionist's receding rear-end and considering the engaging possibilities of nepotism correctly applied, dark clouds were gathering upon the already darkened horizon. Great forces were stirring beneath the Earth's surface, and in a distant part of the galaxy, plans were being hatched that would ultimately threaten the very fabric of universal existence.

Or so it says here.

2

If it's God's will, who gets the money?
Tony O'Blimey

If there is one factor which binds together all the really great religions of this world, it's that God created man in his own image. Many cynical atheists loudly assert that the reverse is really the case, putting the whole thing down to egocentricity on the part of the believer. But then what do atheists know about God anyway? What these doubt- ing Toms have failed to grasp is the hidden truth: God created man in his own image, because he had to.

The erect biped, head at the top, feet at the bottom, wedding tackle about halfway up, represents the universal archetype, when it comes to the 'intelligent' being. This fact has long been known to science-fiction afficionados and UFO contactees. Alien beings, from no matter which part of the galaxy they might hail, inevitably bear a striking resemblance to man. There are the occasional variations in height and cranial dimensions, but for the most part our cosmic cousins are a pretty reasonable facsimile of ourselves. Many even speak good English, often with a pronounced American accent. Such facts can hardly be argued with. They are evidence, should any really be needed, of a cosmic masterplan, and sufficient in themselves to serve friend atheist up with a wok-load of egg. Faces, for the use of.

What it all comes down to, as it so often does, is the very beginning of the universe. This, say the bigheads of the scientific fraternity, all began with a big bang. Wrong! The universe, in fact, began with the sound of a duck call, followed by a whistle and an enormous cosmic wind-break. Had anyone been around at the time to overhear these sounds, they would probably have received a pretty good indication of what God had up his sleeve, amongst other places.

About five minutes after the burst of celestial flatulence, when the air had begun to clear a bit, things began to settle down into the shapes which were most comfortable and efficient for them. And so they remained. No-one has yet improved upon the sphere as a planetary shape, nor the erect biped as its ruling species. That's the way it is. Like it, or lump it. QED.

Certainly, some races evolved mentally a lot quicker than others. The reason for this has come to be known as Duke's Principle, 'a man's gotta do, what a man's gotta do'. Or to simplify it, they evolved quicker, because they had to. It all depends very much upon what a particular planet has to offer in terms of pickable food, huntable animals, farmable lands and whatever. The Trempish of Trempera, for instance, found themselves competing with huge armour-plated reptiles, carnivores with virtually impenetrable hides and seemingly insatiable appetites. If the Trempish hadn't had the ingenuity to dig a series of baited dead-falls, distil an acid from the bark of a rare tree, tip their arrows with it and shoot the trapped beasties in their exposed pineal glands, they would surely have died out. As it was, they hadn't, so they did! Thus proving, that when a man's gotta do what a man's gotta do, he'd better pull his finger out and get on with it.

And so it was with the Phnaargs of Phnaargos. Their

22

'gotta doing' was not immediately apparent. They lived upon a gloriously verdant world, devoid of killer reptiles and flying scorpions, rich in natural vegetation, with a mild climate and some really knockout sunsets. However, to wax biblical, this Eden was not without its serpent. Only here it came in the form of the cathode ray tube. Mankind didn't come across this miracle until its closing moments, but it wasn't so on Phnaargos. For on Phnaargos, the cathode ray tube grew wild. And so, at a time when humankind was still tossing rocks at the hairy elephants and experimenting with DIY in the family cave, the Phnaargs were watching TV.

Now, if it was strange that the cathode ray tube should grow wild upon a planet, then it is surely stranger still that the botanical equivalents of the video camera, the microphone, the mixing desk, the spotlight, the little monocular thing that a really duff director wears around his neck, and all the other paraphernalia necessary to television production, should similarly be blooming away, ready for the harvest. In fact, many might be forgiven for finding it unlikely, to say the very least. But the Almighty moves in mysterious ways, his wonders to perform. And who are we to question his motives?

Now, with all this technology sprouting around them, one might also be forgiven for thinking that the Phnaargs were a 'race blessed of God'. But, you'd be wrong on that one too. For nothing could be further from the truth. The Phnaargs were the first race ever to become irrevocably hooked on television, the first to fall victim to the dangerous and terminally addictive radiations of the cathode ray tube. And once infected at such an early stage in their development, they were well and truly done for.

Within a few short years of their discovery, the planet was literally forested with cultivated TV stations and the

23

Phnaargs, almost slaves. Those not engaged in full time viewing strove to supply the needs of those who were. The needs soon became demands and the demands were wild. For this was a young and primitive stock and it liked its TV meaty!

And so Duke's Principle came into effect upon Phnaargos. The Phnaarg TV execs, finding that supply was far outstripped by demand, were forced to do something. To boldly go where no man had gone before. To seek out new worlds and new civilizations. And televise them.

And such it was, that by a rare freak of chance, which suddenly makes all the foregoing relevant, the Phnaargs came across Planet Earth. Here they found man, still stoning the mammoths, whacking up the murals and generally minding his own business. Had he been allowed to carry on with these trivial pursuits, he would probably be doing so even now. But the visiting Phnaargs were not slow to realize the potential of mankind's development as great TV material. They wasted little time in setting up their horticultural transmitters and getting on with the show. And the rest, like it or like it not, is history.

The series became an overnight success. The Phnaargian viewers took to this 'everyday story of simple folk' like Teds to a tapered trouser, and *The Earthers* became the most popular series in the history of the universe.

Now, on the face of it, this might appear to be harmless enough stuff, a race, hopelessly addicted to television, watching the exploits of another. And so it might possibly have remained, but for the Phnaarg viewing public's fanatical craving for 'a bit of action'. Much against their better judgement, the producers of *The Earthers* found themselves forced to help things along a bit.

24

It all began in a small way, with fire, the wheel and language. The Earthers just didn't seem to be getting the hang of them. And as the series was now running prime-time, there seemed good reason to slip all these into one weekly episode, to get the ball rolling.

The fact that this *was* done has always been vigorously denied by the producers, as have suggestions that they have been doing likewise ever since. Continually tampering with Earth history to keep the ratings up. The Phnaargian tabloids have made scandalous assertions that certain popular figures have been 'reincarnated' over the centuries, and even that some of the major roles have been played by Phnaargian actors dressed up to look like Earthers.

Whether there is any truth in this isn't easy to say, the producers of the series wisely having kept the precise location of Planet Earth to themselves as a simple precaution against nosy parkers. But the fact that next week's episode of *The Earthers* is always previewed in the television papers should be enough to raise the occasional suspicion.

However, by the Earth year 2050 viewing figures on Phnaargos were tailing off dramatically. And viewers, miffed that their favourites had got the chop in the Nuclear Holocaust Event, an episode which achieved the biggest ever ratings and won several much-coveted awards, were switching off in droves. The idea of watching a rather undistinguished cast of scabby-looking individuals, whose lives apparently revolved around watching television, was of very little interest. It was so far-fetched, for one thing.

And so it came to be that on a May morning, when summer was the season, the executive team of Earthers Inc. held a very special meeting. The boardroom perched, high in the spiral leafbound complex. The Phnaargian sun, Rupert, nudged a golden ray or two down towards the broad and membraned picture-window, where, tinted to a subtle rose-pink, they fell upon the exquisite table of Goldenwood which grew in the centre of the room. The room itself was another marvel of horticultural architecture. A masterpiece, designed and grown by the leading 'hortitect' of the day, Capability Crabshaw.

Crabshaw's current passion was for the work of the late and legendary Vita Sackville-West. This was reflected in this year's boardroom 'look'. The chairs were the product of painstaking topiary work, performed upon box hedges. The svelte grass carpeting the floor was sewn with thyme, camomile and other fragrant herbs, which released aromatic essences when stepped upon. *Acacia Dealata* and *Albizia Julibrissin* flowered in weathered terracotta pots, arranged in pleasing compositions to every corner of the room. It was all very much just so. But whether the members of the board, hunched sullenly in their box-hedge baronials, had any appreciation whatsoever for this Sissinghurst in the sky, must remain in some doubt. For these were desperate men. And he who had the most to lose was the most desperate of them all.

Mungo Madoc, station controller, surveyed his troops with a bitter eye. Mungo was 'Earthish' to the very nostrils. But for the greenly-dyed mustachios, waxed into the six points, befitting to his status, and the extraordinarily lush three-piece, clothing his ample frame, one might have taken him for an Earthman any day of the week. Except possibly Tuesday.

Of the executive board, little can be offered to the reader in terms of their variance from established Earth type. They averaged around the six-foot mark, some corpulent, others of that lean and hungry look once alluded to by a certain Phnaargian copy-writer of days gone by. There were six of them in all, and a right surly-looking bunch they were too. It may be of interest to note that while, at this time, all media on Earth was run by females of the species, here on Phnaargos, male chauvinism held sway. And a woman's place was in the greenhouse.

Mungo tapped his trowel of office upon the shining table-top. All conversation ceased as he drew breath and launched straight into the meat of the matter. 'Gentlemen,' he said, his voice having the not unexpected nasal quality of one addicted to the pleasures of orchid sniffing, 'gentlemen, we are in big schtuck here.'

Executive heads bobbed up and down appropriately. At the far end of the table Diogenes 'Dermot' Darbo, naturally bald, but resplendent in a vine-hair-toupé said, 'Yes, indeedy.'

'Viewing figures have sunk to a point beneath which even the Fengorian Flatworm might find squeezing a somewhat hazardous affair.' There were some nervous titters amongst those few who hadn't heard the remark before. 'And so I'm holding this special council, that you may favour me with your propositions for the revitalization of the series.'

Mungo's team made encouraging faces. But nobody spoke.

'You will offer me your proposals, I will mull them over and almost upon the instant decide who remains on the team, enjoying all the privileges, and who seeks new employment turning compost in the nursery beds, enjoying the fresh air.'

The heads remained nodless but the brains within them pulsed with activity.

27

'I'm waiting, gentlemen.'

Hook-nosed Gryphus Garstang rose tentatively to his feet and raised an arm, gorgeously encased in spring-flowering cyclamen. 'What do you say to another war?' he asked brightly.

Mungo Madoc eyed the young man almost kindly. 'Another war?' said he, tucking a soft green sapling behind his left ear. 'If it hadn't been for your brilliant concept of World War Three to celebrate the arrival of the twenty-first century, we wouldn't be in this mess now.'

'I seem to recall that being a corporate decision,' Garstang replied, rattling his foliage in an agitated manner.

'And I seem to recall you insisting that you accept the TV awards at the celebration dinners.'

The hooknose reseated himself as Mungo continued, 'Garstang, you have been on the team for, how long is it now?'

'One hundred and eighty-seven Earth years.'

'And during this short period there have been no less than three world wars.'

'They've been very popular with the viewers.'

'That's as may be, but it surely can't have escaped your attention that the Earthers are a little hard-pressed for weapons at the moment. What do you suggest they do, sling food tins at one another?'

Gryphus Garstang maintained a sulking silence.

'I think we should go for the love angle.' The voice belonged to Lavinius Wisten, a pale willowy wisp of a man, with the bearing of a poet and the sexual habits of a Fomahaunt Marshferret. 'Passion amongst the shelter-folk. My team and I have come up with a scenario in which two proto-embryos become separated accidentally at the sperm bank. They grow up in separate shelters, then meet and fall in love, finally to discover that they are twins. I'm also working on the possibility that they have a genetic mutation that makes them immune to radiation. They leave the shelters and repopulate the Earth. I thought we might call it *Earth Two, The Sequel*.'

Mungo Madoc sank into his chair and made plaintive groaning noises.

'Well, I think it's got everything going for it.'

'But it's not in the plot.'

'We could weave it in.'

'Weave it in?' Mungo raised himself up to an improbable height and blew exquisite pollen from his left nostril. 'How many times must I remind you that this series has an original script?'

'Oh, that again,' said Garstang, and immediately wished he hadn't.

'When our founder drew up the original script for *The Earthers*, it was written into the contract that, although a certain degree of creativity was allowable, the basic plot wasn't to be tampered with in any way. This, you will recall, is referred to as Holy Writ.'

'And if I recall,' sneered the hooknose, 'it ends with a world war.'

'And if I recall,' said Calvus Cornelius, who felt that it was his turn to stick two pennyworth in, 'it was scheduled to end in the Earth year 999.'

There was a long silence; this was one of those things that it was not considered seemly to touch upon. Cornelius could suddenly hear the call of the compost beds. 'Or so Garstang is always saying,' he said rapidly.

'I never have,' Garstang rose with a flurry of heart-crossing.

'Gentlemen, gentlemen, this is getting us nowhere. Surely one amongst you has something constructive to offer.' Mungo Madoc gazed at the blank faces. His eyes soon caught upon that of Fergus Shaman, which appeared a little less blank than the rest. It was smiling broadly.

'Fergus,' said Mungo, 'Fergus, do you have something to tell us?'

Fergus nodded brightly. He was a curious fellow. Somewhat lop-sided of face and bent of body, he carried about with him a mysterious air which, real or imagined, gave him a certain authority. Mungo Madoc could never quite bring himself to call him Shaman, at least not to his face.

'I have the solution,' said Fergus Shaman. 'That is all.'

'Then the floor is yours.' Mungo reseated himself, clasped his fingers before him on the tabletop and smiled the sweetest of smiles.

'Whether or not *The Earthers* was scheduled to end in 999, I don't know; neither in truth, do I care.' Ignoring the raised eyebrows, he continued, 'One thing I do know, is that it remains very much in all our interests to see that it doesn't end in the foreseeable future.' Eyebrows lowered, heads nodded slowly. 'The so-called Armageddon sequence must be postponed for as long as possible. Indefinitely, if needs be.'

'But the viewing figures . . .' said Mungo.

'I am, of course, well aware of our dilemma. The viewing public is a fickle creature, it loves its heroes and hates its villains. Through the medium of constant re-runs it is also well aware of the story so far. Let's not pretend that we haven't tampered with the plot. We have, time and time again.'

'Out of the purest motives,' said Mungo Madoc.

'Be that as it may. What I'm suggesting will come as a shock to some of you, but we are in a desperate situation. It's a somewhat revolutionary approach, but I think it will pay off in the long run.'

'Go on then,' said Mungo, 'say your piece.'

'I'm proposing that we skip back one hundred years and change the plot.'

There is always a silence before the storm and indeed there was one now. When the ensuing storm broke, it was a real belter. Sheltering beneath an umbrella of facts, only known to himself, Fergus Shaman weathered it out.

'How?' said Mungo, when he was finally able to make himself heard.

'In the simplest terms available, we pick upon a popular character of the time, allow him to view the future, his own in particular, and offer him another chance.'

'Go on.'

'Well,' said Fergus, 'back in the 1950s there was a certain Elvis Presley. Perhaps you recall him?'

'Big fat Northern Irish fellow, always shouting "down with the pope".'

'No,' Fergus shook his head, 'that was someone else entirely.'

'Sorry, they all look the same after a while.'

'This Elvis Presley was a leader of the nation's youth. In 1958 he joined the American Army. Many historians agree that this was the downfall of his career. The expression "sold out" was one in popular use at the time. However, in my new scenario, Elvis refuses to take the draft. He is arrested and spends a short time in prison. But the outcry from the teenage population is so great, that he is soon released. He becomes a figure in American politics and in 1963 becomes president of the USA.'

31

'I know this Presley,' Garstang pipped in, 'he was a wally, by any account.'

'I have no wish to be flippant,' Fergus replied, 'but I hardly see why that should affect him becoming president.'

Mungo chuckled. 'Sounds like a president in the grand tradition to me. But I don't see how this Presley can be held responsible for the events in the latter part of the twentieth century.'

'Simple politics,' Fergus said. 'If Presley had never joined up, nor would half a generation of the nation's youth. There would have been no war in Vietnam, the Americans being unable to raise an Army. You can't fight a really decent war without conscripts.'

'It still sounds a bit iffy, even if it was possible, I can't see how we are going to get away with it.'

Fergus did a bit of smiling. 'Back in the eighties there was a soap opera on Earth. It was very big indeed, but the producers made a grave mistake by killing off one of its most popular characters. In order to revive viewing figures they did likewise to him a series or two later, by simply having him turn up in the shower one morning as if nothing had happened. It was then revealed that the last umpteen episodes had just been his wife's bad dream.'

Looks of disbelief were passed around the table. Someone said, 'Come on now.'

'As true as I'm standing here,' said Fergus, 'I won't mention the name of the series, but the Earthers are still watching it now. Although it is presently set in a millionaire's bunker and has only three characters left. My plan is a case of life imitating art. After all the viewers consider *The Earthers* to be a real-life drama.'

'Which it is,' said Mungo Madoc.

'And so there you have it. Presley for president, the Nuclear Holocaust Event postponed for another hundred years, the Armageddon Sequence for another thousand. I'm not saying that this Presley is the all-round good guy; on the contrary, his reign as president will be a colourful affair. Plenty of sex and drugs and rock and roll.'

Wisten grinned enthusiastically. 'Sounds good to me.'

'Sounds good to me,' Mungo agreed. 'But I foresee certain small flaws in the scheme. Firstly, as we all know, the Earthers are a contrary bunch. One can never rely on them to carry the plot. We come up with all kinds of grand scenarios but they inevitably cock it up. Sometimes I wonder who is running this show, them or us.'

'There are no absolutes in this business, I agree, but I have done my research, and barring some, dare I say it, act of God, I'm certain that it will work. I have all the facts and figures right here. You are all welcome to look them over.'

'As indeed we will.' Mungo stroked the table-top with a wan digit. 'But there is one minor point that I should like to raise. It's a small matter, but one which I think shouldn't be overlooked.'

'Oh yes,' said Fergus, 'and that is?'

'That is the simple matter that time travel is an impossibility, you craven buffoon!'

Fergus shook his head. He was still smiling. 'Not any more,' said he, winking lewdly. 'Not with the latest miracle of modern horticulture.'

He dug into his trouser pocket and brought out a spherical green object, which he reverently laid before him on the table.

'Gentlemen, please allow me to introduce you to THE TIME SPROUT!'

'Pleased to be here,' said the vegetable in question.

33

3

A stairway to oblivion is better than no stairway at all.
The Suburban Book of the Dead

The interview with Ms Vrillium went remarkably well, all things considered. Rex put this down to the element of surprise. He had evidently earned some big kudos in getting past the receptionist. Now he listened with growing interest as the nature of his post was outlined to him.

'Religious affairs correspondent,' said Ms Vrillium. 'As you are no doubt well aware, Buddhavision is the biggest of the Big Three stations. We are a religious organisation, linked to Buddha Biological and Buddha Wholefoods International. It is our duty to bring enlightenment to the masses. This we do by providing superior entertainment, embodying elements of theological doctrine couched in terms that the layman can understand. Am I making myself clear?'

'Absolutely,' said Rex. What an ugly woman, he thought.

'You are practising, aren't you?'

'I'm trying my hardest.' Their eyes met. 'Ah, I see, a practising Buddhist. Yes, cross my heart.'

'Adherence to doctrine must forever be uppermost in your . . . mind.'

It was only a slight pause, but Rex got the message.

'Clear as a temple bell,' said he. What an exceedingly ugly woman, he thought.

'Unfounded accusations have been levelled at us by the other channels, that we pander to the lowest instincts of the vox pop.'

Rex tut-tutted and shook his head, 'Get away.'

'It has been suggested that *Nemesis*, hosted by—' Ms Vrillium's gaze wandered towards the ceiling; Rex followed it with his own, but couldn't see what the attraction was, '—hosted by our divine holiness, the one hundred and fifty-third reincarnation, the Dalai Lama.'

'God bless him,' said Rex. 'The man is a saint.'

'It has been suggested that the high mortality rate amongst contestants on the *Nemesis* show and the explicit sex between the presenter . . .' Ms Vrillium's gaze went skyward once more, but Rex gave it a miss '. . . the Dalai Lama and his hostess is in some way immoral.'

'Sounds like religious bigotry to me. That new lady Pope on the *Auto-da-fé* show is hardly reticent when it comes to putting the torch about.'

Ms Vrillium made an even more unpleasant face. 'And look at the way she does her hair. And those vestments, do they, or do they not, clash with the set?'

'I've never watched it,' said Rex, who had no intention of being caught out that easily. 'But they do say it's a man in drag.'

Ms Vrillium didn't smile. 'As I was saying, by demonstrating the joys of pure love and the punishment of sin, within the boundaries of a single show, *Nemesis* provides the viewer with an experience which is ecstatic, cathartic and instructional. That is the essence of good television.'

'It certainly is,' Rex agreed. 'Now, about the job?'

'You will concern yourself with fringe factions.'

'Fringe factions?'

The ugly woman looked at him thoughtfully. 'Fringe factions. Divine enlightenment is the preserve of but a happy few. Most grope in the darkness, blindfolded by misunderstanding and misinterpretation. They wander along paths which lead towards fragmentation and chaos.'

'You want me to go out and spread the good word then?'

'Hardly. We are not expecting you to act in a missionary capacity. After all, what do you know of the higher truths.'

As that was a statement rather than a question, Rex said, 'I'm perplexed.'

'Subversive religious elements exist. Underground organizations practising all manner of unsavoury rites and damnable heresies. We wish merely to learn names, details, locations of chapters, meeting houses and so forth. You will furnish us with such information, so that the Dalai can remember these unfortunates in his prayers and meditations. In the hope that salvation might ultimately be theirs. Are you following all this?'

Rex removed the finger which was ruminating in a blocked nostril, and nodded enthusiastically. 'Bringing the lost sheep back into the fold.'

'Sheep? What has this to do with sheep?'

'I was speaking metaphorically.'

'Indeed. Well, if metaphor is your forte, then just let me say that the station does not require any dead wood.'

'You can rely on me.' Rex straightened his shoulders. 'Just lead me to my office.'

'Office?' The ghastly noise which came from the woman's throat bore a vague resemblance to laughter. A very vague resemblance. 'Do you have your own transport?'

Rex shook his head.

'Then we will issue you with some. You will report in from the in-car terminal hourly. Hourly, do you understand?'

'What if I have nothing to report?'

'You will nevertheless report in. Company vehicles are very expensive. Should an operative fail to report in, it will be assumed that he has absconded with the vehicle. The mother computer will therefore immobilize the vehicle and reverse the environmental controls. Simply a precaution which in your case, I trust, will never be applied.'

'Indeed not.'

'Do you have any questions?'

'We haven't discussed salary, hours or expenses, as yet. Perhaps these matters should be thrashed out now, to save you any inconvenience at a later date.'

Ms Vrillium held up a small transparent cube. 'This will furnish you with all the information you should require regarding your first assignment.' She tossed the thing to Rex. 'You will be paid on results, legitimate expenses will be covered.'

Rex turned the cube upon his palm, he was not altogether convinced. 'Is my sister Gloria about?'

'Gloria is far too busy to speak to you now. But if it's anything important I might mention it to her tonight. We live together, you know.'

'How charming,' said Rex. 'Do you think I might use your lavatory?'

4

Everything for the state, nothing outside the state.
Mussolini

Careful with that axe, Eugene.
P. Floyd

Half an hour later, Rex Mundi sat at the controls of company vehicle 801. It was a spartan little craft, two speed, closed environment, single seater, automatic guidance. Powered by a nuclear reactor the size of a matchbox. 'A child could fly it,' he had been unreliably informed. The dashboard housed a computer console, but to Rex's chagrin, lacked a TV terminal.

Rex delved into the breast pocket of his radiation suit and drew out the small transparent cube. He slotted it into its housing and the narrow console screen sprang into life. It formed the station logo, three tiny tadpoles chasing each other's tails, then crackled uncertainly with the outspeak of its selective memory. 'Rex Mundi, religious affairs correspondent seven, please identify.' Rex pressed close to the screen. 'Identification confirmed. Work schedule one. Proceed to section four, north quarter. Investigate recent unconfirmed reports of cannibal cult Devianti.'

'Cannibal?' Rex punched the co-ordinates into the

directional guidance system and the knackered craft lurched aloft.

'Hourly reportage to be strictly observed,' the voice from the console continued. 'Credits allotted for this assignment as follows: informer twenty-seven, acolyte thirty-five, high priest one hundred. Have another day.'

'High priest, one hundred credits.' Rex's eyebrows rose to meet his spirits. 'Further rehousing, with access to the state nympharium thrown in.' A big bonus indeed.

The car swung up and Rex peered down at the blasted landscape. He could make out the Nemesis Bunker, which wasn't difficult as it covered about thirty acres, the subway terminal, the ranks of hardly-built rehousing, the rubble-strewn roads. A grim enough vista. He hit the clouds at about 500 feet and travelled a while in darkness. Rex considered circling Odeon Towers, just to see what it looked like from above, but the thought of one hundred credits kept his mind firmly on the job. He had definitely fallen on his feet here. A job with prospects, firm's car, expense account. This was the big time. Good old Gloria, and he had thought she didn't like him much. It was, of course, all far too good to be true.

A series of diminishing circles appeared upon the blued screen of the console. The voice said, 'Descent locked. In case of malfunction please remember that we are all part of a cosmic masterplan and that even in the moment of your extinction you are following your Karma and that the Dalai's thoughts are with you. Let's both sing together, *Om-mani-padme-hum . . . Om-mani-padme-hum . . .'*

'Thanks a lot.' Rex switched off the console as the car fell heavily towards the overgrown car park at the back of the Tomorrowman Tavern. Here it struck the ground with a sickening thud. Rex felt at his teeth, none seemed any more loose than usual. He screwed on his weather-dome, released the canopy and stepped out to view the hostile landscape.

The pub looked about as wretched as any he had encountered before. A jumble of corrugated-iron sheets, welded together and sealed against nature beneath a plasticised acid-proof shell. A neon sign winked on and off, lamely advertising the establishment as 'The morroma Tav'.

Rex wandered across the car park. Two other vehicles were parked. One, a rather snappy Rigel Charger, probably the perk of some TV bigwig, the other, a clapped-out Morris Minor converted into a half-track, anyone's guess.

The airlock and decontamination systems at the To-morrowman seemed to be largely symbolic in nature. A double plastic entrance-flap, between which crouched a lounge boy, who tossed tubs of anti-bacteriant at the visitor as he passed through. The grim expression upon the lad's face informed Rex that job satisfaction wasn't part and parcel of the post. Inside, the bar was everything that might reasonably be regretted. It was low and long and loathsome. Rex sought a mat to wipe his feet on, but there was none, so dripping profusely, he cradled his weatherdome and put on a brave face.

Several patrons hunched before the bar-counter, sipping dubious-looking cocktails and staring into TV terminals, Rex found a vacant bar-stool and climbed on to it. The barman behind the jump regarded him with passing interest. He was scabious fellow, in leathern apron and gloves. He lacked an eye and glared at the world with that remaining in a manner which, Rex felt, lacked a certain warmth.

'Good day to you,' said Rex encouragingly.

'Possibly your definition of the word differs from my

own,' replied the barman, idly dabbing at the counter with a rag unfit to swab latrines. 'But if you're buying liquor it's all the same to me.'

'Quite so.' Rex drummed his fingers upon the counter-top. 'Now, what shall I have?'

'The beer tastes like bog water and the liquor is distilled from rat turds.'

'Do you have a personal favourite?'

'Tomorrowman Brew is perhaps less noxious than most.'

'A double then.'

'As you please.' The barman decanted a small measure of the demon brew. 'Eyeball the terminal. Those I find to be without credit generally leave the establishment with a dented skull.'

Rex stared into the counter screen and much to his surprise it flashed up twenty credits to his favour.

'A man of means,' said the barman, punching in Rex's account to date. 'Drink your fill.'

Rex placed the cup to his lips and took a tentative sip. It wasn't as bad as all that and the nausea which inevitably followed any kind of intoxication didn't come.

'Cheers,' said Rex, raising his cup. 'Will you have one yourself?'

The barman eyed him with curiosity. 'You are asking me to take a drink at your expense?'

'Certainly.'

'The mad shall always be mad, such is the way of it.' He poured himself a large measure and knocked it back with a single movement. 'So,' he said, wiping his mouth with the bar-cloth. 'What do you want to know?'

Rex finished his drink and stared into the putrid bottom of the cup. 'I'm a wanderer, a seeker after truth, if you like.'

'I don't like, but continue.'

'I'm driven by a single compulsion. An unquenchable thirst for religious dogma in its each and every form.'

'Then watch the screens,' said the barman, 'there's dogma enough for anyone there, crap it all is.'

'Quite so, but a whisper has reached me that there are others hereabouts of alternative persuasions. Non establishment.' Rex gave the barman a knowing wink.

The barman shook his head. 'I would know nothing of such matters. I merely serve the drinks and kick out the drunks.'

'I'm willing to pay handsomely for such information.'

'Ah,' the barman grinned, fearsomely, 'then you have come to the right place. Comparative religion is my life's work. I run this bar as a sideline.'

'Indeed. Then we understand one another.'

'That remains to be seen.'

Rex leant forward across the counter. 'The Devianti,' he said.

The barman's eye rolled into his head, leaving only the ghastly white. 'I must be off about my business.' Snatching up his bar-cloth, he limped down the bar to serve a dwarf, who was noisily rattling his cup.

'He won't tell you nothing mister,' said a voice at Rex's elbow. 'Scared shitless he is.'

Rex looked down at the wretch, ill-clad and foul smelling. His skin was toned a vile yellow, crudely rouged at the cheeks. 'And who might you be?'

'Josh is the name, mister. Rogan Josh. Your offer still hold good?'

Rex nodded. 'It does, but there is one small matter I feel you should know.'

'Oh yes?'

'I suffer from an unstable mental condition which

manifests itself in bouts of psychotic violence when I find myself being incorrectly advised.'

The wretch flinched. He had that wasted, haunted look, which wasn't uncommon. Pulling at his single lock of hair, he said, 'I can set you straight, mister. Honest.'

'Then kindly do so.'

'It'll cost you.'

'Say your piece then and I shall endeavour to place an accurate monetary value upon it.'

'These Devianti. I know where they hang out.'

'Hang out?'

'Where they live, take up residence, co-exist, assume a non-transient occupancy. The dunghole where they do their butchery.'

'Go on.'

'They're bad boys, mister. They eat people.'

'I'd rather gathered that.'

'So you'd better take a food parcel, unless you wanna be on the menu.'

'Do you want another drink?' asked the barman, who had been edging back, all ears. 'Or do you want kicking into the street?'

'One more for myself,' Rex nodded towards Rogan Josh, 'and one for my companion, that will indeed be all.'

'Oh, thanks very much,' sneered the wounded barman. 'Would it be of any interest to learn my considered opinion of yourself?'

'None whatever.'

'Not that I consider you the accidental outcome of a homosexual relationship?'

'One for myself and one for my companion.'

The barman splashed two foreshortened measures of Tomorrowman into as many glasses, overcharged Rex's account and stood with his arms folded, grinding his tooth.

Rex steered his informer away to a side table. Here he spoke in whispered tones. The barman, whose hearing was considerably less acute than his temper, slouched off, muttering beneath his breath.

'Now,' said Rex, 'all I require are names and locations.'

The wretch eyed him with open suspicion. 'Who are you, mister?' he asked.

'Rex Mundi is the name. Whenever you think of four credits, justly earned, you will think of me.'

'If you dispense credits as liberally as you do words, then I shall be happy enough.'

'Quite so. Then let us begin with the local high priest. Always best to go straight to the top, I always find.'

'Thinking to pay him a visit at home, are you?'

'Certainly.'

'Then as you won't be coming back, you won't miss another five credits for the information.'

'I tend towards the optimistic,' Rex replied, 'but your point is well taken. I shouldn't wish my murderer to gain financially from my demise. My cash is at your disposal.'

'Good, then I will tell you all you wish to know. There are some old warehouses about a mile north of here.'

'How will I know them?'

'You'll not miss them. They are surrounded by barricades. But don't let this deter you, just walk straight up and knock.'

'Assuming that I have somehow avoided the attentions of the snipers who no doubt guard the place, who should I ask for?'

'Assuming that this miracle has occurred, then Rambo Bloodaxe is your man.'

'Rambo Bloodaxe?' Rex crumpled in hilarity. 'Don't wind me up.'

'I'm serious, mister. They've all got names like that. Brad the Impaler, Deathblade Eric.'

Rex shook his head. 'Might I suggest, that in your certainty for my forthcoming extinction, you are presuming to take liberties with my not inconsiderable intellect? I feel the red mist coming on.' Rex clutched at his head and made a ferocious face.

'Hold on, hold on mister. I'm telling you the truth. I wouldn't lie to a dying man.' Rex peered through his fingers. 'Anyway,' the wretch continued, 'if you return to prove me wrong then . . .'

'Then it wouldn't go well for you.' Rex looked at his watch. Whether or not Rogan Josh was telling the truth, or even a small part of it, seemed a matter for grave doubts. But it was something at least, and this was his first day on the job. If he screwed up, he would learn by his mistakes. Rex pulled a three credit piece from his purse and tossed it towards the wretch.

Josh stared at it in horror. 'But you said . . .'

'I lied.' Rex took up his weatherdome and walked.

He returned to his car and punched the name of Rogan Josh into the console. If he never got any further than dealing with informers, he should still be able to turn a handsome profit. But what about Rambo Bloodaxe and his anthropophagous acolytes? That was another matter. But then, what did it matter? If the whole thing was simply down to the Dalai remembering a few lost souls in the meditations, surely he could punch in any old name.

Rex pondered long and hard on this one. He wasn't slow to conclude that the same thought must no doubt have crossed the mind of his predecessor. Rex hadn't bothered to ask what became of him, assuming that he had found promotion. Now he wasn't too sure. Perhaps no-one ever got out of this job alive.

Rex shook his head, he was just being morbid. Probably the drink. But he would do well to be shrewd until he knew, for certain, exactly how the land lay.

A flicker of movement caught Rex's attention. Someone had left the tavern and was coming across the car park. Rex sank low in his seat and peeped into the wing mirror. It was Rogan Josh.

The wretch, who suddenly didn't appear so wretched, strolled across to the Rigel Charger, disarmed the anti-personnel device and climbed aboard. There was a roar of engines, a cloud of dust and a great whoosh as the car sped skywards.

Well now, thought Rex, smacking the battered 801 into drive, the plot thickens. 'Confirm identity and report destination,' said the console.

'Rex Mundi.' Rex glanced at the screen. 'In pursuit of Devianti informer.'

'Identification confirmed. Have another day.'

The Rigel Charger sloped off through a bank of low cloud and Rex followed, the 801's guidance system locked into the heat pattern of its exhaust. Rex sat back in his seat. It was dead exciting, all this, just like the sci-fi videos he had grown up on. 'Zoom zoom,' said Rex Mundi. 'And away we go.'

Exactly why the 801's computer failed to recognize the high-voltage power cables ahead as a possible hazard to low-flying aircraft, and take the appropriate evasive action, was a matter for the company crash crew and the accident investigators to file reports on later.

For now, the mother computer simply recorded that a blip had vanished from the main-screen, and pronounced, 'Car down, nuclear hazard, no survivors. Repeat no survivors.'

5

There's one reborn every minute.
Dalai Dan

'Shame,' said Haff Ffnsh, 'I had high hopes for him.'

'Closedown on that one, I'm afraid. Do you want me to cover the crash? It's quite unexceptional.'

'No.' Haff stroked an organic module and the screen's membrane darkened. 'Fade up on the Dalai and we'll check the day's doings.'

'Dull, dull, dull.'

'Mr Madoc's directive. We are but pawns in the game.'

'This station could do with a change of management. If I was at the helm, things would be different.'

'Your views on the subject are well known to me. Constant repetition does little to improve my opinion of them.'

'Just one week,' said Jovil Jspht, 'or even a day, you'd see some viewing figures, I can tell you.'

'What, killer maggots from the Earth's core? Do me a favour.'

'I've circulated my memorandum. It's legitimate material, Holy Writ stuff.'

'Mr Jspht, you are assistant controller of the largest network production in the galaxy. Many would envy you your position. Many, in fact, seek to take it. Why can you not simply do the job you are paid so handsomely for?'

49

'No-one recognizes my true talents; come the revolution . . .'

'It did come. Perhaps you were at lunch, you so often are.'

'One day the whole world will know my name,' said Jovil Jspht.

'Very possibly, but few will be able to pronounce it. Kindly manipulate your module.'

> 'This is the time
> This is the place
> The time to face
> What the fates have in store
> It's double or drop
> Do or die
> And here's the guy
> We've all been waiting for
> He's the man with the most
> The heavenly host
> The holiest ghost
> In the cosmic drama
> And here he is
> The shah of showbiz
> The Dalai . . . Dalai . . . Dalai
> Dalai . . . Lama.'

'A catchy little number, I think you will agree.' The musical director raised his violet mohawk from the keyboard and smiled hopefully towards Gloria Mundi.

'It's crap,' she replied, 'but I suppose it will have to do.'

'There's another verse . . .'

'Have the Lamarettes rehearse it and I'll get back to you later.' Gloria turned upon her seven-inch heel and strode off across the studio floor. The musical director watched her depart. Certain words formed upon his pale blue lips, but they are better left unrecorded.

The *Nemesis* studio was by far and away the most lavish that any the Big Three stations possessed. *Nemesis* was the most successful gameshow in pre-recorded history.

The original formula had been conceived as long ago as the 1950s, possibly even earlier. But it held together now as well as it ever did. Take one charismatic host, several thinly-clad lovelies and a star prize. Then add a never-ending stream of contestants, willing to debase themselves in the holy cause of avarice. Stir well and serve weekly.

No matter what variations the whim of fashion dictated, the original formula never failed. But with *Nemesis* it had been brought to its apotheosis.

Nemesis had its genesis in the closing years of the twentieth century. These were pretty grim times, by any reckoning. Toxic pollution had finally succeeded in dissolving the ozone layer, the natural barrier that shielded the planet from the adverse effects of the sun's ultra-violet rays. This triggered some very unpleasant changes in the Earth's eco-system. Crops failed and sun-bathing became a pastime for the suicidally inclined. Doomsday looked very much to be on the cards.

Plans had existed for years to construct vast underground food and medico synthesisation plants. But successive governments, daunted by the costs, had each in turn quietly shelved them. Now, with public unrest running hand in hand with spiralling inflation, it was quite out of the question.

However, there is nothing like a good war or natural catastrophe to bring out the religion in people. And while the governments were growing bankrupt, the major churches of the day suddenly found that they had standing room only and that their coffers, so long empty, now brimmed to overflowing. Hence the underground plants, which synthesised food and medical products from waste and probed deeply into the Earth's core to tap new sources of mineral wealth, came to be built by the Big Three.

The Buddhists, the Fundamentalists and the Jesuits.

Of course, it's to be doubted whether these plants could possibly have supplied the needs of the Earth's continually increasing population. So when the Nuclear Holocaust Event occurred, and production suddenly outstripped demand, many attributed this to the foresight of God. And the Big Three, now sole suppliers of the world's needs, felt no need to contradict them.

The governments of the post-NHE world sought bravely to regain control, but found themselves in for some rather unpleasant surprises. In Washington, Supreme Commander North threw open the doors of the Nuclear Emergency Supply Silo to reveal a million cable-television sets. Outgoing President Wormwood's legacy to the post-nuclear age.

In an attempt to restore the status quo, he called together every remaining member of the American Armed Forces. The minutes of their meeting remain on record. But what the thirteen men had to say to one another doesn't make for an entertaining read.

As a fully paid-up Buddhist, Supreme Commander North wasn't slow to realize upon which side his synthabread was buttered. A quick call on the hotline to Buddha Biological and the re-allocation of one million TV sets secured him the token position of President Elect for life.

For their part, the boys at Buddha, incapable of distributing a million TVs worldwide, struck up lucrative deals with Fundamental Foods and Jesuit Inc. to dispose of two-thirds of their unexpected windfall. Shortly thereafter, these found their way into the bunkers of the holocaust survivors. And the rest is history.

The EYESPI modifications were added a few years later, 'In an attempt to raise standards and morale, offer incentive and engender healthy competition.' And competition, healthy or otherwise, was something that the Big Three, now each with its own TV station, had become increasingly more involved in. And it was the game show that became the hub of this competitive universe.

The Jesuits' *Auto-da-fé* show had its followers and the Fundamentalists' *Whoops, There Goes an Atheist* made a reasonable showing. But it was *Nemesis* which really caught the public's imagination.

Hosted by the Living God King himself, and hailed by its PR department as the Ultimate Terminal Experience, it was gameshow magic in the grand tradition. And often a great deal more.

Gloria Mundi pushed her way between the females who milled about the studio floor, mounted a short flight of steps and entered the Green Room. Here, in a somewhat soiled saffron three-piece, sat the golden boy himself.

Dalai Dan was looking a little the worst for wear. With difficulty he focused upon Gloria, his bloodshot orbs speaking eloquently enough of the previous night's revels, without going into any of the sordid details.

'You look like death,' Gloria observed. 'Been burning the temple candle at both ends again?'

'Piss off,' said the Dalai Lama, 'I'm meditating.'

'I would have thought you'd had enough warnings. You can't carry on like this.'

Dan stroked his shaven head. It needed a shave. 'Go fly a kite.'

'Pope Joan's ratings are up again. You're slipping.'

'I recall ordering a Tampa Sunrise.' He picked a nubbin of wax from his left ear.

'No more drinkies, you're on in five minutes.'

Dan turned the ball of wax between thumb and forefinger. 'Drink not only water, but take a little wine, for thy stomach's sake.'

'Wrong denomination, dear.' Gloria seated herself, across from the hungover holyman. Dan's eyes wandered as she crossed her impossibly long legs. She was painfully attractive. Tall, sleek, elegant and quite deadly. The kind of woman that left all but the most heroic of men drooling hungrily from a safe distance. Her skin was toned a soft powder blue, a perfect match for her eyes. Her black hair tumbled away to a waist, about which the thumb and forefingers of God's most favoured might almost meet. The remaining portions of her body all conformed to the unreasonable standards set for the heroine of some sword and sorcery novel.

'You are a prize schmuck,' said Gloria Mundi.

Dan pulled his eyes away from her legs. 'I never chose to become the Dalai Lama, you know,' he said with some bitterness. 'It's a burden rather than a pleasure. But I'm the real McCoy, and I would thank you to show a little respect once in a while.'

'Respect has to be earned,' Gloria replied, as the phrase has always been a favourite amongst women. 'The winning couple from last week are here. Don't you think you should speak to them?'

'What for? We aren't thinking of letting them survive another week, are we?'

Gloria shook her beautiful head. 'Do you remember

your eighty-second reincarnation?'

Dan made a thoughtful face. 'Vaguely, that's when I had to do a runner from the Red Chinese, wasn't it?' Gloria nodded. 'I remember wearing foolish glasses and giggling a lot, and,' Dan turned his third eye upon Gloria, 'I remember that the Maharishi got all the best girls.'

'I've got you on video, you used to talk a lot of sense back then.'

'What are you getting at?'

'What I'm getting at, as if you don't know, is that even in exile you were worshipped by millions as the Living God King.'

'I still am.'

'You had responsibilities. You still have.'

'Oh, very funny. The one hundred and fifty-third incarnation I might be, God's chosen representative on Earth I might be, but a cabbage I ain't. If you wish me to fulfil my responsibilities then allow me to go into spiritual retreat for about thirty years.'

'Duty then, you have a duty to the station.'

Dan closed his eyes and drew his trousered legs into a full lotus. He began to hum gently and before Gloria's eyes, slowly levitated towards the ceiling. It was a spectacle Gloria had witnessed before, but this made it no less unnerving.

'I'll talk to the winning couple myself,' she said, making a rapid departure from the Green Room.

She slammed the door and stalked back across the studio floor. As she approached the winning couple she was further distressed to find that the Dalai was already with them. He raised his Tampa Sunrise to her and smiled sweetly. 'Gloria,' he said, 'what kept you? Not been talking to yourself again I hope?'

6

And a rose smells sweetly when it's growing in manure.
Ivor Biggun

Back on Phnaargos the Time Sprout was holding court.

'Sixteenth generation, eobiont engram modification,' the wily veg explained, 'utilising the transperambulation of pseudo-cosmic anti-matter.'

'The what?' asked Mungo Madoc.

'Curve of space,' said the sprout. 'Time doesn't travel in straight lines. I thought everyone knew that.'

Executive heads bobbed up and down. 'Yes, indeedy,' said Diogenes 'Dermot' Darbo.

'Well, it's the first I've heard of it,' said Mungo.

'You see time doesn't really exist, it's an illusion. Relative of course.'

'Oh. Of course.' Mungo turned to face Fergus Shaman. 'Fergus, if this is a practical joke, I shall not be responsible for my actions.'

'Could be ventriloquism,' Garstang suggested. 'An uncle of mine had a singing turnip. Went distinctly quiet once the old bloke had kicked the bucket.'

'Yes, yes!' Mungo beat upon the table with his fists. 'My patience is not inexhaustible.'

'When you're all quite finished,' the sprout bobbed up and down, 'I will gladly enlarge upon any concepts that you might find . . . trying.'

'He has a certain eloquence,' said Lavinius Wisten. 'I like that in a sprout.'

Mungo Madoc made digging motions with an ethereal compost shovel. 'The floor is yours,' he told the loquacious veg.

'Well,' said the sprout, 'I'll keep it brief, it's all to do with the microcosm and the macrocosm. As above, so below, that sort of stuff. The infinite atom, the sprout, the planet, the sun, all spheres you see. You are all, no doubt, conversant with Phnaargian dogma, that the entire universe is nothing more than a pimple upon the nose of the deity.'

All present, barring the sprout, made the sacred sign, pinching their thumbs and forefingers to the tips of their noses.

'Then you will no doubt wish to expedite matters before the great one chooses to lance his boil.'

'Point taken,' said Mungo. 'We need waste no more time regarding the mechanics. Can you, with accuracy, convey a member of our team back to an exact location, at an exact time, on Earth?'

'A piece of peat. Although there may be one or two minor biological problems for the traveller accompanying.'

'Ah,' Mungo nodded meaningfully. 'Now this does surprise me.'

'Ironic extrapolations are quite wasted upon me. I merely state fact. The Phnaargian isn't designed to travel through time. He's the wrong shape for one thing. He will "pick things up" as he travels along.'

'What? Like germs, do you mean?'

'Knowledge,' said the sprout. 'We will be travelling at the speed of thought. So therefore on the same wavelength. He'll pick it all up, centuries of it. The accumulated knowledge of every intelligent being in the galaxy, that has ever lived, possibly even ever will live.'

'So when do we leave?' Mungo asked. 'Best get off, eh?'

'Slow down, the man who takes the trip and picks up all this knowledge will become . . .'

'Godlike,' said Mungo Madoc.

'Barmy,' said the sprout. 'Stone bonkers.'

'Ah,' said Mungo. 'I see.'

'As a hatter,' the sprout continued. 'Off his kookie, out of his tree . . .'

'Quite so.'

'Basket case.'

'Thank you.'

'Loony, dibbo, round the twist . . .'

'Thank you very much. And this will happen as he makes the journey back?'

'The journey back into the past is OK; it's the journey forward that will do for him. Blow his mind, freak him out, spring his . . .'

'Thank you! This matter will require a good deal of thought. Fergus, kindly take your little friend down to the lobby. I'm sure he'd like a glass of water, or something.'

'Virtually self sufficient, chief,' said the sprout. 'Metabolic rate merely ticking over, pseudopodium catered for.'

'The lobby!' shouted Mungo and he meant it.

The door sealed upon a sullen Fergus and a complaining sprout. Mungo smiled down at this team. They returned his gaze, with varying degrees of apprehension.

'This is a conundrum,' said Mungo Madoc. 'One, in fact, quite new to my experience. But it has potential. I like it.'

'But it isn't going to work,' Gryphus complained. 'In fact it's a load of old . . .'

'Now, now. I can see the problems. To achieve our end, we must dispatch one of our number back into the past. On his return he will be a headcase.'

'With delusions of Godhood,' sneered Gryphus.

'A Godhead case,' tittered Diogenes 'Dermot' Darbo. 'Indeedy.'

'Every problem has a simple solution. This one is just a matter of expendability.'

A great silence fell upon the boardroom. Silent prayers were offered up.

'It's all right.' Mungo raised a hand. 'I don't consider any of you expendable. We need a volunteer. Someone whom the station won't miss. Some insignificant little nonentity with ideas above his station.'

'Showtime,' said Jovil Jspht. 'For what it's worth.'

> 'He's a friend to the foe
> The star of the show
> The man we all know
> By his king-sized karma
> He's a breath of spring
> He's the living God King
> He's the Dalai . . . Dalai . . . Dalai
> Dalai La . . . ma . . .'

The Lamarettes were tonight stunningly clad in silver lamé slingbacks, matching gloves and diamanté ear-studs. Anything more and they would have been grossly overdressed.

As the Dalai materialized on stage, the applause lights flashed and the audience synthesiser went overboard. In homes above ground and homes beneath, prayer wheels span like football rattles and ring pulls popped from a million cans of Buddhabeer. In the control room Gloria bit her lip.

'Blessings be upon you.' The Dalai twirled upon his heel and made 'peace' signs. 'Inmost One here saying a real fine howdy doody and a big Buddha welcome to . . . wait for it . . .'

The vox pop crouched upon the edges of their make-shift seats . . .

'N E M E S I S!'

Lights flashed, sirens wailed, gongs were beaten. The Lamarettes fussed about the Dalai, who had fallen to the floor, as if possessed. 'Back to my suite, girls,' he giggled, 'I'll give you something king-sized to meditate on later.'

'I think I'll take my lunch hour now,' said Jovil Jspht. 'If you don't mind.'

'As you please,' Haff Ffnsh replied. 'But don't be late back.'

Jovil Jspht left the control room of Earthers Inc. and wandered down the organic corridor. Ahead of him the doors of the executive lift opened and Fergus Shaman, wearing a grim expression and cradling something in his arms, slouched out. The two men didn't exchange pleas-antries.

Jovil eyeballed the open lift doors. He'd never actually seen the upper floors of the spiral complex, his status didn't allow it. Jovil halted, the doors would close in a matter of seconds. Was it worth the crack? If he was discovered it would be a big number. Demotion. Goodbye pension scheme, hello compost shovel. In this world, as upon any other, chances were only taken by the nerveless few, success their preserve alone. To quote the motto of the Phnaargian Special Service 'Who Dares Wins'.

Jovil shook his head. The lift doors closed.

Mungo Madoc sniffed at the Destiny lily which grew from his lapel. 'So we are all agreed, it is a one-way trip for the chosen operative.'

Diogenes 'Dermot' Darbo made foolish chortling sounds. Gryphus Garstang rubbed his hands together. 'Sounds good to me,' he sniggered.

Lavinius Wisten raised a limp hand. 'How are we to ensure that the operative in question doesn't return from nineteen fifty-whatever-it-is?'

Mungo Madoc twirled his outrageous moustachios in a manner much beloved of old-time villains about to foreclose on the mortgage. 'Garstang, let me have your thoughts.'

Gryphus Garstang grinned wolfishly. 'Shouldn't be too hard to arrange, a neat little "magic box" with the words "return to Phnaargos" printed on it and a single button. He presses the button and . . .'

Outside in the executive corridor, a certain Jovil Jspht, hearing the buzz of conversation, pressed his ear to the boardroom door.

'All right.' Mungo Madoc took himself over to the picture window and gazed down upon sunny green Phnaargos. 'We are all agreed. We need a hero. A brave and fearless Phnaargian, willing to travel back into the past and change history. Prepared to risk all for truth, justice and the ratings.'

From where his ear was pressed, Jovil Jspht wasn't able to hear the laughter, only the applause.

'So,' Mungo continued, 'suggestions, gentlemen.'

'I think I know the very fellow.' Grypus Garstang held up a certain memorandum, which had appeared upon his desk, as upon many others, that very morning. 'If

I was to mention "Killer Maggots from the Earth's Core".'

Outside the boardroom Jovil Jspht puffed out his chest. So this was it, recognition at last. He had always known that his time would come, that his talents would one day receive the merit they deserved. This was going to be one in the eye for Haff Ffnsh. Oh, happy day.

'The ideal pillock,' said Mungo Madoc, but by this time Jovil Jspht was well on his way to the canteen.

There may very well be a moral here somewhere. But in the light of future events, it would be extremely hard to pin it down accurately.

Mungo Madoc buzzed down for some executive nose-bag and a magnum or two from the reserve stock, Jovil Jspht blew his whole week's luncheon vouchers on a belly-buster of heroic proportions and down upon Planet Earth certain others took their midday repast.

'Luncheon,' said Rambo Bloodaxe, 'and pre-cooked.'

Deathblade Eric poked around in the wreckage of Rex Mundi's burned out air car. 'The reactor's still intact. Non-contaminated meat. Shall I carve?'

'Certainly not, Eric. I can't abide dining alfresco. Kindly haul him back to the hotel.'

Rex Mundi's mortal remains were unceremoniously dragged from the crumpled cab and deposited in the back of Rambo's in-town runabout, a vehicle constructed from corrugated-iron and charred timber, camouflaged to re-semble a thrown-together transient's hut. Side slits housed hidden armoury and the whole caboodle was powered by a nuclear reactor, not dissimilar to the one Eric had now commandeered from Rex's defunct 801.

Rambo keyed the ignition and the hidden wheels plied their way along the rubble-strewn street, en route for the

Hotel California. Headquarters, high temple and Holiday Inn hideaway of the Devianti.

'A few prime cuts and then it's into the freezer for this boy,' said Rambo, swerving the vehicle to clip something which might have been a cat. 'That Rogan Josh is a decent enough cove.'

Eric opened Rex's purse. 'Ten credits, Josh said our lunch owes him!'

'Give him the lot, Eric. Money is the root of all evil, you know.'

'The lifeforce of God in action in the material world.'

'Forever the philosopher, Eric.'

'It's a gift,' said Deathblade Eric.

They were a likeable pair of rogues, these Devianti flesh-eaters. Well spoken, nicely mannered, and decently turned out. Personable young men.

Rambo was of old Sussex stock, with a triple-barrelled last moniker. Eric, the hereditary heir to the Lambton Lairdee, his extremely great great-grandfather having slain the famous Worm and been bunged the title in perpetuity by the king. Three hundred years of selective inbreeding had left its inevitable hallmark, but whatever they lacked in the chin department was adequately compensated for by their deportment and ingrained sense of style.

For instance, they always wore their radiation suits beneath their clothes, a vogue which hadn't as yet caught on amongst the general public, acid rain having the tendency to play havoc with one's mackintosh.

The Devianti favoured striped shirts, club ties, grey cords, Hunter wellingtons and Barbour jackets. Beneath their weatherdomes jaunty-looking tweed caps were the order of the day. Despite their unconventional lifestyle they considered it essential to keep up appearances. The manufacture of such upper-crust-schmutter had, needless to say, ceased fifty years before and so its 'just-bought' look paid a posthumous tribute to the exclusive tailors of old London Town.

It might logically have been presumed that the warrior bands of social outcasts currently stalking the streets would have come from the 'lower orders'. But not a bit of it. The 'lower orders' were all safely tucked up at home watching television. It was Rambo and his ilk who had become subject to Duke's Principle and were forced to take to the streets.

The upper classes had fared rather badly in the post NHE world. Without Wimbledon, the Royal Tournament, three-day events and *Gardener's World*, they couldn't actually bring themselves to watch TV. And so they became non-participants in the great EYESPI credit race. Those of them who left the bunkers made futile attempts to reclaim their ruined estates. But you just couldn't get the staff.

Soon, like closing credits, they faded from the screen.

The young, for their part, took to the antisocial behaviour which was their birthright, and bands like the Devianti were formed. Within their ranks, they maintained a strict social order, reasoning that when society was eventually restructured, it would be for them to reassume their natural place at the top and govern it. The fact that they had become the complete antithesis of this society totally escaped them.

These were, as the Bard of Mersey had once unknowingly predicted, 'strange days indeed'.

Rambo swung the car towards another cat, but the six-legged moggy danced nimbly aside. The in-town runabout bumped over the mangled wreckage of something which had seemed very important at the time it was built and trundled up to the door of the Hotel California.

'Home again, home again, jiggedy jig,' sang Eric, shinning down from the cab. 'Oh shit!'

'Language.' Rambo joined him at the rear of the runabout. It was empty.

'Well, bless my soul,' said the cannibal chief. 'This is most unexpected.'

'This is most unexpected,' said the smiling Jovil Jspht. 'Now let me see if I have it right. You have chosen me to travel back into the past and alter the Earth's history.'

Mungo Madoc nodded sagely. When put like that it did sound pretty ridiculous at best. 'We think you are the man for the job.'

'And indeed I am. So, I manifest myself as an angel before this Paisley.'

'Presley, Elvis Presley.'

'Convince him not to join the Army and then come straight back here.'

Mungo patted him upon the shoulder. 'What could be simpler?'

'Gosh.' Jovil flushed with sheer pride. 'An angel.'

'We will issue you with everything you will require. There are several videos in the archives made after Presley's death. They will say it all to him. Frankly we don't mind what you say to him. Just convince him not to join the Army. Leave the rest to us.'

'And once I'm done, I just press this little button.' Jovil reached for the black box which lay before him on the boardroom table.

Garstang hurriedly drew it beyond his reach. 'That's right, but not a minute sooner and only when you are a considerable distance away from Presley.'

Jovil looked puzzled. 'Why?' he asked.

'Because . . . because why?' Mungo gazed about at his execs. 'Because why, Garstang?'

'Because you must be on your own,' said the sprout, who had twigged exactly what was going on. 'Transient photons causing a cross polarisation of the interstellar overdrive. Anyone standing nearby would get sucked into the positronic trans-dimensional warp factor five graphic equaliser.'

'Exactly.' Mungo nodded approvingly.

'Sounds very complicated.'

Mungo nodded again. 'Oh, it is. Very.'

Jovil turned to the sprout. 'But what about you though?'

'I'll find my own way back, don't worry about me.'

'So, Mr Garstang here will fill you in on all the details, issue you with the bits and bobs and whatnot. Do you have any questions?'

Jovil shook his head, 'I can't think of any.'

'Good, well if you do, I'm sure Mr Garstang will set you straight. Won't you, Mr Garstang?'

'Indeed I will, sir.'

'So now,' Mungo drew Jovil to his feet, straightened up and saluted him. 'Good luck soldier. The future of the series rests in your hands. We applaud you.' The executive team put their hands together. On Phnaargos applause was considered the highest compliment or accolade that could possibly be paid to an individual. It meant that you had really made it. On twentieth-century Earth, the nearest equivalent would have been a guest appearance on *Wogan* or a libellous attack on your sexual habits by a Sunday newspaper.

'You can count on me.' Jovil Jspht stood rigidly to attention. There was a tear in his eye.

To further applause he left the boardroom in the company of Gryphus Garstang, who was carrying the black box at arm's length.

'Don't forget this,' Mungo plucked up the sprout and tossed it after them.

The boardroom door sealed and Mungo rubbed his palms together. 'I think that went remarkably well.'

Fergus Shaman shook his head doubtfully. 'I really must protest. You are going about this all the wrong way. It will end in disaster.'

'You would rather make the trip yourself, then?'

Fergus shifted uneasily. 'I'm not saying that. But blowing him up . . . something might go wrong.'

'The thing that worries me,' said Lavinius Wisten, 'is the fact that he never asked once whether the mission was dangerous.'

'He trusts us.'

'It will end in tears,' said Fergus.

'And another thing,' Wisten continued, 'that sprout, he cottoned on to what was on the go a bit fast. I wouldn't trust him as far as I could kick him.'

Mungo nodded vigorously. 'Now on that we are both agreed. I think we will have a little surprise waiting for friend sprout when he gets back.' He made knife and fork motions with his fingers.

Fergus leapt to his feet. 'You can't do that. The Time Sprout is a marvel of horticultural science. It will open up new vistas, whole new worlds.'

'It is a loose end,' said Mungo Madoc in no uncertain tone, 'and it will go down a treat, lightly boiled with just a dash of melted butter.'

Fergus Shaman buried his head in his hands and wept bitterly.

*

As the lift slithered obscenely down the yielding membrane tube, Jovil Jspht made little clicking sounds with his tongue and popped his fingers. It was true that he hadn't touched upon the possible dangers of the mission. But this was simply because he hadn't even given them a moment's thought. Far greater issues were at stake here. And anyway, how could anything possibly go wrong? He had become the Chosen One. The Saviour of the Series. The Man with the Mission!

And Jovil already had the whole thing planned out. He would return to the 1950s and sort out this Presley character, put him on the right track. There was no real problem there surely. And even if there was, he could always bung Presley the little black box, let him go and see for himself the mess he'd got everyone into. No problem. After all, he had no intention of using the black box himself. Once the Presley business was out of the way, he meant to get down to the real task at hand. The revitalization of the series! His own personal rewrite of the script!

Jovil did a big ear-to-ear job. And all set in the 1950s, it couldn't have worked out better if he had planned it himself. His very favourite period in Earth history. The golden age of science fiction. *Forbidden Planet, Them, The Quatermass Experiment*. Those were the days. The skies were full of UFOs, and every secret research establishment had a radioactive mutant skeleton in its cupboard. It was just perfect.

He'd give the Phnaargian viewing public something they would long remember. The rating topper to end all rating toppers. He could already see the blurbs.

Mankind faces its greatest ever threat.

Spawn of the nuclear age . . . Born of
the Bottomless Pit . . . can nothing
stop . . .
THE KILLER MAGGOTS
FROM THE EARTH'S CORE???

This was no accident of fate, no mere chance or coincidence. He had been singled out for this. It was Divine
intervention.

'Thank you, thank you, God,' chirruped Jovil Jspht,
pressing his thumb and forefinger to his nose and making
the sacred squeeze. 'Thank you very much.'

Above and beyond all this, the deity in question examined the tip of his holy hooter in a shaving mirror the
size of a billion galaxies. 'You're a ripe-looking little
bugger,' he said.

7

All the world is just a stage and all the men and women merely players.

Elvis Presley

Rex Mundi peeped out of the discarded bio-hazard drum where he had taken up temporary residence. He saw Rambo Bloodaxe kick the rear of the in-town runabout. He saw Rambo Bloodaxe kick the rear of Deathblade Eric and finally he saw Rambo Bloodaxe kick at the rear of a six-legged moggy, miss and fall heavily to the oily sod. Rex stifled a snigger and felt himself for probable fractures. He appeared to be in remarkably fine fettle, all things considered. His radiation suit was somewhat charred, but its heat-resistant inner lining had spared him a roasting. His weatherdome was badly cracked, though, and the rancid stench of the outside world was all too apparent to his recently-rooted nostrils.

Through the dome's blackened glass Rex watched Eric help his chum up from the dirt. The two Devianti gazed bitterly up and down the ruined highway. Threw up their arms, cursed profusely and slouched into the Hotel California. Breathing as shallowly as possible, the lad in the toxic drum considered his lot. It wasn't much of a lot. He had a rough idea as to which 'major redevelopment area' he was in, and it was a long hike from Nemesis Bunker. And although he was hidden, he was still inside the grounds of the Devianti headquarters, which was no cause for immediate merriment. The area might well be guarded by any number of fiendish devices. Sonic wave press-pads that could shake a man's brains down his nostrils before he even realized that he had been rumbled. Invisible laser-mesh fencing, one step forward and you were diced meat. Rex's imagination rose to new heights of improbability. He was in deep shit here and no mistake. He gave his chronometer a bit of perusal. It was jammed at two-thirty p.m. which meant that at the very most he had an hour before darkness fell and the night rains began. And God knows what came out to feed. He was in an unholy mess and no mistake about it.

Rex had never had a lot of truck with religion. The pre-packaged theology beaming endlessly from the terminal screens seemed to him just a trifle unconvincing. Whether he was alone in this or whether the entire viewing public shared his doubts, Rex had no idea. Perhaps he was the last atheist. If so, then God was about to be well chuffed.

'Dear old God,' prayed Rex Mundi. 'Please get me out of here.'

It had been considered essential by Mungo Madoc that Jovil's departure towards the 1950s be accompanied by the correct amount of fuss and bother. Or the least as much as could be inexpensively mustered up during the few short hours it took to copy the archive footage of Elvis's sorry last years and program them into a portable monitor. Thus the board hobbled together certain new orders of merit and scrolls of honour from what immediately came to hand. These were solemnly presented to the would-be time traveller with much due reverence and many a hearty hand-clap.

The actual send-off was a somewhat private affair, Jovil's offer to have the entire event broadcast live across Phnaargos being politely, yet firmly, declined. Amidst thunderous applause he climbed on to the boardroom table, sprout in one hand, black box in the other, portable monitor and packed lunch in a jaunty knapsack slung across his shoulders.

'In order that this momentous occasion be long re-membered,' quoth the young buffoon. 'I have prepared a short speech.' Beneath their smiles the executive board ground its collective teeth. 'For such a cause I go fearlessly backwards.' Jovil gestured with his box-bearing hand, which had the board clutching at their failing hearts. 'Mere words cannot express my gratitude for your having chosen me to go upon this mission. Thus I will let my deeds speak for themselves.'

The dangerous ambiguity of this escaped the board, who sought successfully to drown out the remainder of his speech with further thunderous applause.

'Then I go.' Jovil raised the Time Sprout above his head and stuck a noble pose.

'You do indeed, chief,' the sprout added. And indeed he did.

'Gentlemen,' said Mungo Madoc, tapping his trowel of office upon the table top, 'gentlemen, we are in big schtuck here.' Executive heads bobbed up and down in agreement. At the far end of the table Diogenes 'Dermot' Darbo said, 'Yes, indeedy.'

'Viewing figures have now sunk to a point beneath which the . . .' Fergus Shaman turned the first page of his minutes and viewed with great interest the words he had but minutes before penned upon them. They came as something of a revelation to him.

It had been his conviction, now amply proven, that

upon the sprout's departure into the past all memories of it here in present would be instantly erased. After all, if the sprout was in the 1950s then the year 2050 hadn't yet occurred, or something like that. It was all extremely complicated and Fergus didn't pretend to understand the most part of it. This was only an initial experiment and its full potential had yet to be fully realized. But so far he appeared to be correct. He scanned the pages of notes and nodded in silent satisfaction.

Mungo for his part, continued with the speech, which unknown even to himself, he had previously made several hours before. Fergus listened to it with interest. But the more the speech unfolded the more an un-comforting thought began to nag Fergus. And the more it nagged the more Fergus tried to reason with it. But the more he reasoned with it, the louder and clearer did it nag. 'If the mission to 1958 had been a success,' nagged the thought, 'and the series successfully revived, then this meeting shouldn't be taking place and Mungo shouldn't be saying all the things he is still saying. So therefore the mission can't have been a success. In fact something must have gone disastrously wrong.'

'Oh dear,' thought Fergus Shaman, 'oh dear, oh dear, oh dear.'

A cold bead of lime green perspiration crept from his hairline across his forehead and down to the end of his nose. Here it captured the light of Rupert and shone like a rare jewel. What on Earth had happened?

Elvis Aron Presley, the man and the legend, looked upon all that he had made and found it good. The King of Rock and Roll raked his manicured fingers through his magnificently greased coiffure and adjusted his quiff. Just so. 'Uh, huh,' said he, winking lewdly

74

into the rhinestoned shaving mirror. 'Mighty fine.'

The time was a little after nine of the evening clock. The evening in question being that of the twenty-third of March, the year being 1958. Just twelve hours before Elvis would take the draft, chuck up his credibility and take that first big step towards a terrible end. But for now he was young, snake-hipped, gifted and sublimely rich: Elvis smiled crookedly in the manner that had weakened the knees of an entire generation of American girldom. Not a dry seat in the house, as one wag most tastefully put it. Curled his lip and confirmed that every thing was, 'Mighty fine.'

But then it happened. The impossible, the unthinkable . . . the noble brow crumpled with anguish, the handsome features were clouded, the sensual mouth gaped in horror. It couldn't be . . . it couldn't . . . The King's eyes focused, blinked, refocused. He leant forward, gazed with undisguised fear and loathing at the terrible sight made flesh before him.

There was a zit on his chin!

Elvis fell back from the mirror and sank blubbering into a gold lamé guitar-shaped lounger. Twelve hours away from the cameras of the world's press and this. He'd have to cancel. He couldn't face his public with a hideous pus-filled bubo hanging off his famous face. He groped for the house phone, there was still time for surgery; his personal skin specialist was downstairs in the medical wing.

There was a bang. It was small by many standards but quite to the point. Elvis was blasted backwards from his lounger, his monogrammed slippers spiralling away upon separate trajectories. Horrid garish fixtures and fittings, all of which will remain undescribed to spare the reader, rocked and tumbled, many mercifully breaking beyond all hope of repair. Several unopened sacks of fan-mail burst asunder to fill the room with a papery snowstorm. You'd better not mess with the US mail, my friend.

Jovil Jspht rose to his feet, coughing and spluttering. 'Hello there,' he called. 'Mister Paisley, I bring you greetings from a distant star. Mister Paisley, are you there? Hello?'

The board meeting at Earthers Inc. finally broke up amidst the usual turmoil of accusation, recrimination, acrimony and general beastliness. Suggestions had been forthcoming from the board but Mungo wasn't impressed. He gave them a single day to come up with something positive, or avail themselves of a pair of heavy boots and a manure shovel.

Fergus edged away down the corridor and made for the archives. He had to know what had happened. If anything actually had. It was possible that the sprout hadn't made it back to 1958. It was possible that the whole thing was a delusion. It was possible that he was going out of his mind.

Fergus pressed his palm to the security panel, the door retracted and merged with the living wall. Fergus passed into the wonderworld which constituted the beating heart of Earthers Inc. and indeed the very planet. The complex was vast. Even though Phnaargian horticology sought ever towards the miniaturization of data storage, the task of reseeding millions of previous episodes was one too costly and gargantuan even to contemplate. The cellular pods, housing the countless centuries of human history, down to the most personal detail, spread away into hazy perspective. Rising to every side in shimmering spires. Billions of brightly shining globes blossoming one upon another. Pulsing gently, maintained at a constant temperature and lovingly tended by numerous minions, trained from birth to know no other life. Organic walkways flowed between the spires merging into one another.

Fergus rode down the central throughway. Here and there he passed the minions, long of beard and wild of eye. Each was dedicated to some particular year, month, day or hour, dependent upon their grade. They never conversed with one another and they paid not the slightest heed to Fergus. As he drifted downstream towards 1958, Fergus pondered upon the wonder of it all. But as that soon gave him a headache he jacked the bugger in.

The year in question rose up before him and Fergus stepped from the throughway to enter its core. Light flowed into it in many coloured shafts, kniving down between the shimmering globes. Ridley Scott would have been very much at home. Ahead, seated before his console with his back to Fergus and the coming and going amidst the light show, was the year's custodian.

'Good day.' Fergus affected a cheery smile. Getting anything out of these lads was always a serious struggle. 'I really must apologize to you for this rude interruption. But something of a most serious nature has come up.' The custodian ignored him. 'Hmm.' Fergus crept slowly forward and lightly tapped the gent upon his padded shoulder. 'If I might just trouble you for a moment.'

The custodian turned slightly in his chair and then slid gracefully from it to assume an uncomfortable twisted posture upon the floor. His eyes looked up at Fergus but they saw nothing. The custodian was quite dead. A feeling of terrible panic welled up within Fergus as he knelt to examine the corpse. Its fingers were charred and the hair stood up upon the crown of its head. Electrocuted? Circuit malfunction? Static overload? Fergus rose to view the console screen. To his horror the graphics spelt out the very date he had come to review. And across the centre of the screen big red letters flashed on and off. They read:

ACCESS DENIED. ALL FURTHER 20TH CENTURY DATA IS NOW BEING ERASED. FAILSAFE IN OPERATION. DON'T TOUCH THAT DIAL.

8

A good performance is more important than life itself.
Iggy Pop

'Surely you can get something.' Ms Vrillium's hatchet nose sliced the air. 'Those air cars cost a packet. What was the last report he made before he went off-screen?'

Maurice Webb, who was quite new to this kind of thing and who had only got the job because word of his remarkably large willy had reached the ear of the female operations manager, scratched at his groin and looked worried.

'We had his final report at—' he tapped at his terminal '—two o'clock, the name of Rogan Josh and a request that twenty-seven credits be placed in his account. He called in from the car park of the Tomorrowman Tavern.'

'And then?'

'And then he flew north for about five kilometres and apparently struck some overhead powerlines.'

'Which weren't logged into the in-car computer.'

'Apparently not.'

'And why might that be, do you think?'

Maurice cringed. 'Lack of interdepartmental co-operation perhaps. I haven't been able to identify the culprits as yet.' Ms Vrillium cracked her knuckles meaningfully. 'But,' Maurice went on, 'I wasted no time. I immediately dispatched two search vehicles to seek out the wreckage and any possible survivors.'

'Very good.' Ms Vrillium patted the young man on the shoulders. 'Very fast thinking.'

'Yes,' Maurice agreed. 'I thought so.'

Ms Vrillium smiled. The effect upon Maurice was very much what it had been upon Rex. 'And these search vehicles, they have the location of the powerlines pro- grammed into their guidance systems, I trust.'

'Ah,' groaned Maurice Webb. 'Now that you come to mention it . . .'

Rex heard the sounds of the approaching craft. He peeped from his toxic hideyhole and saluted the murky heavens. 'Bravo God,' called Rex. 'You don't waste a lot of time, do you?'

The two explosions came fast upon one another. A double mushroom cloud rose beyond the Hotel California. Rex Mundi, the noted atheist, took to his heels. He climbed into the cab of the Deviantis' in-town run- about, jiggled the joystick, thrummed the controls and made a very well orchestrated getaway.

Deathblade Eric and Rambo Bloodaxe, galvanized into action by the sounds of more falling fodder, issued from the hotel just in time to see Rex making off with their car. Rambo kicked himself in the ankle.

'Fair gets a fellow's dander up, does this,' he observed as he hopped about.

'It surely do,' his companion agreed, 'it surely do.'

Merrily he rolled along. Rex whistled station ditties as he steered his way between this and that, and around the other. Luck, if not God, seemed for once to be actually on his side. The two approaching craft, he rightly surmised, had been sent out by the station in search of his remains. As they had met with a fate similar to his own, it seemed reasonable to assume that the crash hadn't been his fault. He wasn't going to get the blame for blowing up one of their precious air cars. In fact he would probably be able to claim some kind of compensation. The situation held all manner of engaging possibilities. Once he was safe back at Nemesis, of course.

The grim monotone of the old town sector passed him by on either side. The buildings were ancient, their faces blurred by the acid rains. Rex knew nothing of this area other than it, like everywhere else, was scheduled for redevelopment. It was evident, even from the sorry ruins which remained, that this had once been a thriving neighbourhood. But what it had once been called and where it in fact was, in relation to anywhere else, was anyone's guess. Geography was a dead science.

Rex recalled the time that his Uncle Tony had shown him something he referred to as 'A Map of the World'. He had pored over the coloured splodges, saying that these were countries and that millions of people had once lived in them. 'Different races,' he said. The whole concept had had Rex enchanted. That a sheet of paper could represent anywhere that it was possible to go, and somehow show you how to get there. Rex had asked the old man how large he thought the world might be. But Uncle Tony merely shrugged helplessly and replied that he had really no idea. And when Rex asked to be shown exactly where they were on the map, he had shaken his head, saying that he didn't know. Then he had wept.

Rex couldn't remember the map in any detail, and possession of such artefacts was illegal anyway. So it was still a mystery. All he knew of the world was that it was flat, rectangular and being redeveloped.

Rex hunched over the controls and squinted into the gloom. Perhaps there never had been countries. He felt sure that if he just drove and drove all he would ever find was simply more and more of just the same.

He switched on the spotlight atop the vehicle. Night was beginning to fall. And so now were his spirits. Rex swerved suddenly to avoid something scaly and un-wholesome which limped across the trackway before him. He was growing very tired and coming to the dire conclusion that he was also growing very lost. The night rain began to sizzle upon the vehicle's roof. It spattered on to the windscreen, drawing blackened tearstreaks down the plexiglass. Further travel would soon be out of the question. Habitation, sanctuary or whatever, was now very much the order of the evening. Rex squinted. It was growing as black as closedown. No lights, not a nothing. Press on a little, what else could he do? The runabout trundled into a pothole and Rex felt some little nagging doubts regarding his future. The filters on his weatherdome had given up the ghost and he had no replacements. The night didn't smell good.

The rain now fell in poisonous torrents. Lightning zipped and flashed, offering chances Rex felt disinclined to take. He pushed the runabout out of gear and switched off the fission drive. He was buggered.

'God,' said Rex, 'about this afternoon . . .'

But he didn't get any further. In between the lightning breaks something else was flashing. Colourfully. Rex didn't take it in at first, but when he did, a grim smile found its way amidst his damp stubble. The light went

on . . . off . . . on . . . off . . . on . . . off . . . the way some
of them do. And this one spelt out MORROWMA TAV.

The sweeping drive up to Gracelands was chock-a-block.
Glorious 1950s black and white police cars were parked
where they had slewed. Front wheels deeply dug into
the plastic turf. Lots of flashing lights flashed, pressmen
in trenchcoats with big cameras and fedoras milled about
the mock Grecian pillars and asked to be 'given a break'.
Ambulances stood, their rear doors yawning. Fat policemen, or cops, as they were then known, displayed their
armpit sweat and called everyone 'mac'. It was all jolly
good fun, although the attention to period detail left
much to be desired. One pressman lit his cigar with a
disposable gas lighter, which was wrong for a start. And
the aerials on the police cars were too modern. The cops'
hair was too long, but you have to expect that.

Elvis Presley didn't have much to say for himself. But
under the circumstances, he could hardly be blamed. He
had been bound tightly, hand and foot, gagged with a
lurex sock and hooded with a US mailbag. He lay face
down in a flower-bed, where for those who are interested,
certain flowers bloomed completely out of season.

Jovil Jspht pressed aside the leaves of a privet im-
aginatively pruned into the shape of a guitar. Behind this,
he and the captured king were hiding. 'There seems to
be no end of fuss going on,' Jovil observed.

'Can't see from down here, chief. Give us a hand up,
eh?' Jovil picked up the sprout and pointed him towards
the confusion. 'Pardon me for saying this, chief. And
shoot me down in flames if you think I'm on a wrong'n,
but surely that is a 1965 Harley Davidson.'

Jovil nodded thoughtfully. 'There's something wrong
all the way round. None of this rings true. What do you

reckon?' The sprout hesitated so Jovil gave it an urgent squeeze. 'Well?'

'Well, give me your impression. What does it look like to you?'

Jovil bit his lip. 'It looks like a film set,' he said slowly.

'Don't it just? And check out the hedge.' Jovil did so. 'Artificial.'

He made a perplexed face. 'I don't get it. We are in 1958, aren't we?'

'We're in 1958. But I don't know if it's the real one or not. It's more like a memory than the real thing. Perhaps when you actually go back in time things aren't the way they are supposed to be. Possibly when the present becomes the past it sort of decays. Gets all jumbled together. Fragments. The further back you go the more confused you find it has become.'

'Sounds feasible,' Jovil agreed. 'So what about him?' He gestured with his free hand towards the hooded Presley, who was starting to put up a struggle.

'He certainly looks like the real Mr McCoy. But listen, I really do think that now might well be the time for getaway rather than conjecture.'

'Yes, I think you're right.' Jovil thrust the sprout into his top pocket, dragged the prone Presley to his feet and bundled him across his shoulder. He stooped to pick up the black box and the portable monitor. Struggling manfully beneath the combined weight, he limped down a gentle incline towards further outcroppings of ersatz hedgery.

'Now why do I just know that there is an empty car with the keys left in the ignition, just beyond that hedge?' Jovil asked.

'Probably for the same reason I do, chief,' came the muffled reply.

84

'Best go with the flow, eh?'

The executive bar at Earthers Inc. was yet another triumph from the trowel of Capability Crabshaw. A splendid neo-gothic gazebo of a place, which swelled in carbunclesque fashion from an upper region of the great spiral tower and chased the sunlight. It was divided into elegant bowers, each made gay by delicate fountains. These cast scented water across a myriad tiny glass domes. Each of these emitted a soft melodic tone. But the beauty of all this was currently lost upon Fergus Shaman. Like the legendary 'lawn' joke of old, Fergus was half-cut. He peered into the bell of his cocktail lily and sighed plaintively. Fifty floors below him a custodian lay dead before a violently flashing console.

Someone had committed murder within the headquarters of the biggest TV station in the galaxy, and introduced . . . what? Fergus pondered on it. Introduced some kind of virus, perhaps, into the cell system. And that someone had to be Jovil Jspht. There could be no other plausible explanation. And the only individual upon the entire planet who knew this terrible truth was he, Fergus 'Oh, God's nose, what have I done?' Shaman. And what had he done? Jovil was obviously a basket-case, barking mad.

A waitress clad in a single figure-hugging sheath of vat-grown moss approached. 'Would you care for another, Mr Shaman?' Under normal circumstances Fergus would have made instantly with the improper suggestions, being something of a ladies' man. But tonight he was just not up to it.

'Same again,' he mumbled, without looking up. 'And make it a large one, please.'

The siren turned huffily upon a five-inch root heel and

wiggled away in a purposeful manner. The lost soul sank into further miseries. Big trouble was coming. Had already come, for all he knew. With no way to access the storage cells there was no way of knowing what Jovil might be up to. Had been up to. The waitress returned, displaying considerably more cleavage and a good deal of uncovered thigh. She slid his drink towards him. Fergus gazed up between her bosoms. 'Do you watch *The Earthers*?' he asked.

The siren shrugged. 'It's not compulsory, is it?'

'No, I just wondered.'

'I do some times. But . . .'

'But what?'

The young woman stretched. As she did so the sheath of moss parted in certain key areas. It was eroticism unfettered.

'Well?' Fergus asked.

'Well. It's dead dull, isn't it? All those scabby people in those ghastly little bunkers. There's no glamour, no romance. It just goes on and on and on . . .'

'Hold it right there,' cried Fergus. 'What did you say?'

'I said it just goes on and on and on.'

'Nothing's changed.' Fergus sprang to his feet and did a foolish little dance. 'Nothing's changed. Did you see it today?'

'Yeah. I caught the end before I came on shift. Wanted to watch *Nemesis*. The Dalai is the only thing worth watching.'

'Nothing's changed.' Fergus punched at the sky. 'He can't have done anything. Perhaps he got killed on the way.'

'No, he was on tonight. There's a new theme song. It goes: this is the time . . . this is the place . . . the time to face . . .'

86

'You really do have a cracking pair of charlies,' Fergus observed. 'What time do you get off your shift?'

'Ten,' the siren replied.

The car was exactly where Jovil knew it would be. Opening the boot, or trunk, as it was then known, Jovil deposited his struggling cargo therein. Slamming down the lid he joined the sprout, who was propped upon the dashboard.

'Where to?'

'Go with the flow, chief.' Jovil did so. He twisted the key and pressed the car into gear. 'It's a dream,' he said as the 1960-Pontiac Firebird sped along the deserted highway. 'I couldn't know how to drive this car, could I? It's got to be all a dream.'

'I have been giving the matter some considerable cogitation. But as yet I'm unable to form any convincing postulations. There is a turn off to the right along here. I believe.'

'I think so.' Jovil spun the wheel and the car sped down another deserted road. Rain began to fall. In the distance a dark building loomed. A sign flashed on and off. It said THE BATES MOTEL.

Rex Mundi steered the in-town runabout towards the flashing sign and entered the car park of the Tomorrowman Tavern. He drew to a halt next to a certain Rigel Charger. The property, he now knew, of a certain Rogan Josh. Near at hand was also a Buddhavision security craft. Broad bodied, black and sinister. Its darkness relieved only by the station logo. Three red tadpoles chasing each other's tails. 'A-ha,' thought Rex Mundi. 'A free ride home unless I am very much mistaken.'

Rex smiled crookedly. Things were going to work out

OK. As he was a little loath to brave the elements in his present condition he rooted about in the cab's storage compartments. A pristine-looking Barbour and one of Rambo's best caps came to the half light. Quite the business. Rex put them on over his radiation suit. Very dashing.

He was about to scramble down from the cab when he saw them. Light flared through the open doorway of the tavern. Figures moved. Two burly forms dragging a far lesser form between them. The lesser form was struggling but his cause was a lost one. A burly form clubbed him from behind and he stumbled forward to splash into the muck.

Rex cranked down the side window to get a better look. The fallen figure was unmistakably that of Rogan Josh. The others Buddha security. One of these stepped forward and performed a quick sadistic act upon the fallen man. Rex winced. Then the two thugs dragged Rogan to his feet and as Rex watched, dumb with disbelief, began to rip off his clothing. Josh pleaded for his life, but his cries were ignored. The acid rain fell unceasingly. The now naked man began to scream. In the lightning flares Rex could see his attackers laughing beneath their weatherdomes.

Rogan stumbled about trying to protect his naked flesh from the scalding rain. Rex watched in horror. Blood began to flow. Rex sank down in his seat and covered his face. And then there was a crash against the front screen. Rex looked up fearfully and stared full into the face of Rogan Josh. Bone showed through the torn skin of his cheeks, one eye appeared melted in its socket. Rogan's fist drummed against the windscreen. Then weakened. The face sank away and was gone. The rain smashed down. Rogan Josh was dead.

The side door of the runabout was torn open. A terrific figure thrust the barrel of an automatic weapon into Rex's face. A voice spoke on the open channel. 'Rambo Blood-axe,' it said. 'We've been looking for you.'

9

When you hear music, after it's over, it's gone into the air.
You can never capture it again.
Eric Dolphy

His divine holiness. The umpteenth reincarnation. The living God King and golden boy of the moment, Dalai Dan, rolled back his sleeve collar and pressed a silver disc to his left wrist. The chemical compound penetrated his skin and was absorbed into his bloodstream. Dan sank back into the settee cushions and took a deep breath. Coloured balls popped behind his eyes and a landscape of unformed shape rolled out before him into oddball odd. His right hand sought out the headset and he dragged the slim grey crescent over his head, feeding the dark end-beads into his ears. The holophonic sound gave him headbutts. Upon the turntable of the antique holophon a disc of black plastic turned at seventy-eight revolutions a minute. The system's pick-up arm moved gently up and down and fed its sonic messages into the bank of electronical hocus-pocus. Enhancing, upmoding, restructuring. What came out of the dark beads and entered the holyman's head was a whole new world.

'Well since my baby left me, I've found a new place to dwell,' sang a voice which was ribbons of ice, frayed at the ends and breaking into wavering star clusters. 'It's down at the end of lonely street at Heartbreak Hotel.'

*

'We don't get a lot of visitors now. What with the new highway and all,' said Norman Bates. 'You can have any room you like.' He turned pensively and selected a key from the board. 'Number three.' There was a stuffed owl on the wall. Somehow Jovil knew that Norman was an amateur taxidermist.

'All on your own here?' he asked. But Norman appeared distracted.

'Just get the key,' whispered the sprout. 'And let's get that sucker out of the trunk before he suffocates.'

Norman Bates parted with the key and then parted company, wandering off towards a large old house which stood halfway up a hill.

Jovil opened the trunk. Elvis was still there, bound and gagged. Only now he was dressed in a gold lamé suit, the hood was gone and his hair was in perfect shape.

'This is all making me very uneasy.' Jovil hauled the hostage from the car and dragged him into the motel room. The room was grim enough. There was a chair, a bedside table with lamp. A single bed, a worn rug. All were in shades of black and white. The ensuite bathroom was spotless, but the shower lacked its curtain.

'I'm going to take off your gag.' Jovil sat Elvis upon the bed. 'If you make a fuss I will strike you hard. Do you understand?'

Elvis nodded. Jovil removed the gag. Elvis spat out flecks of lurex.

'Who the fuck are you?' he asked.

'I am Jovil Jspht.' The time traveller bowed slightly. 'I come from a distant star.'

'You scrubbing around the guardian angel bit then, chief?' a muffled voice enquired.

'Seems a mite redundant under the circumstances.'

92

Elvis listened to this exchange. He was more than a little confused. 'You some kind of schizo?'

Jovil shook his head and pulled out the Time Sprout. 'I come from another world. Honest. Don't you ever go to the movies?' He placed the sprout on the pillow.

'Where's your ray gun, then?'

'My ray gun? Oh, I see. Just stay there a minute and I'll show you something that might convince you.' Jovil strode from the room, leaving Elvis to spit sock. He returned to the car where he pulled out his knapsack. As he clicked the driver's door shut, he paused for a moment. The car was now a 1958 Plymouth. Jovil made a worried face and hurried back to the motel room. Here he swept the nasty tablelamp aside and set up the monitor. 'This is going to come as a bit of a shock to you but I feel you should see it just the same.'

'Is that a General Electric or one of those new Jap jobs?'

'It's an Abendroth Triple D,' said the Time Sprout informatively. 'Self-contained bio-system. Audio and visual through binary intrapolation of pseudopodia. It's organic yet non-sentient. Although there are well-founded arguments in favour of it enjoying some primitive state of being.'

'Thank you.' Jovil tinkered with the monitor. 'But I think your explanations will like as not confuse him. They do me.'

A sudden look of enlightenment appeared unexpectedly upon the King's youthful face. He leant towards Jovil and whispered into his ear. 'If you untie me, I will help you kill the . . . you know . . .'

'I do?'

Elvis made eye movements towards the sprout. 'The alien. I'm getting this now, it's got you under some kind of mind control. Just untie me. I know Karate.'

'Roll the movie chief. Let's get this over and done with.'

Jovil stroked a module and stepped back from the monitor. Light whirled up forming a broad image which hung in the air.

'Holy shit,' croaked Elvis. 'I gotta get me one of these doodads.'

'Just watch.'

Elvis did so, and what he saw during the next half hour he didn't like one little bit.

The room Rex Mundi now occupied was tiled throughout with octagonal mirrors. It lacked furniture but for the steel chair into which the naked Rex was strapped. The floor was also mirror, but reflection was made difficult by the large amount of congealed blood splashed about it. The room smelt bad. It smelt of stale sweat, it smelt of fear. Rex stared up at his own image. It didn't please him. Small white discs adhered to sensitive areas. These shone out amongst the grime which coated his body. He felt terror but also a strange self-loathing. A sense of total worthlessness.

A voice crackled down to him through an unseen intercom. 'Bloodaxe, Rambo Bloodaxe. High priest of the sub-cult Devianti. We have no wish to prolong this interview. So to spare yourself the prolonged agony and we the inevitable arguing with the management over waiting time, it might just be simpler all round if you answered the questions without delay.'

'As elected representative of the interrogation and security sub-committee I take exception to that remark,' came a second voice. 'There is no need to hurry. Give the gentleman a jolt or two as a little taster.'

'Hold on,' cried Rex. 'I'm feeling in a particularly talkative mood at present.'

'Good boy,' said the first voice. 'Now your chosen moniker is Rambo Bloodaxe, yes?'

'Well, actually no. There seems to have been some mis—' The pain hit him from every side. Every nerve ending was being torn from his body at the same time. 'Yes, yes,' Rex screamed, 'Bloodaxe, yes.'

'Good boy. Easy when you've got the knack, isn't it?'

'You had the volume turned right down,' the second voice said. 'He couldn't have felt a thing. Whack it up a couple of notches.'

'No. No.' Rex yelled back. 'It's working just fine, honestly. What else would you like to know?'

'How many in your chapter?'

Rex could only guess. 'About twelve?'

'Good,' said the first voice, which pleased Rex no end. 'Names?'

'Deathblade Eric . . .'

'Yes.'

'Er . . .' Rex came apart at the seams. Pain comes in many colours; this came in all of them. 'Vile Tony Watkins . . . Killer McKee . . . Syd the Slayer . . .' Where they came from Rex had no idea but they poured from his mouth in a great unstoppable torrent. When he was done the voice said, 'Correct.'

Rex bit his tongue, his body shook uncontrollably. Correct?

'Now we come to the important part. What do you know about . . .'

Rex spoke rapidly. 'Get-my-sister-Gloria-Mundi-you-have-got-the-wrong-man-I-don't-know-anything-about-any—' His unseen tormentor cranked up the volume and then the pain left Rex. It occurred to him almost at once that he was dying. Had died. Everything was gone.

He was staring down at himself. But he wasn't alone. A cool soft palm stroked his forehead. A face stared into his. And such a face. She was beautiful. A golden aura encircled her head.

'An angel,' Rex gasped.

'You're such a pet,' the Goddess replied.

'And that's about it.' Jovil Jspht switched off the monitor and the motel room fell back into monochrome. 'Do you want to see any of it again?' Elvis shook his brain-stormed head rapidly. 'A dismal end by any account,' sighed Jovil.

'Gross.' Elvis spoke in a strangled whisper. 'How did I get that gross? And that sweaty?'

'Not a pretty sight, eh? Listen, do you want something to eat?'

'No, I don't! Something to drink.'

'Good idea. I'll go round to the reception and see what I can find. While I'm away the "alien" here will put you straight on the plan. Then you can do as you please really.' Jovil slipped the gag back over Presley's mouth. 'Nothing personal,' he said.

Jovil locked the motel room door behind him and slipped down the darkened veranda. A wan light showed through an unwashed window. There was a chill in the air. Jovil knocked at the door. The sound echoed, hollow. Norman Bates must have turned in for the night. Jovil tried the door. It swung in. A single naked lightbulb dangled above the reception desk. Jovil checked the place out. Beneath the desk he unearthed a bottle of Kentucky Bourbon. This was either half full or half empty depending how you felt about it. Jovil unscrewed the cap and took a slug. Wiping the back of his hand across his lips he went 'ah' and took another.

Just along the darkened veranda an old woman with a blood-stained kitchen knife turned the pass key and pushed open the door to room number three.

Rex refocused his eyes. 'Gloria?' His sister struck him a second time.

'Wake up,' she demanded. Rex did so. The security men were removing the white discs from his skin, leaving behind horrid red weals. 'Get him up and hose him down. He smells disgusting. Oh God, he's messed himself.'

The security men hastened to oblige, looking far from happy.

'Is this going to affect our bonus payments?' one asked. Gloria glared at him daggers.

Rex had never taken a bath before. Never even seen one except on the Food Operas. If this one was typical, then baths were a very lavish thing indeed and it wasn't surprising the vox pop never got a look at them. He lazed in the hot scented water. The bath was a bulbous glass dish set into the opaline floor. The bathing chamber was sumptuous. Carven sofas of ancient design swelled with plush cushions. Amber light fell in rich pools. Welcoming towels hung upon heated chromium tubes. A large terminal with an elaborate EYESPI broadcast news. Rex felt disinclined to watch. His current interest lay with his feet which floated magically before him. Rex sank lower into the water. Squeezing soap deliciously between his palms. The froth overflowed his fingers. The image of the tiny pills of caked fat which arrived with the weekly provisions, hands and faces for the use of, clouded his pleasure for but a moment. He allowed his body to float to the surface and applied soap to his penis.

'When you've quite finished wanking,' said the voice of Gloria Mundi, whose face now occupied the terminal screen, 'your presence in my apartment would be appreciated.'

Rex submerged slowly. All things must pass, he thought, philosophically.

He gnawed upon an exotic viand. Savouring another sensory mind blast.

'Is this meat?'

'Fresh meat.' Gloria watched him dispassionately. 'I wouldn't advise over-indulgence. Your digestive tract won't be able to cope.'

Rex wiped a sweetly-smelling knuckle across his mouth and reached for his wine glass. Gloria drew it beyond his reach. 'I would like a full report. In detail.'

Rex grubbed up sweetmeats and thrust them into his mouth. 'I've had a rough day,' he mumbled. 'How's yours been?'

Gloria leant back in the high quilted chair and sipped wine. She wore a wide-shouldered jacket of black antique leather gathered at the waist by a braided silk belt. White silk trousers, her feet were bare. Gold rings encircled several toes. The room was dressed much after the style of the bathing chamber. Early Opulent. Long windows looked out upon a flawless blue expanse of nothing. Rex gestured towards them.

'What is out there?'

'The sky.' Gloria sipped more wine.

'The sky is blue?' Rex peered at her suspiciously. 'How might that be?'

'The sky has been blue for a decade. However ground conditions are maintained as they have been and will continue to be for an indefinite period.'

'You are telling me that the cloud cover is artificial?' Rex couldn't believe what he was hearing.

'We are restructuring society. An agreement exists between the Big Three. When restructuring is complete then the cover will be lifted. Are you shocked?'

Rex chose his words carefully although his head swam. 'I'm surprised naturally. But high-echelon decisions are just that. Who am I to say?'

'Who indeed?' Gloria speared a tasty titbit with a 200-year-old eel fork. She ran her pointed tongue about her painted lips. 'The Living God King knows his own business best.' Her unguarded smile wasn't lost upon Rex, although he pretended otherwise. He was altogether shaken by this staggering disclosure. 'But how can such a secret be kept. If those living below were to find out . . .'

'But they won't, will they Rex? The air cars are programmed to fly no higher than the cloud cover. Only the tips of the Big Three's bunkers pierce the murk. Only the élite see the true sky.'

'But is it safe?' Rex recalled his Uncle Tony telling him about an 'ozone layer' which had been destroyed during the previous century.

'Quite safe. And it's quite safe with you, isn't it brother?'

Rex nodded numbly, his injuries were making themselves felt in a big way. And he felt very sick indeed. 'Might I use your toilet?' he asked.

The sound of the revving engine and the wheel-screeching departure of the Plymouth drew Jovil's attention away from the Bourbon bottle. He lurched out on to the veranda to watch the tail lights dwindle in the rain-swept night. He stumbled to the open door of room number three and gazed inside. There were signs of a violent struggle. The monitor was smashed upon the floor. Table and chair upturned. Across the wall above the bed was a garish streak of red. Elvis and the Time Sprout were nowhere to be seen. The deadly black box was nowhere to be seen.

Jovil slumped on to the bed and buried his head in his hands. A stranger in a strange land. And now one with very unfavourable prospects.

Jovil Jspht groaned dismally and vanished from the plot.

10

NOTICE IMPORTANT. PLEASE FOLLOW CAREFULLY THE INSTRUCTIONS FOR THE PLAYING PLEASURE AND HAPPY USING OF THE KOSHIBO HOLOPHON 2000.

Note One. The KOSHIBO *2000 is designed and built as same for your happy using to the highest standards as yet. To this purpose recommendation is made that all surfaces must be clean for use and not touched with hands nude or otherwise uncovered. Or with dust on.*

1) *Place the record with the playing side uppermost upon the playing deck. With hand in glove.*
2) *Closed the top must be for the playing.*
3) *Play in order with button marked for* ON.
4) DANGER TO HEALTH. *Do not unjack plug until the play is done with.*
5) THE KOSHIBO CORPORATION *accepts no responsibility in the small print.*

Holophon instructional manual 1993

Discomforting but inevitable successor to the augmented CD, the Holophon 2000 now offers the enthusiast by far the greatest ever opportunity to burn out what few remaining brain cells he, she or it may still possess. Latest in a long line of trial-by-error technology intended to augment audio playing through the introduction of analogued sensory stimuli, which create what the manufacturers refer to as Inner Visuality, this is another turkey. The flaw in this particular system, as in all those previously marketed, is that the analogue frequency remains fixed, with the result that no two listeners experience the same image patterns.

Regular readers will recall the brilliant article by Sir John Rimmer, Telepathy: Food for Thought Unfit for Human Consumption?, *which explained that telepathy is impossible between most humans due to the unique (fingerprint) brain frequencies of each separate individual, telepathy being only conclusively proved between identical twins who share the same alpha and beta brain-patterns.*

Thus a system broadcasting upon a single fixed frequency can only offer you the opportunity to play Russian roulette with your brain.

So not one for the Christmas stocking, kiddies.
High Tech Review 27.7.93

Dalai Dan wormed the small plastic beads from his ears. Sickly yellow gobs of unappealing wax now clung to them. He touched a sensor and wrenched the jack from its socket. Two minutes and twenty-two seconds, or it could have been several lifetimes. It was all the same in there. He reached out for the highball glass and missed. His brain was still vibrating and he had no sense of perspective. The room before him was a flat canvas. To the left of the picture a door vanished sideways and the cut-out of a woman swelled to encompass the greater part of the room. Yet she appeared to get no closer. Most curious.

Gloria gazed into the face of the God King. 'That is disgusting,' said she, 'I've seen you do some pretty revolting things, but both pupils in one eye, that's a new low, even for you.'

Dan blinked violently and rubbed at his eyes. 'Mirror! Mirror!' Gloria delved into her sharkskin handbag and brought out the vanity. The flat room vanished to be replaced by Dan's flat face. His right eye was blank and white. His left . . . 'Goddamn,' howled the high lama, 'what have I done?'

'By the smell of you, you've done your underwear.'

'No control of bodily functions in there.'

'Ah.' Gloria understood. 'You've been in the holophon. You will kill yourself in there. Don't come crying to me when you do.'

'Oh, ha bloody ha ha. My eyes, woman.'

Gloria sighed. 'You jacked out of the system before it closed. If you must persist with this madness, you really should read the instructional manual. You'll be all right in a minute or two.'

'Hand me my glass.' Gloria pressed it into the shaking hand and closed the fingers.

'What were you playing anyway?'

'Classical music. Black disc.'

Gloria raised a manicured eyebrow. 'A vinyl recording, you've got one of those?'

'Circa 1950 something.'

'Elizabethan. How did you come by that? Those things are almost . . .'

'Icons? This one was . . .'

Gloria's flat face left the picture. Dan tried to turn his head but the effort made him giddy. Gloria bent over the holophon. Beneath the squat dome upon the system's deck lay the ancient seventy-eight, encased within a two-centimetre protectrite shell. 'Do you know what it says on the label?' Gloria asked.

'It is by SUN.' Dan clutched his skull. 'The script is old English. I thought antiques were your speciality.'

Gloria lifted the dome and ran a finger reverently across the protectrite. 'And you've played it. Heard it play. Does it play?'

'Impressed, aren't you? It plays, I've heard it.' Dan laughed painfully. 'I've experienced it. You wouldn't believe what's in there.'

Gloria sniffed. 'Probably a fake. I've seen more than one.'

'Check it out.'

Gloria did so. Imprinted upon the protectrite was the seal of the Antiquities Federation. 'Goddamn,' said Gloria Mundi.

Dan ground at his eyes. Normality was returning. 'So what do you want here, anyway? Come to get yourself laid?'

Gloria stuck her tongue out and made a face. 'Something has come up. Something important. Where did you get this?'

'None of your business. What something has come up?'

Gloria closed the dome and turned upon the Dalai. 'She has been here again.'

'She? What she is this?'

'The she who makes you wake up screaming. The she you call Christeen.'

'Rubbish.' But they both knew it wasn't.

'We've got her on tape this time.'

'Interview is it? Don't wind me up.'

'Not exactly. Listen . . .' Gloria seated herself upon a Persian pouffe. 'I know we've had our differences in the past . . .'

'And in the present. My precognitive senses advise me that the future looks no rosier.'

'You get right up my nose.' Gloria's knowledge of twentieth-century vernacular was impeccable.

'Please,' Dan grinned, 'I prefer the missionary position.'

'Clearly the matter is of no interest to you. I shall be going.'

'Sit down.' It was a command, not a request. Gloria sat down.

'How many seconds of activity on the tape?'

'Thirteen.'

'The exact number of seconds that your brother was brain dead.'

'The same thirteen seconds. What do you mean? You knew about those gobshites torturing my brother. You let it happen and did nothing until they killed him.'

Dan raised his eyes. The pupils were correctly rehoused but appeared to be lit from within. 'I see everything, Gloria. I am the Dalai Lama.'

'But you let them put my brother through that when you could have stopped it?'

'It was a controlled experiment. Anyway, your brother is alive and kicking.' Dan touched the centre of his forehead and closed his eyes. 'No, correction, alive and shitting. He is currently venting his bowels into your bidet.'

Gloria opened her mouth to release invective. Dan held up his palm.

'Save it until you are alone. I will hear it then. All in all I don't think your brother has had an unsuccessful first day. I think he deserves a little bonus. Have him come up to see me tomorrow at ten sharp. And Gloria—'

'Yes.'

'You can bugger off now.'

11

The term Universal Law is meaningless. In universal terms no absolutes can possibly exist. Each truth mankind discovers is inevitably modified by another which ultimately disproves it. And bearing this in mind we turn to the vexed question in point. 'Do the Gods exist?' In universal terms the question is unanswerable because the word 'exist' has no absolute definition.

So to rephrase the question, 'In terms understandable to the human mind, do the Gods exist?' This is somewhat easier. The answer is yes. The Gods of men exist. Whether the Gods that the great apes of Africa worship, when they dance beneath the full moon, exist, I don't know. Whether the Fish God of the Sargasso to which the eels make their yearly pilgrimage exists, I don't know. Whether the nameless winged spirit, to which all birds sing their hymns each dawn, exists, I can't say. But the Gods of men, they are certainly real. I know this because I have met one.

The Suburban Book of the Dead

Rex snored soundlessly in his battered armchair. Before him the terminal flickered, the EYESPI scanning his sightless pupils and feeding points back to MOTHER. Rex's expulsion from Gloria's apartments had been abrupt, undignified and sadly lacking in fond farewells. His bodily functions had figured large in the tirade of abuse which had issued from his sister's mouth. In fact her manner was so threatening that Rex considered it prudent to avoid the subject of her bed, on to which he had recently thrown up. The only thing that saved the evening for Rex was the kindness and camaraderie shown to him by the two security men who found him wandering, half-naked and drunk in equal part, about the maze of corridors. They had fitted him out with a new radiation suit, loaded its pockets with beer and ciggies, made profuse their apologies for the little misunderstanding and finally flown him home to Odeon Towers.

Rex dreamt about the woman of his dreams. The lady he had seen in his dying vision. They were alone running through fields of tall waving brown stuff. And they didn't have any clothes on. Rex was dead peeved to be awoken by the violent rapping at his chamber door.

Mungo Madoc rarely slept. Being the product of some pretty snazzy genetic engineering, he merely topped up his system every day with a cocktail of vitamins, proteins and things of that nature. A tiny implant in the base of his skull calculated exactly which doses were required to maintain equilibrium and fed the data to a graft set into his left wrist. Here the information appeared as a graphic readout. Mungo merely followed the dictates of his wrist and swallowed whatever he was told. And thus he ran on and on, much after the fashion of the well-oiled machine.

On this particular night Mungo's wrist was pleading for a megadose of tranquillisers. The wrist's owner was in a veritable fug.

'Erased? Erased?' screamed Mungo. 'That is impossible. Inconceivable. Do you hear?' The less modified board members, who felt the need for their full eight hours' shut-eye, shuffled about in their jim-jams nodding and mumbling.

'It is sabotage,' cried Gryphus Garstang.

'It is iconoclasm,' agreed Lavinius Wisten.

'It is the end of civilisation as we know it,' Diogenes 'Dermot' Darbo pinched at his hooter. 'Oh yes, indeedy.'

'Shut up.' Mungo raised a shaking fist. 'Shaman. Where is Fergus Shaman?'

Fergus cowered to the rear of the pyjama party. 'Here, sir.' He raised his hand. Mungo grabbed it and hauled him forward.

'Shaman, an entire year has been erased. I want it back, do you understand?'

During his many years on the board Fergus had managed to side-step many an impossible demand. This time it didn't look all that simple. 'I . . . how?' was about all he could muster at such short notice.

'I don't care how. Just do it.'

'If I might just interject.' The voice belonged to Jason Morgawr. Jason was tall, young, well-favoured in the face department, a genius in bio-genetics and founder of the Earthers Inc. Amateur Dramatics Society. The executive board hated him to a man.

'I regret,' said he, 'that it can't be done. The virus has destroyed all the cells relating to the Earth year of 1958. But surely this is the least of our problems.' Those who witnessed the look upon Mungo's face had it firmly ingrained into their memories from that day forth.

'Least of our problems?' roared Mungo Madoc.

'This sabotage was only discovered an hour ago, but it is clearly apparent that the virus is already spreading. If it's not stopped it will continue to move forward. It will eventually catch up with the present day.'

'What are you telling me?' Mungo sank into his chair.

'I am telling you that if it catches up with the present day we will go off the air. *The Earthers* series will close down.' Mungo's mouth opened and closed and went on doing so.

Garstang turned upon Jason. 'Do you have a solution?'

'We can try to isolate the infected area, shut down all the cell systems surrounding it.'

'Then do it. Do it.'

'We are trying. But nothing like this has ever been attempted before. The storage cells aren't separate units. They all compose microcosms of the whole. If we start tampering too much with them we have no idea what might happen.'

'And the saboteur? Murderer?'

'All evidence points towards one Jovil Jspht.'

Fergus flinched.

'He was seen in the archives earlier today. Showed a fake security pass and has since vanished without trace.'

'I know that name,' Mungo said. 'He's the maggot man, all those memos.'

'We'll track him down.' Gryphus made martial fists. 'I'll get my men on to it at once.'

'It could take years.' Mungo began to giggle most queerly. 'If he's gone off-world we may never find him. Maggots . . . maggots . . .'

Gryphus Garstang wasted very little time in assuming control. He organized a search of Jovil's rooms, offered Jason unrestricted funding to search out a solution and summoned the house physician. The now gibbering Mungo was led away.

'Gentlemen,' Gryphus addressed his troops. 'This is a crisis situation.'

110

12

*. . . the God had been drinking heavily all day. In my line
of business, which is one of extortion, you get to see a lot
of bars and you get to recognize the regular faces. If you
want to see your old age, you do. So, I first notice the God
in Fangio's on East 32nd. I was collecting 'dues'. A half
hour later on West 13th I walk into Johnnie's Bar and Grill
and he is there also. Then he is in Laughing Sam's and
then again in the Cool Room. So either this guy has a lot
of twin brothers or something is going down. I don't figure
him for a Fed, you get a nose for those guys and when he
came across to me I knew he wasn't looking for a handout
neither. He asks me do I do the horses and I says sure, so
then he sticks a racing sheet in my paw and says, be lucky.
And then he just kind of shuffles out. Now I've been around
some and a little more and I reckon I know all the angles
but I check the sheet out. He's got doubles ringed and
outsiders and a whole accumulator based on a single dollar
stake. All looks pretty crazy to me and I go to bin the rag.
But something inside says to me, what's a dollar good for
anyway, so I make a call and place the bet. Biggest damn
mistake I ever made in my life.*

The Suburban Book of the Dead

'Enjoying the job?' the Dalai Lama asked. Rex looked up
from the floor. He had but recently been thrown there by
the two security men who had called to collect him when

he missed the Dalai's appointment. The one Gloria had failed to mention. 'The job,' said Dan. 'Enjoying it?'

Rex climbed to his feet. Having endured the previous day an air crash, potential death from the knives and forks of the Devianti, witnessed a cold-blooded murder and all but been tortured to oblivion, Rex wondered whether perhaps he had misunderstood the question.

'It gets you out and about,' he said warily.

'And the pay is very good. You certainly came up trumps in the bonus department.'

'I don't think I'll bother with the pension plan.'

The inmost fellow waggled a cautionary finger in Rex's direction and exercised his fingers on a terminal keyboard. They were in Ms Vrillium's office. It looked no better at a second viewing. 'How did you come by these names?' Dan gestured towards the screen. 'Very enterprising, the entire Devianti gang it would so appear.'

Rex slouched over to the desk and viewed the terminal without enthusiasm. Bloodaxe and Eric were known to him, but as to the rest . . .

'How *did* I come by them?'

'Under questioning. Would you like me to play back the extract?'

'No,' Rex replied, 'I wouldn't.'

'Well, nevertheless you named them all.' Rex shook his head. He couldn't think of a convincing lie so he thought of the credits.

'I'm on my way to becoming a wealthy man.'

'You certainly are. A little tampa perhaps, I understand you missed breakfast.'

'My thanks.' Rex watched the Dalai as he ordered up the meal. He looked much taller than he did on the TV But powerful men always appear taller than they really are. Except for the short ones, of course. But the charisma

112

was undeniable; there was an almost fearful presence about him. This was a man who wasn't to be messed about with.

'Did you know that you were brain dead for thirteen seconds?'

Rex shivered. 'I knew something had happened . . . brain dead . . .'

'You saw something during this time? Felt something?'

She was beautiful. Her eyes the palest of blue. The smile soft upon the full red mouth. Her breath smelled of violets. A golden glow surrounded her and her hand was upon his forehead. Rex trembled.

'I can't remember. I'm cold.'

He looked up. The Lama was staring deeply into his eyes. 'It doesn't matter, Rex. Ah, here comes the nosebag.'

A dull body in station fatigues knocked and entered bearing a chrome tray. He placed this on the desk and backed away, head bowed.

'For what we are about to receive,' intoned Dan, 'you can thank me in person.'

Ms Vrillium massaged Gloria's breasts. 'You're very tense, dear.'

Gloria looked up through half closed lids. 'Something is occurring.'

Ms Vrillium lowered herself on to Gloria's nakedness and chewed upon a blood-red nipple. 'What thing?' she asked between delicious bitings. Gloria rolled back her head and gasped.

'Something big. Something powerful. I can feel it. Ouch. No, don't stop.' Ms Vrillium slid down Gloria's body. Her long tongue flickering across the taut perfumed flesh, dwelling upon special places, savouring the exquisite tastes. She thrust her face down between the

113

outspread legs. Gloria moaned, arched her back, her hands clawed the pillows.

The bedside console chimed. 'Hope I'm not interrupting anything.' The voice belonged to Dalai Dan. 'Come straight up to my office will you?'

Gloria distinctly heard the undisguised chuckle before the line went dead. 'Bastard,' she shrieked.

Ms Vrillium broke surface. 'Sorry, dear. Were you talking to me?'

Rex sought invisibility. His sister looked far from cheerful.

'Gloria,' smiled Dan. 'And to what do I owe this pleasure?'

'You called me?'

'I did? Oh yes, of course I did.'

Gloria was poised in the doorway. She wore a jumpsuit wrought from some rubberized material. A tight cap of likewise confection encased her head. The boots were French calf, although Rex didn't know that. The heels were of glass and lit from within. Today's all-over colour, saving the boots, was crimson. The effect was dramatic, to say the least.

'I want you to arrange another air car for your brother. I want him issued with a stun suit and other appropriate items of self-protection. He has a busy day ahead. So, get your finger out, would be my specific advice to you at this time.'

'Hold on there,' Rex spoke with his mouth full. Gloria made a pained expression. 'What do I want a stun suit for? Where are you proposing to send me?'

'Special mission, Rex. I want you to go back to the Hotel California.'

'Oh no.' Rex shook his head with some ferocity,

spraying breakfast. 'Not this boy. Not back there.'

'Be at peace there.' Dan raised a palm. 'You will be quite safe. No danger to life and limb.'

'But they'll eat me.'

'Not this time. You will come, as it were, under a flag of truce. Do you know what that is?' Dan ignored Rex's shaking head. 'You will issue to the Devianti word of my personal amnesty.'

'Amnesty?' Gloria couldn't believe her ears. 'These are subversives. They eat human flesh.'

'Are you questioning me, Gloria?' Rex saw the fire in the holyman's eyes.

'No.' Gloria turned away. Rex watched her go. His eyes remained fixed upon the open doorway. This was no laughing matter. These lunatics could get him killed. And he just beginning to value life. To consider possibilities. He had seen the sky. He looked up at the Dalai.

'The Devianti. How could I convince them?'

Dan patted him upon the shoulder. 'You will find a way, my son. You are a young man of infinite resource. And you appear to have a charmed life. My thoughts will go with you.' Rex had the feeling that they certainly would.

'Bring back Bloodaxe. I don't care how you do it.' He handed Rex a transparent cube. 'It's all here. The power-lines have now been programmed into the in-car. You'll find the bonus to your liking. Consider the pension plan, you might choose to retire tomorrow.'

Rex turned the cube in his hand. This way lay madness. He was putting his life on the line. For what? For credits? But something compelled him. It seemed like a soft voice whispering in his ear. It said, 'Do it.'

'OK.' Rex shook the Dalai's outstretched hand. 'I'll do it.'

The oily-fingered engineer at the motorpool led Rex towards the air car. 'You will be bringing this one back?' he asked, eyeing Rex suspiciously.

Rex shrugged. 'Who knows? The guidance system has definitely been reprogrammed, hasn't it?'

'It has now,' replied the demoted Maurice Webb, nursing certain tender parts which had received the unwelcome attention of security truncheons. 'Drive carefully, won't you?'

'Have another day.' Rex saluted and climbed into the cockpit. He closed the canopy, slotted in the cube, eyed the EYESPI.

The car lurched up into the overhanging gloom, above which, Rex now knew, was open sky. His potential winnings filled the screen. Rex's elementary knowledge of mathematics didn't enable him to 'name that sum', but it looked very impressive indeed. He used to have a calculator on his watch. Rex tapped the moribund thing on his wrist. Two-thirty it said. The car droned on, creaking and rattling and performing certain stomach-turning manoeuvres, which Rex assumed correctly to be the product of incompetent reprogramming. Finally it went into a steep incline and landed with a thud inside the compound of the Hotel California.

Rambo Bloodaxe didn't observe Rex's arrival. He and his followers were knelt in prayer before the bewildered-looking man in the golden suit. This fellow was staring vacantly into his cupped hands. Here rested a green spheroid of vegetable extraction.

'Lord.' Rambo extended a platter of barbequed man meat. 'Will you take sup with us?'

Elvis Presley appeared to awaken from his trance.

'Where the fuck am I?' he asked, which was reasonable enough to his way of thinking.

'The Hotel California, Lord.'

'California? California never looks like this.' Elvis clutched at his nose. 'This smells like Philadelphia.' Knowing nothing of W. C. Fields, that particular remark was lost upon the Devianti, amongst others.

'We are your servants, Lord.'

'Then cut the Lord crap, buddy. I am the King.'

'It's definitely him, Rambo,' whispered Deathblade Eric. 'You were not incorrect in your assumptions.'

'He seems a trifle confused though,' Rambo replied. 'The temple lights are on but the congregation doesn't appear to have shown up. The sideburns are a killer, though, and we all saw him materialize before us out of thin air.'

'Now see here, buddy, if this is one of those religious cult things then you have got the wrong boy.'

Rambo looked at Eric. Eric just looked blank. Rambo said, 'We are your disciples.'

'Disciples? Fans, do you mean? Shit, I've gotta be dreaming. What the hell am I on?'

'Dreaming,' Eric nodded. 'Men are but the dreams of the Gods, I've read that.'

'Listen, I gotta use a phone, get Colonel Tom to send a limo or something.'

'Someone should take down his words.' Eric wrung his hands. 'The Revolution begins. Although we may not understand his words future generations may. This is scripture, Rambo.'

Rambo tugged upon the lobe of his right ear. 'It doesn't sound much like scripture to me, old bean. Shouldn't he be saying thee and thou and the like?'

'Anyone got a dime?' Elvis asked. 'Or I can call

117

collect? Where's the phone booth?'

'I'll do it phonetically.' Eric picked up an appropriate tablet of fallen stone and began to scrawl upon it with charcoal. 'Dime, now that sounds straight forward. Some kind of religious artefact, do you suppose?'

A look of dire perplexity wrinkled the King's noble brow. 'Are you telling me you don't know what a dime is?'

'Not as such, Lord King.'

A look of supreme enlightenment, of the kind that the reader will come to recognize, flashed upon Elvis Presley's face. 'I'm in Moscow,' he groaned. 'The Commies have got me. You'll never get a word out of me. God bless America . . .' Elvis placed his hand over his heart and began to sing.

'Excuse me chief,' came a voice from his left hand. 'If I might just have a word.'

'The miracle of the talking hand.' Rambo flung his forehead to the floor. 'Make a note of that, Eric.'

'Will do.' Eric scribbled away like a good'n.

'I hate to interrupt chief. But if I had thumbs they would now be pricking. Big trouble is heading our way.' Elvis ceased his singing. The door creaked open and Rex Mundi stuck his weatherdomed head through it.

'Cooee,' he called. 'Hello there, anyone at home?'

'Idolater.' Rambo sprang up. 'Kill the idolater.' The Devianti rose to its collective feet. Weapons were drawn.

'Hold on,' Rex cried. 'Don't be hasty, I bring good news.'

'Slay the idolater. By Godfrey, it's yesterday's lunch!'

'I think that now would be as good a time as any to take our leave, chief,' the sprout advised. 'Whilst they are otherwise engaged I'd make a break for it, if I was you.'

'I am me.' Elvis thrust the Time Sprout into his top pocket. 'Up and away.'

'Hold it easy.' The Dalai Lama peered into the terminal screen. 'We don't want to rush this.' Gloria leant closer. 'Let him get clear.'

'Of course, I mean your brother no harm.'

'I've got a fix,' said a nondescript menial, who had got a fix. 'Two fixes in fact. But there's no way of telling who they are.' Dan and Gloria watched the little red spots on the flickering mud-brown screen. 'They're crossing the compound,' the nondescript continued. 'There, see the heat signature of the air car? They've entered the air car.'

'Must be Rex then.'

'And he's got one of them with him.'

'Bring them back on automatic,' Dan ordered.

'It's basic stuff.' The Time Sprout checked out the dashboard. 'Turn the key, give it some revs and pull back the joystick.'

'It's a fucking spaceship!' said Elvis Presley.

'They're up.'

'Take out the entire quadrant.' Dan raised a knotted fist. 'Nuke it out.'

'Nuke it out?' Gloria fell back from the screen. 'What are you doing?'

'Call it involuntary euthanasia.'

'Co-ordinates fixed,' said the menial, 'Counting down.'

'You can't do this, you'll start a war.'

'Home territory, Gloria. A terrorist headquarters. The newscast will say that they blew themselves up with a bomb of their own making.' Dan turned to the menial. 'We are all prepared to video the explosion, aren't we?'

'Yes, Inmost One.'

'But . . . a warhead. That's a bit drastic, isn't it?'

'Something is occurring Gloria. I can feel it. Accuse me of being overcautious, if you wish. No, scrub that, accuse me of nothing. I'm the Dalai Lama.'

'The air car is free of the drop zone, Inmost One.'

'Then launch.' Dan made with the sweeping gestures. *'Om-mani-padme-boom.'*

OM   MANI   PADME   BOOOOOOOOOOOOOOOOOM

. . . thirteen thousand. I kid you not. Thirteen thousand dollars. For a one dollar stake. I sat in Fangio's all the next day just waiting for the God to show. I figured he'd want his share or something. But I guess I figured a whole lot more. Like how he'd picked me out of the teeming millions. How he'd come to do that. All kinds of stuff. I had the whole day to do it in. Around six he comes by. He was drunk but he was smiling. He says that he's sorry he's late, like as if we'd arranged something, which we hadn't. He asks if I'm feeling lucky again, except the way he says it, it doesn't seem like a question. Then he hands me the day's sheet. The first five of the evening's races out at the coast are ringed. I'll need a new bookmaker, says I. He hands me a list of names. When you're on a million, says he, we do Wall Street. And we do.

The Suburban Book of the Dead

The firestorm loosed itself. Brick melted, concrete became carbon. The canopy of flame flung itself up at the cloud cover where it whirled and twisted as if in agony. The shockwave spread, ionising the ether. Crushing and distorting, spreading its circle of death.

'Nice shot,' said Dalai Dan.

Time passes quickly when you're having a good time. It goes at a fair old lick while you're asleep. What it does once you're dead is anyone's guess. Rex wasn't dead. Betrayed and dumped upon from a great height. But not dead. He awoke in a great blackness, which was not altogether encouraging. Nor was the smell. He groaned, as one might, and felt about at himself in order to gauge how much, if anything, remained. The basics were all in place. Groaning once again for good measure, he tried to rise.

'Easy now.' The voice wasn't his own. Nor was the smell of violets. 'Who, I, where, what?' Rex floundered about. A soft light grew before him. And she was there smiling. 'You. You saved me . . .'

She nodded. The golden corona about her head became brighter. 'And I have watched over you for nearly eight hours. Now come with me. You will be all right.'

'Showtime.' Dan rolled down his sleeve. 'And bring on the dancing girls.'

> 'This is the time
> This is the place
> The time to face
> What the fates have in store
>
> It's double or drop
> Do or die
> And here's the guy
> You've all been waiting for
>
> He's the man with the most
> The heavenly host
> The holiest ghost
> In the cosmic drama
>
> And here he is
> The Shah of Showbiz

The Dalai . . . Dalai . . . Dalai
Da-lai La-ma . . . '

The Lamarettes high-kicked and made with the grinding pelvic movements. The cameras closed in upon golden pubic regions and then swung out to frame the grinning face of He-who-knows-what's-what-in-the-great-metaphysical. 'Hello and howdy doody,' crowed the lad himself. 'And welcome to *Nemesis.*' Cue applause. Cue reprise.

Lights flashed. Buzzers buzzed. The station logo chased its tails.

'And a really special show we have lined up for you tonight.' The bunker-bound, following the holy writ, popped cans of Buddhabeer and intoned the mantra of the day: 'Give us an Om. Give us a Mani . . .' and so on ad infinitum.

'This is no ordinary show tonight. Not that any show could ever be called ordinary. Oh no, siree.' Dan ran his hand down the naked thigh of an untried Lamarette. 'We have a young man with us tonight who I know you're going to love. Flew right into the station today. Says that he hails from Tupelo, Mississippi, and calls himself the King.'

The Lamarettes went, 'Ooooooooooh.'

'Exactly. And how many kings can wear a single crown? No, don't struggle over it. The answer is one. But this boy says he's the one and only, so it looks like we're gonna have fun. So ladies and gentlemen, I know you want to meet him. The King . . . come on down.'

Encouraged by a twentieth-century farming contrivance, known as an electric cattle prod, Elvis Presley took the stage.

As the spotlight hit him the King of Rock and Roll

underwent a dramatic transformation. From bewildered schmuck to figure of greatness. Many and various are the wonders of this world, explainable for the most part they ain't. 'Bring the band on down behind me, boys,' said the big E, 'where's my geetar?'

'Welcome to the show,' crowed Dan, spinning full circle upon a mirrored heel. 'Mr King, is it not?'

'*The* King. Call me *the* King.'

'Well "The", we're sure as makes no odds glad to see you here. And what would you like to answer questions on?' Several of the Lamarettes had, to Dan's annoyance, detached themselves from the throng and were now fawning about the young man with the killer sideburns. Straight for the chop this boy, thought Dan. 'Come on now girls,' he crooned, 'give the boy space to breathe.'

'Ooooh and aaaah,' went the Lamarettes.

'Kindly desist!' Knowing which sides of their bread had yak butter uppermost the wayward nubiles grudgingly withdrew. Pouting for the greater part. 'On with the show,' cried Dalai Dan.

'Where's my geetar?' asked Elvis Presley.

'I'll get it, chief,' said a small green voice.

'Not quite tuning into you there, boy. What would you like to answer questions on tonight?'

'Questions? I just did "Love Me Tender" on Ed Sullivan. If there's gonna be questions I gotta square it with Colonel Tom.'

'This is *Nemesis*.' This boy isn't dealing from a full deck, thought Dan. 'Marion, can I have the questions? Any questions?'

Marion's appearance on stage always drew standing ovations from the male members of the bunker-bound. Which you may take as you will. No woman could really look that good, but Marion did anyway. Even a conservative description of her bodily charms would be gratuitous. Elvis whistled. 'Baby,' he said.

'The questions, Marion, please.' Marion made free with the questions.

'The questions are on Rock and Roll,' she husked. Elvis strummed a chord upon the guitar he was suddenly holding. 'Have I missed anything, chief?' the sprout asked.

Marion parted with the plastic questioncard and swayed precariously from the stage. Elvis watched her go.

'OK, Mr King, the questions.'

'Uh, just one minute.' Elvis whispered something into his top pocket.

'Outrageous,' the sprout replied. 'But good for a laugh. I'll give it my best shot.' Words and actions rolled into reverse. Marion returned to the stage walking backwards in a fast action re-run. She took back the question card. Elvis took Marion in his arms and did young and healthy things to her. Refastening his fly, at length, he said, 'On with the show, small buddy.'

Time rolled forward and Marion left the stage a second time. Now in a state of disarray. She was wearing a very large smile.

'Slight technical hitch,' Dan spluttered. Something was going very wrong indeed.

The cavern was stone-tiled and ancient. Unspeakable things oozed through gratings and dripped into a sea of blackness. But all Rex could smell was violets, all he could see was the beautiful woman. She was there in the middle of the foul lake. Standing. Her bare feet didn't touch the water.

'Who are you?' Rex asked. 'What are you?'

125

'I am Christeen, and now is my time.'

Rex shook his head. 'I'm confused. I don't understand.'

'You will, all in good time. I have chosen you. We are in the End Days, the final times.'

'I don't doubt that.'

'There are many pasts but only a single future.'

'Where am I?' Rex asked.

'On the edge of tomorrow. Will you join me?'

'I surely will.' Rex Mundi walked upon the water.

'And that is the correct answer.' Dan grew slightly damp about the brow. 'Which leaves you with just one single question left.'

'No sweat.'

'But before I ask you this question, let's bring back Marion to tell us about tonight's Special Star Death.'

'Yeah, let's do.'

Lights flashed. Applause cued. Marion once more took to the stage. A golden envelope in a gloved hand. 'Tonight's Star Death is a real killer,' she purred, opening said envelope and reading as one does from the card. 'It's a chance to be . . .

'Brutally slain.'

ooooooooh and aaaaaah.

'Ritually disembowelled.'

aaaaaaaah and oooooooh

'And literally torn to pieces in a frenzy of sexually crazed bloodlust.'

'Well all right,' yelled Dan, 'and we want to see it.'

'Hey, fella.' Elvis flexed his manly shoulders and adjusted his guitar strap. The magical guitar was worrying Dan no end. 'Hey fella, I don't think I get this.'

Dan winked at the viewing public. 'What don't you get, boy?'

'Well. Now see here. If I answer the question wrong then I get . . .' He drew his right forefinger across his throat. Dan nodded enthusiastically.

'And if I get the question right, I still get . . .'

Dan's head bounced up and down. 'That's the way we play the game.'

'Ah. No sweat then. Just didn't want to look a jerk in front of my public.'

'No problem. Now just stand on the spot there. We want all the viewers to see you.' Elvis stood on the spot.

'OK. Right on. The question.' Dan waggled his finger at the mythical studio audience. 'And no helping out there.' The crowd synthesiser roared with laughter. 'Can you complete the following? Well since my baby left me . . . I've found a new place to dwell . . . it's . . .' Dan's words trailed off. Holophonic images swam in his brain. Black vinyl in a protectrite shell. Worlds colliding. Time collapsing at the edges.

'It's down at the end of lonely street at Heartbreak Hotel,' sang Elvis Presley. Dan backed away from him. The aura surrounding the singing man was unreadable, unbearable. But the voice . . . the voice.

'SUN,' mouthed the Dalai Lama. 'You are SUN.'

Elvis was alone in the spotlight. The bunker-bound looked on in awe. Something was occurring. Certain board members, domiciled upon a distant planet swapped incredulous expressions. 'That's what's-his-name,' gasped Gryphus Garstang. 'You know . . .'

'Paisley,' said Lavinius Wisten. 'Ian Paisley. How in the nose of God did he get there?'

14

*. . . and the God says to me, it's a restructuring job.
We're putting the world to rights and that can't be wrong,
can it? No, says I. The Lord giveth and the Lord taketh
away, says he. Too true, says I. We had a deal of property
by then and were extending into the entertainment
industry. All legit, I might add. Or looked to be. The Lord
giveth and the Lord taketh away. I remember that. Because
it seemed like a lot of people were being taken away.
People who got awkward or too nosy or whatever. I never
saw where they went but went they did. He was restructuring and I was living high off the hog. Praise the
Lord, says I.*

The Suburban Book of the Dead

Is this the real life or is this just Battersea?
Freddie Mercury

'Fergus, I would like your opinion on this.'

Fergus Shaman's eyes flickered towards Garstang, then
back to the screen. 'Well, he's singing, isn't he?'

Gryphus Garstang leant back in Mungo Madoc's chair.
He was smoking one of the lime-green cheroots from
Mungo's private stock. 'Why am I getting this strange
kind of *déjà vu*?' he asked.

Fergus shrugged nervously. 'I really couldn't say. The
continuation of the genetic code throughout succeeding

generations argues for the existence of ancestral memory. Your grandfather possibly . . .'

'If that is the case then I must be one of Garstang's distant cousins,' Diogenes chimed in, 'which I'm not.'

'You never can tell.' Fergus tried hard to sound convincing.

'Presley.' Cried Wisten. 'Elvis Aron Presley, born January the eighth, 1935. Joined the US Army twenty-fourth of March, 1958.'

Garstang sprang to his feet and pawed at the intercom. 'Get me Jason Morgawr,' he demanded.

Morgawr's handsome face appeared a moment later upon the deskset. 'You rang?'

'Do you have access to the exact date on which the virus was inserted?'

'Twenty-third March, 1958,' Jason rattled it out. 'In-grained into all our memories, I would have thought.'

'Quite so.' Garstang blanked Jason's face from the screen.

'A curious coincidence,' Fergus suggested.

'What's that?' Lavinius Wisten pointed to the enlarged image of Presley.

'What's what?' Gryphus followed the pointing finger.

'Up there, sticking out of his breast pocket. It looks almost like a . . .'

'Sprout,' said Gryphus Garstang. 'It looks like a sprout. Fergus, where do you think you're going?'

'I'm going to be sick,' Fergus replied.

Elvis bowed towards his viewing millions. 'I wouldn't wait around for an encore,' the sprout advised. 'I think we had best be away.'

The security men burst into the studio. All stun suits, mirrored visors and weighted truncheons. They plunged from either side of the stage to meet head-on in an orgy of unrestrained violence. But the punishment they meted out was only inflicted upon their fellows. Of Elvis Presley and his little green buddy no trace whatever remained.

It all went down very big with the viewing public of at least two worlds. Tune in next week, they most certainly would.

Dan crouched on his sofa. The cocktail glass was never very far from his mouth. Gloria paced the floor behind him. Her thoughts were not music to the Dalai's inner ear. 'Stop pacing, damn you. You're giving me a headache. Look, look.' Dan re-ran the video yet again. 'There, see it? He just vanishes. Gone. Here, see it again.'

'I have seen it. Seen it till my eyes crossed. You have really fouled up this time.'

'Me? How was I to know?'

'I thought you knew everything.'

'Well I do. Almost.'

'You kill my brother and you let this clown make a fool out of you on your own show. I'll bet Pope Joan is splitting her raiments.'

'Shut up! This is serious. Don't you realize who that was?'

'I don't know and I don't care.'

'It was SUN.' croaked Dan, emptying his glass into his throat and reaching it out for a refill. 'It was SUN himself.'

'SUN?' Gloria looked perplexed. 'What do you mean? On the vinyl, that SUN?'

'That SUN. I knew something big was happening.'

'But how? I mean it's impossible. He must have died before the NHE.' Gloria flung herself into a chair, breathing heavily. 'It can't be.' She chewed her lower lip. 'I want to hear it,' she said suddenly.

'What, hear the vinyl? Through the holophon? Certainly not, you couldn't take it.'

'I want to hear it.'

Dan gazed at her strangely. 'It's all connected somehow.' His voice lacked any tone. 'Something between he and I and it is in there somewhere.'

'Then I want to hear it.'

'All right. Perhaps you should.' Dan took up the headset and wiped the plastic beads. 'I should have killed him the moment we found him in Rex's air car. I should have realized then.'

'So why didn't you?'

Dan adjusted the headset over Gloria's hair and fed the beads into her ears. 'I don't know,' he replied with disarming frankness. 'Are you ready?' Gloria nodded. Dan jacked in and set the level to its minimum. Gloria nodded again. Dan pressed the 'on'.

A thin white line of static became wafers of light with each pop and crackle. Presley's voice came from a million miles away and was suddenly within Gloria's head.

WELL   I'VE   PLACE   DOWN   OF

   SINCE   FOUND   TO   AT   LONELY

     MY   A   DWELL   THE   STREET

       BABY   NEW   IT'S   END   AT

       LEFT

       ME   HEARTBREAK
              HOTEL . . . .

The words sloped and slid and within each one there was

a face or shape. Beacons flashed. Men ran. A woman with a knife loomed. Time ran forwards and sideways. Men burned. Flame spiralled.

EVER   SO   LONELY   YOU   COULD   DIE

jack out.

'You're all right now, dear.' Ms Vrillium dabbed Gloria's forehead with something cool. 'Look at the state she's in. What did you do to her?'

'Ask her what she saw?'

'Not now. She's messed herself all over. Go away, can't you?'

'I must know, it's important.'

'She can't talk now, can she?'

Dan turned upon his heel and strode from Gloria's apartment, slamming the door dramatically behind him. Gloria raised herself up on an elbow and tossed back her hair. It was speckled with vomit.

'I'll run you a bath dear.' Ms Vrillium stroked Gloria's forehead. Gloria nodded towards the door. With a knowing smile upon her far from winsome features, Ms Vrillium tiptoed across the room and dealt the aforementioned a thunderous blow with her fist. The ensuing cry of pain didn't come from her. Dan limped away down the corridor, clutching his ear and muttering blasphemy. Ms Vrillium examined her knuckles and sniggered terribly.

'Thank you.' Gloria swung her long legs down from the bed. 'I appreciated that.'

The Phnaargian sun, Rupert, balanced upon the horizon as if savouring the final dying moment of the day. The two moons, Elsie and Doris, were already on the up and up, electroplating the spires and cupolas of Vance. The brilliant flash of green as Rupert was swallowed away by the night failed to raise the spirits of Fergus Shaman. Fergus was a worried Phnaarg. Events had now gotten well beyond his control. The manure shovels were calling out his name. Fergus sat in his office before the shimmering window membrane. The stars were coming out. And around one of them circled a little blue planet called Earth.

Fergus made a helpless face. It wasn't his fault. Well, some of it was. A great deal of it was, in fact. But not all of it. It was that madman Jovil Jspht who was at the back of it all. And it was Mungo Madoc who had put Jovil's name up in the first place.

But Mungo Madoc was currently banged up in the company floatarium. No doubt presently communing with the big-nosed one himself. And it was he, Fergus, who was going to carry the watering can for the whole big mess. Garstang was piecing it all together. The board were starting to remember. But how could they? The answer to that was in the top pocket of a gold lamé suit. The Time Sprout was back in the present day bringing all memories back with him. But what was Elvis doing there? And what about Jovil? Had he pressed the black button? Had he told Presley what he was supposed to? No, he couldn't have if things hadn't changed. But then perhaps they had changed. How was he to know?

Fergus considered the gentleman's way out. Board members generally took the window when things got too much for them. Fergus shuddered. So it had come to this.

The office door spread in all directions and the doomed man looked up to meet the gaze of Jason Morgawr. 'Glad

134

to catch you,' Jason said cheerfully. 'There have been some developments.'

'Oh yes?' Fergus found his eyes wandering towards the window. Eighty floors and all of them down.

'The virus.'

'You've stopped it?'

'Sadly no.'

Fergus visualized the ground coming up to meet him.

'The virus is still spreading. But we seem to have discovered something more.'

'Go on.' Fergus went splat upon the pavement. It hurt. He considered poison.

'There is a curious mutation in the cell banks. It doesn't appear to be damaging the cells but it's subtly altering their form. Sounds crazy I know, but it's almost as if the cells are receiving new information, coming in from the early 1960s. But history can't change, can it?'

Something fast-acting, Fergus thought, and very very toxic indeed.

'Well, what do you make of it, Mr Shaman?'

'Have you re-run any of the mutated cells to see if you can spot the changes?'

Jason gave Fergus a cautious glance. 'Well, we can't, can we? If we do we simply accelerate the spread of the virus. And even if we could, we have no other records of the period to compare. It's certainly queer though.'

'It certainly is. Have you mentioned this to anyone else? On the board, I mean?'

'Not yet. I was just on my way up to tell Mr Garstang.'

'Ah,' said Fergus. 'That really might not be such a good idea.'

'Oh, and I don't see for why.'

'I was only thinking of you. Mr Garstang may perhaps

be a little upset by this new development. He is a somewhat temperamental fellow. In fact he might even hold you directly responsible.'

'What?' stormed Jason Morgawr. 'I don't see how he could come to that conclusion.'

'Don't you?' Fergus was all smiles. 'Best leave it, eh?'

Jason Morgawr seated himself deliberately upon Fergus Shaman's desk. 'I'm an ambitious man.'

'Get your arse off my desk.'

Jason was unmoved. 'I said that there had been further developments. That meant more than one.'

Fergus shifted uneasily, Jason continued, 'During my investigations I visited the research labs. It must evidently have been there that Jspht constructed the virus. So I did a little probing, and what do you think I found?' Fergus shook his head, Jason ignored him. 'I found that large amounts of company funding had been channelled into a project under your authority. Project Sprout.'

'Oh, dear me,' said Fergus Shaman. 'The game would seem to be up.'

'You disappoint me, Mr Shaman, I thought you would want to make more of a fight of it. Denials, cries of innocence, offers of bribery.'

'Offers of bribery?'

'What did you have in mind?' Jason asked.

'Something in middle management perhaps?'

'I had my sights set a little higher, as it happened.'

Fergus Shaman thought aside the poison bottle and considered the sharp young Phnaargian. 'Such would require a great deal of mutual back scratching, I so believe.'

'Through time?' Ms Vrillium rinsed Gloria's hair and sponged her back. 'But how could that be?'

136

'I don't know, but it's in there. In the vinyl, in the holophon. And he knows it too.'

'He'll be listening to us now, I'll bet.' Dan certainly was.

'Let him listen.' Gloria dandled her fingers in the scented water. 'I told you something big was happening. It's all linked together somehow, and he is getting desperate.' She shouted the final four words toward the ceiling.

Ms Vrillium's hands were beginning to wander. 'I'm sorry about your brother,' she said.

'Don't be. He was an irritating little tick.'

Ms Vrillium climbed from the bath and held up a warm towel to Gloria. 'She came to your brother, didn't she?' Gloria ran her long fingers through her sleek wet hair. 'She came to him. I know it. She is real.'

'Then now is the time of the Rapture. The End Time.'

'It would seem to be that way.' Gloria let the towel fall from her shoulders. 'So perhaps we should put what time yet remains to good use.'

The cultured orchids upon the bedside table broadcast the following hour's sexual gymnastics to the receiving beds of Phnaargos where they went down very well before an audience of some thirteen billion.

A mile beneath Gloria's heaving bed Rex Mundi made love to a Goddess.

15

. . . where did it all go? All those millions? Into the foundation, I suppose. It was somewhere in California, although I couldn't tell you exactly where. But the killings we made on Wall Street and all the others. Vegas, for example. All above the line profits went straight into the foundation. Laying the stones, the God says. And he never put a foot wrong. Never high profile. Always the same suit and always drunk. I learned fast, never ask questions and never try to pull a fast one. He kept it all in his head. No written records. So when the IRS caught up with us there wasn't a damn thing they could do. The God had it sewn up tighter than a drum. He knew when they were coming, what their names were and which of them would take the bribe. Some operator.

The Suburban Book of the Dead

'My son. My dear boy. I don't know what to say.' Dan seemed genuinely lost for words. 'Does your sister know you're back?'

Rex shook his head. 'I thought I had better come up to see you first, sir.'

'Quite right. But let me just get this straight. You say that you got blown into some sewer or whatever, wandered about for hours on end and then found yourself in the sub-basements here at the bunker?'

'That's about the size of it.' Dan closed his eyes and

studied Rex's aura. The lad appeared to be telling the truth. 'Remarkable. And fortuitous.' Dan topped up his glass. 'Another.'

'I don't mind if I do.' Rex held out his glass for a refill.

'And you met no-one during these wanderings?'

'No, sir.'

'Dan,' said Dan. 'Call me Dan.'

'No-one, Dan.'

'Quite remarkable.'

'I was wondering, Dan, if there might be any chance of me putting in for a desk job. I really don't think I have the makings of a religious affairs person.'

'Not a bit of it,' Dan leaned across his desk and gave Rex shoulder pats. 'You were born to the job. Believe me, I know these things.'

'People keep trying to kill me,' Rex complained. 'This I find most upsetting.'

'These are difficult times for us all. Come over here and let me show you something.' Dan led Rex to an alcove and drew aside a red damask curtain. A glass panel afforded a view into an inner chamber. Here upon a bed of ample proportions two untried Lamarettes disported themselves.

'Naked ladies,' said Rex approvingly. 'Why are they painted orange?'

'Saffron, my dear boy. What do you think?'

'Very nice.'

'A little bonus. Call it perk of the job. Why not go in and amuse yourself for an hour. We can talk later.'

Gryphus Garstang decided to keep Rex's performance in. But only for comic relief.

The Phnaarg in question paced the boardroom of Earthers Inc. Beneath his feet herbs released pleasing

140

fragrances into the overcharged atmosphere. 'It's all coming back now,' he stormed. 'Is it all coming back to you, Fergus?'

'In dribs and drabs,' answered the unhappy one.

'Time Sprout.' Garstang ceased his pacing and waggled a menacing finger beneath Shaman's nose. 'Time Sprout, Fergus.'

'Yes indeedy,' crowed Diogenes. 'Indeedy do.'

Lavinius Wisten flexed his sensitive fingers. 'If we had gone with my original idea of love amongst the shelter folk none of this would have happened.'

'But that is the point,' argued Fergus. 'Nothing has really happened. The virus will be stopped. I have Jason Morgawr's word on that.' Morgawr, who was sitting in on the meeting, glared him daggers. 'I really can't see what all the fuss is about.'

Garstang touched a module on the Goldenwood table. A frozen image of last night's *Nemesis* 'special' filled the far wall. Fergus shrank into his leafy chair.

'Are you absolutely sure you can't see what all the fuss is about?'

'Well, it looks like he dodged the draft, didn't he?'

'But he shouldn't be there, should he?'

Fergus shook his head doubtfully. 'But see,' he went on, 'he isn't there any more, is he? He's gone now and probably for good.'

'Sure of that, are you, Fergus?'

'Certainly,' lied Mr Shaman. 'The mechanics of it all are returning to me now. We won't see him again.'

'The ratings are up,' said someone. Garstang glared about the table. Heads were nodding, some thoughtfully, some solemnly, although it was hard to tell at a glance which were which.

'Up?' Garstang reseated himself in Mungo's chair.

141

'Up.' Lavinius Wisten prodded skyward.

'Let me see those figures.'

Diogenes opened his briefcase and tinkered with a small technical thingamebob. A holographic image sprang up above the table. 'All the excitement,' Diogenes explained. 'Rex Mundi has rather captured the public's imagination with all his thrilling escapades. Escaping alive from the crashed air car, then the nuking of the Hotel California and Elvis turning up on the *Nemesis* show. It's all good stuff.' Graphs and pillar charts rotated before them. 'It's all on the up and up.'

'The up and up.' Garstang pinched at his nostrils.

'A case of giving the public what they want to see. Plenty of sex, violence and intrigue. The viewers are switching back on. We are talking mega millions here.'

'See,' said Fergus.

Garstang made a conspiratorial face. 'How much of it is down to us?' he asked.

'Ah,' went Diogenes, 'you mean field operatives, script advisers, that kind of thing?'

'The kind of thing which doesn't go beyond this boardroom,' Garstang stared pointedly towards Jason.

Morgawr smiled his winning smile. 'My lips are of course sealed,' said he. 'We are all on the same side here.'

'Quite so. Well, Diogenes?'

Diogenes thumbed his controller and two holographic heads floated in the air to revolve slowly.

'God's Nose,' cried Fergus. 'Are they ours?'

Diogenes nodded and then tittered foolishly. 'And the beauty of it is that neither of them knows about the other.'

'Oh, very clever.' Garstang laughed. 'Very clever indeed. Isn't that clever, Fergus?' Fergus Shaman nodded. It certainly was very clever, but with all the loose ends kicking about, it was also potentially very dangerous indeed.

Rex Mundi lay on the bed of ample proportions, plucked a curly orange hair from his teeth and sighed deeply. The two beauties had long since departed and he was now alone with his thoughts. These were, however, in the light of recent events, somewhat confused.

He felt sure that he had lied through his unwashed molars to the Dalai regarding his wanderings beneath the Earth. But for the life of him he couldn't recall a moment of it. His memory was quite blank. Rex gazed up into the mirrored ceiling. He dearly needed another bath.

The bedside console purred. 'Rex,' the Dalai's voice was slickly sweet, 'sorry to bother you but I dearly would like another word in your ear.'

I bet you would, you fly-pecked dump of rat's do, thought Rex. But he was now learning to guard his thoughts so well that those the Dalai received said, Certainly sir, I'll be right there.

'Certainly Dan, I will be right there,' said Rex Mundi.

Dan wore a dapper line in quilted loungewear, embroidered all over with symbols Rex neither understood nor cared about. 'You feeling a little better now?' the perfect master enquired.

Rex nodded and laboured with some difficulty to remove the idiot grin which was firmly plastered across his face. 'Very much so, thank you.'

'Good. Then on with God's business, as it were. A little matter has come up and I would like your assistance with it. Sit yourself down.' Dan indicated the floor. Rex seated himself, with never a wayward thought.

Dan tapped his desktop terminal and a hard photographic copy peeled into his outstretched fingers. He examined it for a moment before handing it to Rex. 'What do you know about this man?'

Rex peered at the portrait. 'The man in the golden suit. He was at the Hotel California just before . . .'

'Before the enemy missile struck.'

'Enemy missile?'

'The Fundamentalists. Out to destroy my mission of mercy.'

'So that was it.'

'We tried to warn you,' Dan continued. 'Picked up the missile on radar, buzzed straight through to your air car. We must have missed you. Then we picked up a trace on the air car's monitor, assumed it was you and brought it back on automatic.'

'Oh,' said Rex. 'I see.'

'But it wasn't you in the air car. It was him.'

'So, who is he then?'

'That is what I want you to find out.'

'You want me to interrogate him? That is hardly in my line.'

'Not interrogate, Rex. I regret that he is no longer on the premises.'

Rex shook his befuddled head. This was already beyond him.

'He was here. In fact, he made a special guest appearance on the *Nemesis* show.'

'Ah,' Rex drew a finger across his throat. 'Then he's . . . yes, well communication with the dead is surely more your field than mine.'

Dalai Dan gave Rex a withering look. This man is a saint, thought Rex hurriedly. Dan's face softened. 'Quite so,' said he. 'There was a slip-up. Interdepartmental. The

144

unions plague me, Rex, they demand and demand and they cock up. This person was allowed to leave the building unchallenged. I should very much like to know his present whereabouts.'

'I remain a little confused about this. How did he leave the building? Did he take one of the company cars?'

'Impossible.'

'Then he had his own transport.'

Dan shook his head.

'Then he stole a radiation suit and walked out.'

'No such suit has been reported missing. We have made extensive checks.'

'Did anyone see him leave?'

Dan drummed his fingers upon the desk top. 'Not as such.'

'Well, with no suit and no air car, he didn't simply walk out into the night rain. He must still be in the building.'

'But he's not.'

'Am I missing something? I don't think I quite understand.'

'Then understand this. He escaped from the building. We don't as yet know how. He is at large somewhere out there and I want to know where.'

'Yes, but I don't see how . . .'

'Bring him back for me, Rex. Or simply tell me where he is and you will be amply rewarded. Do I make myself clear?'

Rex smiled broadly. 'Would that include further indulgences with the saffron women?' Dan nodded wearily.

'Right then, Dan. I am, as ever, your man.' Rex leapt to his feet. 'I shall require one or two small favours.'

'Go on then.'

'I'd like to take the photograph with me.'

'Take it with my blessings.'

'Thank you. And I'll need an air car.'

'Of course.'

'But not one with the hourly check-in system.' Dan looked doubtful.

'Of course you can monitor my movements.' Dan nodded in agreement.

'And one further thing. I will want access to MOTHER.'

'That,' said Dad, 'is quite impossible.'

'For a limited period. Say twenty-four hours.' Dan scratched his shaven head. I will do anything to help this great man, thought Rex.

'Twenty-four hours then. And keep me informed of your progress.'

'Of course, sir.'

'Good then.' Dan wrung Rex's hand between his own. 'Go with God.'

Rex inclined his head. 'It's an honour to serve you, Inmost One.'

Dan gave him an encouraging wink. 'Good boy.'

As Rex backed from the room, Dan pondered upon the wisdom of his decision. Giving any unauthorized person access to MOTHER was an extremely hazardous affair. To be on the safe side he would monitor all Rex's requests for data retrieval.

You are certainly welcome to try, thought Rex, but I wouldn't rate your chances.

The lads at the motorpool were quite warming to Rex Mundi, what with there being ever fewer air cars to service and everything. When news reached them that Rex was taking to the air once more they were not slow to open a book on the outcome of his latest jaunt. The

146

young-fellow-me-lad who escorted Rex across the tarmac even asked for his autograph. 'Have another day,' he called gaily as Rex climbed into the cockpit. 'Drive carefully now.'

Rex closed the canopy and eyeballed the dash. 'Rex Mundi. Special assignment. Destination Odeon Towers.'

'Identification confirmed. Kindly fasten your safety belt.'

Rex did so and the car lurched into the murk.

Rex set the car down on the flat roof of Odeon Towers, to spare it the dismantling it would inevitably receive in the street below. He lifted the roof hatch and climbed down the short metal ladder which led directly to his own landing. Very convenient, thought Rex.

'Mr Mundi has his own private aerodrome you know,' he said in mock conversation with some station swell. Rex disarmed his door and went into his rooms. The grim hovel had about it almost a refreshing air of normality. Well, almost. Rex had seen too many things over the last two days to ever fully come to terms again with his accustomed squalor. He slammed shut the door and took himself over to his homemade armchair, tossing his weatherdome into a not so far corner.

His plan was simplicity itself. How the Dalai hadn't thought of it was beyond Rex. Although Dan, in Rex's opinion, wasn't all the God he cracked himself up to be. Feet of clay, or something like.

Rex tweaked the controller and the TV terminal lit up. The EYESPI took up his identification and prepared to log viewing points. Rex switched to the data channel and punched in a series of instructions at the console beneath the screen. He worked with flawless precision. Calling up MOTHER he requested security clearance and was given it after a moment or two's delay. Rex tapped at the console. REQUEST IDENTIFICATION OF SUSPECT THROUGH IRIS PATTERNS. The computer granted his request. Rex held up the photograph to the EYESPI unit. The information exchanged. Circuits mished and mashed. The words UNCLASSIFIED. IRIS PATTERNS UNREGISTERED appeared on the screen. Rex smiled. It was no more than he had expected. He tapped in a further set of requests, this time under a security code of his own invention. Then he sat back. Presently the words PRESENT LOCATION UNKNOWN came up, followed by SCANNING NOW IN OPERATION.

Rex reached under his chair and brought out a warm can of Buddhabeer. He popped the ring and slurped the muddy liquid. Sooner or later, the mystery man was bound to watch television, even glance at a screen. And when he did, MOTHER would register it and beam his whereabouts straight back to Rex. It was a killer of a plan. He would buzz straight through to the Dalai and get him to despatch a couple of company bullyboys to make the arrest. He had never even to leave his chair. 'Sheer genius,' said Rex to himself. 'Rex Mundi, you sly dog, I don't know how you do it.'

Elvis had been watching television for nearly three hours. He was, to say the least, fascinated by all he saw. The floor about the set was littered with Coca Cola cans, empty Bourbon bottles, Kentucky Fried Chicken boxes and several Chinese women in varied states of undress. For those who prefer clarity to implication, Elvis was in the penthouse suite of the Hong Kong Hilton. It was a summery day in July. It was 1994.

'Hey, little green buddy,' called the King. 'Bounce over here, they're showing another of my movies.' The Time Sprout lay upside down on the bedside unit. He seemed a mite wilted. 'Sorry, chief,' he gasped. 'A bit puffed here.'

'No sweat.' Elvis fiddled with the remote control and brought the sound up. 'Don't mess with this guy,' came an actor's voice. 'He knows Karate.'

'Goes with the sickle,' the on-screen Presley replied.

Elvis fell back in his chair. 'Goes with the sickle, do you hear that? Goddamn, honey, shift your ass, I can't see the movie.'

'Chief,' croaked the sprout. 'Chief, I think we've got a problem.'

'Look at that jacket. Was I cool or was I cool?'

'Chief, I think I'm about to go to the great compost heap in the sky.'

'You what?' Elvis swung about in his chair, dislodging titties and beer. He stumbled over to the ailing sprout. 'What are you saying?'

'It's all this toing and froing. I think it's done for me.'

'Shit man, I thought you were a higher life form.'

'I am.'

'Then let me get you a glass of water or something. Here, d'you wanna beer?'

'Won't do. I need a bio-enzoic top-up.'

'Then I'll ring down for one. Listen, we're buddies, ain't we? You've got me out of all kinds of shit.'

'Right.'

'And you said you'd let me meet Abe Lincoln.'

'I'm dying, chief.'

'I'll ring down for the bio stuff . . .'

'No good . . . I've got to get back to Phnaargos. Back to the germination beds and re-charge.'

'I'll get us a cab.'

'Wrong, all wrong . . .'

'Don't leave me. Hell, I need you, fella.' Elvis plucked

149

up the sprout and held it lovingly to his cheek. There was no mistake about it, it was definitely starting to pong a bit.

'If I stay here any longer I'll rot. I've got enough energy left to get us back to Phnaargos. You've got to help me when we get there, OK? I'll tell you everything on the way.'

'Right, right. No sweat, OK. Let's get.'

They got.

Elvis Presley's departure from the Hong Kong Hilton was easily as opportune as any of his previous sudden departures had been. On this occasion he outran, literally by seconds, the hotel's security forces, who had just been tipped off that their penthouse guest was none other than the notorious international fivestar moonlight flitter, currently wanted on five continents.

Elvis bucketed through time and space. He was becoming somewhat seasoned to it by now. It was merely a toothbrush in the top pocket number. And for all the Time Sprout's early fears, he showed no signs whatever of ill effect. In fact he seemed to thrive on it. He never got any smarter, though.

There was a crash-bang-wallop and the two fell through a crack in the clouds and wound up suddenly in a certain research establishment at Earthers Inc. 'Quickly,' croaked the failing sprouty. 'The vat at the end of the hyper-ponic bench . . . bung me in or I'm a goner.'

'No sweat, small buddy.' Taking in only a blur of his fantastic surroundings Elvis stumbled along the bench. He never saw the figure crouching near at hand, nor the compost shovel as it arced through the air. It struck him a resounding blow to the top of the skull. As he toppled sideways, the sprout fell from his grip, bounced across the floor and came to rest at the feet of Gryphus Garstang. 'Gotcha,' said that very man.

'Oh shit,' said the Time Sprout. 'And farewell.'

Garstang turned to Jason Morgawr. 'I have to hand it to you,' he said. 'How did you know they'd come back?'

'I just reasoned it out. I went through Mr Shaman's private papers and saw the flaw almost at once. Genetics is my business. I knew that the sprout would have to come back for a top-up and that it would most likely come in the company of Mr Presley. All we had to do was to wait.'

Garstang nodded approvingly. Smart-arsed bastard, he thought. He gazed down at the Time Sprout. 'And you . . .' Gryphus Garstang turned his heel. The Time Sprout became history.

16

*The universe begins to look more and more like a great
thought than a great machine.*

Dr J. B. Rhine

It was 3.35 on the afternoon of 7 June 2050. The sun
wasn't shining.

Rex took to pacing the floor. It had never been a habit
which found great favour with him. Firstly because it
was a waste of valuable viewing time and secondly it
involved a good deal of ducking and diving, if it was to
be achieved without cracking one's head open on the
gilded cherub. Now seemed a good time for it though.
Twenty-three hours had passed and MOTHER had told
him precisely nothing. Surely no-one could go a full
twenty-four hours without watching television. It was
unthinkable. Rex paced and cursed, cursed and paced.
Took it by rote. But it didn't help one jaded jot. Rex
checked his chronometer. Still two-thirty, he'd have to
get that fixed. Heroes always managed to pull off the
big one in the nick of time. Everyone knew that. Old
Adam Earth, lantern-jawed wunderkind of Buddhavision's eternal foodie *New Day Dawning*, always
managed to pull it off anyway. Get the sabotaged food
production line running again just as section so and so
was on the point of starvation and the sneaky rival station

was about to fly in the missionaries with the food parcels. Always in the nick of time.

Of course that wasn't real life, although Rex was beginning to have his doubts regarding exactly what 'real life' was. He gazed about his hovel. Real life was this, and time was running out.

'Come on,' Rex implored the screen. 'Come on.'

A sun called Rupert shone in through a boardroom window. Here it lit upon a company of fellows who sat about a golden table. This company was suddenly called to stiff-spined attention by the unexpected arrival of a portly gent with greenly dyed moustachios. 'Out of my chair, Garstang.' The order was no sooner issued than it was obeyed.

Mungo Madoc seated himself before the assembly and examined faces to gauge the expressions thereupon. Satisfied that, as ever, deceit and treachery numbered amongst his board's more noble qualities, he smiled wanly and began to speak. 'Gentlemen,' he said. 'You will be pleased to know that the company medics have delcared me Category A. In the very rudest of rude good health.' There was much enthusiastic hand clapping. 'And so the captain returns to his ship, revitalized, extensively modified and fully informed as to the wayward vessel's present position and uncharted course.' Mungo dipped into his cigar box. It was empty. He frowned. 'During my period of recuperation, confidential aides have kept me fully informed as to your separate roles in this sad and sorry affair. Oh, truly do I weep for the sons of Phnaargos.'

The board members peeped suspiciously at one another. How much did Mungo know? Who had told him? What whats which they had told him were

154

the actual whats and which were not? And things of that nature.

'The ratings are up,' said Diogenes brightly. 'As you are no doubt well aware,' he added for good measure.

Mungo nodded and said, 'Fergus, what do you have to say for yourself?'

Fergus Shaman straightened the fern fronds securing the wristlets of his tunic. He had come, almost at once, to the precarious conclusion that Mungo was in all likelihood indulging in a little bullshit baffles brainery. Taking a deep breath, and having very little to lose, he set forth to test his hypothesis. 'It is for certain,' said he, in a manner which left no doubt that it was, 'that having been precisely informed upon all matters concerning my role in this affair, you should find me an island of moral rectitude in a sea of infamy. Whatever rewards you should wish to heap upon me I shall accept with just humility.'

Gryphus Garstang's hook nose cut the air as he rose to his feet.

'Rewards?' quoth he. 'You blaggard, sir. Just desserts are all that remain to you.' Fergus looked aghast. And very well he looked it too.

'Mr Madoc,' he said softly. 'I'm sure that I share the feelings of my fellow board members in saying that we will miss Mr Garstang, whose dismissal from the high position, that he has so sadly abused, must surely be on the cards. I, for one, take this opportunity to wish him all success in the more earthy pursuits you no doubt have in mind for him.'

Mungo gazed towards Garstang, loving every moment of it.

Garstang threw up his hands. 'This man,' he spluttered, going purple in the face, 'this man all but wrought

155

complete destruction upon all of us. And now he seeks to cloud the issue by making preposterous allegations against the one who found him out.'

Mungo Madoc snuggled down in his chair. 'Fergus, what of this?'

Fergus made a knowing face at his superior. 'Unfortunately, in your absence Mr Garstang's megalomania has been allowed its full head. The results are not a thing of joy.'

'I stepped in in a temporary capacity as there was none better qualified to do so. I'm the very personification of altruism. My thoughts were, as ever, only to serve the series to the best of my capabilities.'

'Tish, tosh and old wet fish,' said Fergus Shaman.

'Step outside and say that.'

'Gentlemen, gentlemen,' Mungo cut in. 'This is all somewhat unseemly. In such heated debate, truth is rarely the victor.'

'Heated is a word most aptly chosen,' Fergus concurred. 'For even now one of your own cigars, so hastily concealed upon your entrance, smoulders in Garstang's pocket, threatening to heat us all.'

Garstang would dearly have loved to have been able to scream 'liar', but with the blue pall of smoke wreathing about him he wisely chose, 'Incendiary! Knowing his case to be lost he seeks to burn me alive! Pyromaniac! Fire fiend!' He danced about patting furiously.

'Barking mad,' Fergus declared. 'Here, let me put an end to this lunacy.' Thus saying he plucked up the water pitcher from the table and emptied its contents over the smoker.

The silence was brief. It was about one moment long. But it was a very momentous moment. Garstang gaped at his once-proud apparel. Absorbing, literally, the state of its ruination. In this he divined a thousandfold ignominy. Scorn, loss of face, ridicule, insult, humiliation, contempt. They were all there. And a good many more. And they all wore the same face. The face of Fergus Shaman.

How much of it was the conditioned reflex of the professional soldier will never be known, how much of it heat of the moment, how much cold-blooded calculation, it's impossible to conjecture. Whatever the case, Garstang suddenly pulled from concealment a small hand-weapon of advanced design and turned its snout upon Fergus Shaman. Their eyes met over the barrel as it disgorged a single pulse of red energy.

There was a loud report. Rex ceased his pacing and pressed his ear to his chamber door. There appeared to be some sort of commotion going on upon the landing below. Rastas partying again, thought Rex, the sooner I get out of this neck of the woods, the better. His stomach rumbled. He was starving, but couldn't bring himself to open another can of synthafood. He made further imploring motions toward the terminal.

Dan's face was back on the screen with the mid-morning repeat of last night's show. The far-from-holy man dispatching further unfortunates towards whatever uncertainties lay out there in the great beyond. And all for the gratification of the viewing public. Rex shook his head, what a rotten stinking world. He slouched over to the terminal and fingered buttons. Dan's face dissolved into the logo of the data channel. He accessed into MOTHER. Rex exercised his fingers upon the keyboard. MOTHER told him that the search was still continuing, but this time politely added that it would cease in precisely seventeen minutes and twelve seconds.

HAVE ANOTHER DAY MR MUNDI, it put in just for good measure. Dan's maniac grin was once more a small screen filler. Rex slumped into his chair, the very picture of despair. For such an inspired scheme to meet with absolute failure really did seem grossly unfair. He had really begun to believe that he was destined for great things.

'Come on,' Rex shouted. 'Give me a sign, anything.'

Nice bit of timing, cue, coincidence, or hackneyed literary device? Who can say? But in answer to Rex's request, his front door suddenly burst inward from its crumbling hinges and smashed down behind him. Rex turned in horror and gazed fearfully over his chairback. Two figures were framed dramatically in the shattered doorway. Both wore Barbour jackets and tweedy caps. Although one of them appeared now to have only half a head.

'Good morning Rex.' Rambo Bloodaxe inclined his intact cranium. 'Glad to catch you at home.' Eric took from his poacher's pocket a large weapon of antique design. For lovers of handguns it was a .44 Magnum with a San Francisco license number. (Yes, probably that very one.)

Eric viewed Rex down the barrel's not inconsiderable length, enquired whether Rex wished to 'make his day' and then squeezed the trigger.

To Fergus Shaman's credit, it must be said that he was as nimble of foot as he was of mind. Fergus saw the hand of Garstang as it delved into the unscorched pocket. Saw the madness in his eyes and was already ducking for cover as the firing button went critical. The electric pulse knifed the air, passed clean through one of Fergus's raised shoulder pads and took Mungo Madoc's left ear off as cleanly as a surgeon's scalpel.

There was another momentous moment. Two in a single day!

Mungo raised his left hand and felt at his blank headside. Fergus flung himself under the table and scrambled towards the door. Lavinius Wisten quietly filled his elegant jodhpurs. Diogenes Darbo, an old contemptible, and no coward he, swung his briefcase into the face of Garstang. Other board members did other things, but in the ensuing chaos it was hard to make out what. And very few, if any, distinguished themselves in any manner whatsoever. Typical.

Green ichor flowed profusely from Mungo's wounded head, a smell of stale cabbage filled the air. The modified readout on his wrist belled straight down to the company medics. Fergus came up from beneath the table just in time to see Garstang, vacant of eye and green of nose, turn his weapon upon Diogenes Darbo, sending that gallant fellow off upon the final journey, from which none, with the possible exception of the Dalai Lama, ever return. Fergus grabbed hold of Mungo and bundled him through a doorway which had suddenly become all the rage.

As they passed through it, Mungo, down but by no means out, put his fist through the emergency seal. To the raised voice of squealing alarms the door shut with a resounding thud.

The Dalai Lama's face exploded into a holocaust of trailing ribbons. Shards of blistering glass struck Rex fiercely from behind. Had he not still been wearing his radiation suit, his buttocks would now have required major surgery. 'Bother,' came the voice of Deathblade Eric through the smoke and flame. 'A little left of centre, do you think?'

159

'If at first you don't succeed and all that kind of thing.'

Rex was torn between white flag waving and the keeping of the ever-legendary low profile. He settled wisely for the latter.

'Behind the chair, Eric.'

'Okey dokey.' Eric shot the head off the gilded cherub. 'Spot on.'

'Kindly give me the pistol, Eric, you are making a complete pig's earhole out of the entire affair.'

'I have had half my head blown away,' Eric complained. Rambo soothed his companion with a touching little shoulder hug. 'Although this makes you an ideal candidate for a station head, I concede that it might impair your marksmanship. Kindly give me the gun.'

'Oh figs,' grumbled the Deathblade, parting with the smoking pistol.

'Come out, come out, wherever you are,' crooned Rambo.

Rex weighed up his chances. The scales were down heavily on the 'none whatever' side. Clinging to the chair's arms Rex began to edge toward the bathroom. To what exact purpose he wasn't as yet certain. The fetid wash-hole didn't number a window amongst the few points in its favour.

'Can't see a blooming thing.' The voice was Rambo's. 'Eric, go and worm the little blighter out. There's a good fellow.'

'You have the equaliser, you go and worm him out.'

'Oh really, Eric.'

'Oh really yourself.'

'Eric,' said Rambo.

'Rambo?' said Eric.

'Eric, it is a well known and easily verifiable fact, that

160

the man who holds the gun issues the orders.'

'But I held the gun a minute ago.'

'But you don't now, do you?'

'But I . . .'

'Eric, I have a gun and you have half a brain. Now, should the situation be reserved, which one of us would you expect to do the ordering and which the worming out?'

'Sounds like a trick question to me.'

'Eric, worm the blighter out or I shoot you dead.'

'Come out, come out wherever you are,' called Eric, fanning at the smoke and kicking variously about. Rex closed the bathroom door as quietly as possible. Needless to say, the door didn't possess a lock. He leant back upon it breathing heavily. He was in serious trouble here, and no mistake about it.

'Fergus,' said Mungo. 'This is a most regrettable business.' Fergus made with the thoughtful nods and winced as Mungo's medics worried at the raw meat. They were now in the medical unit of Earthers Inc. It looked for all the world like nothing on earth.

'He's holding Lavinius Wisten hostage,' said Mungo. Fergus nodded once more. 'And also my ear.'

'Wisten is perhaps expendable,' Fergus ventured.

'But not my ear.'

'Oh, certainly not, sir.'

'Fergus, please don't take this the wrong way. But I sincerely feel that I should hold you at least partially responsible for all this.'

'Have no fear, sir,' Fergus replied. 'The day will yet be saved. I have a plan.'

A plan, thought Rex, if I only had a plan. He scrutinized

161

the loathsome little cell in search of inspiration. By the crepuscular glow of the neon mirror-light, he could see all there was to see. The room was tiled from floor to ceiling. The ceramics crazed, smeared with generations of filth. The grout supported a flourishing moss garden. Above the chipped enamel shower-tray a single hosepipe thrust obscenely from the wall, beneath a rusted turncock. The lacklustre mirror above the leaky grey basin reflected Rex's thoughts. The room spelt gloom and doom and rhymed appropriately enough with tomb.

Rex cast an eye over his collection of lice repellents and skin toners racked beneath the mirror. Hardly bomb-making equipment. A fist went thud on the door. 'There's another room through here,' came the voice of Eric the half-a-brain.

'Then in you go, Eric, wormy wormy.'

Rex heard Eric put forward, what were, to his mind, several very plausible reasons regarding the inadvisability of sudden entry. He also heard a clunk, which he rightly assumed to be the sound of a pistol butt striking the load-bearing side of Eric's skull. 'Ouch,' went Eric in ready response.

Rex snatched up a can of Peachy Face Pock Filler and brandished it in a menacing fashion. The futility of this wasn't slow in the dawning. Rex swung it at the neon tube, plunging the bathroom into darkness. He climbed into the shower-tray and assumed the foetal position beneath the flaccid hosepipe.

Eric kicked open the door. Rex's terminal was now well ablaze and through the fire and smoke Eric didn't look as pretty as a picture, lit from his bad side by the conflagration. Rex cowered as Rambo joined his chum in the doorway. Firelight danced on the barrel of the .44 Magnum as it nosed into the bathroom, sniffing him out.

For Rex it was the dry throat and the loosened bowel of the condemned prisoner. So this was it. The end. Death was always a squalid affair, but Rex, like all men, had laboured under the cosy misconception that his would have some dignity about it. It's funny just how wrong you can be some times.

'Time to die,' said Rambo Bloodaxe. 'Then time for lunch.'

'Your plan, Fergus, you will kindly favour me with it.'

'Well . . .' Fergus wracked braincells; he was sure that somewhere in his head there was just bound to be a plan. 'The way I see it . . .'

His words were, however, cut off by the timely arrival of Jason Morgawr, who had somehow managed to put himself in charge of security. 'We have a problem,' said he, addressing himself to Mungo's single ear. 'Garstang is making demands.'

The modified Mungo, who now had the capacity to witness an entire planet's destruction, with scarcely the bat of an eyelid, yet who still harboured a certain resentment regarding the loss of his ear, said, 'Oh yes?'

'He says he wants the captive and a safe passage down to the research labs or he will . . .' Jason leant low to Mungo's ear to relay the sordid details of what fate held for Lavinius Wisten.

'And to what end do you suppose, and hang about, what captive?'

Thought so, thought Fergus, he knows nothing. Jason shook his head and feigned ignorance. Fergus put his finger to his lips. 'Elvis Presley,' he whispered. 'Garstang has, for reasons better known to himself, brought Presley here to Phnaargos.'

163

'Here? I mean here, yes in the heat of the moment it had slipped my mind. Your thoughts, Fergus?'

'My thoughts no doubt mirror your own, sir. Garstang obviously hopes to evade justice by escaping through time, taking Presley along for security. He's somewhat more important to us than Wisten, after all. Several more Time Sprouts even now ripen in the research labs.'

'You confirm my own worst fears. Your thoughts yet again.'

'The employment of a soporific gas introduced into the ecosystem of the boardroom might prove advantageous at this time.'

'Uncanny,' said Mungo.

Jason Morgawr bounced before them. 'Further developments. Garstang has locked the boardroom televisual system into broadcast, and he's threatening to make his feelings felt before the viewing public.'

'Then close him down.'

'No can do, sir. The broadcast system in the boardroom overrides all the others. A little innovation of yours, if you recall.'

'But of course. Fergus?'

'My thoughts? The gas, and now.'

Morgawr made with the head-shakes. 'He's already on to that. He's blocked the eco duct, with Diogenes Darbo, I understand. He says that if his demands aren't met within the next five minutes he will expose the entire *Earthers* series as having been engineered by the company. Dirty laundry will be aired, names will be named.'

'Fergus? Fergus? Stop that man somebody.'

Fergus Shaman found the ward door barred to him. 'Now,' said he, as he was hauled back to Mungo, 'is the kind of occasion when I offer up my thanks to the Deity for having blessed us with a station head such as yourself, whom alone is capable of solving a problem, which to we lesser mortals appears quite insoluble. In fact I was just on my way to the company chapel to offer up these very thanks when you called me back. Did you want anything in particular, sir?'

The entire medical crew turned towards Mungo.

'Ah,' said that man. 'Ah yes, indeedy.'

Rex pressed back against the clammy tiles. Rambo cocked the trigger. Rex screwed up his eyes. 'Hosepipe,' came a voice at his right ear.

'What?'

'Hosepipe.'

He knew that voice, the voice of the Goddess, the voice of Christeen. And he knew the time too. That brief five minutes of the day when the heating went on at Odeon Towers. So timed that most of its residents would be out working. Bath time. 'And it's goodbye from him,' chuckled Rambo. Rex reached up for the rusted turncock. Wrenched it around. Miraculously it spun, as if newly greased. Rex clutched the perished hosepipe. The jet of superheated water was fast and furious. It struck Rambo full face, blasting him from his feet into the arms of his dithering henchman. Acting Fireman Mundi trained the jet upon them both, laughing like a maniac. The jet faltered, trickled and died. Rex's water ration for the day was all used up. 'Ooooooooooooh!' Rex leapt to his feet. Rambo was staggering about groaning terribly and feeling for his gun. Rex kicked him viciously between the legs. As he doubled up, the steely toecap of Rex's workaday boot caught him squarely in the sinking chin. Rex snatched up the fallen weapon and leap-frogged over the toppled Devianti. Eric made a half-hearted swing in his direction, but Rex bludgeoned him down with the pistol butt.

Really it was all a most excruciating display of gratuitous violence. But once cut together from the various viewpoints afforded from the televisual moss and lichen in Rex's apartment and beamed out across Phnaargos, it went down very big with the growing audience of some fourteen billion.

'Yes, indeedy,' said Mungo Madoc once again.

Fergus watched the face of the station chief as it ran through its full repertoire of thoughtful expression. This man is barren of ideas, thought he. 'Perhaps you should go up and speak to him yourself, sir.'

'Perhaps I should go up and speak to him myself,' mused Mungo.

Fergus turned his eyes towards the ceiling. He'd cared little enough for the older Mungo Madoc, but this new one didn't do much for him either. 'Perhaps you should.' Fergus agreed.

'So be it.' Mungo rose ponderously from the surgical couch and pulled aside his gown. His wonderful suit was in ruination, but he simply sighed it away. Like the warriors of old, Mungo Madoc girded up his loins and went forth to do battle.

There was a lot of effing and blinding coming from the boardroom. A knot of special service men crouched about the doorway, weapons at the ready. One of them rose to salute Mr Madoc as he arrived. 'Ranting away in there like a stone bonker,' was the considered opinion on the matter.

Mungo pressed him aside and addressed the boardroom door. 'Garstang,' he shouted. 'This is Mungo Madoc.' There was a snap, a crackle and a pop. An electric pulse seared through the door. Something pale and fleshy bounced on to the corridor floor.

The now earless Mungo Madoc turned to Fergus Shaman. 'Your thoughts on this?' he asked.

17

Let's get serious, no let's don't, let's mime the hard bits.
Frank Zappa

Rex didn't pause long in his burning apartment. He snatched up his weatherdome and tore away a small section of flooring. From the hidey-hole revealed he drew his most valuable possession, *The Suburban Book of the Dead*. He thrust the book into a pocket of his radiation suit and made off at the hurry up. Up the iron ladder went Rex, through the hatch and on to the roof. The air car stood awaiting his whim. Smoke began to rise through the roof hatch.

Rex bundled into the air car, slammed shut the canopy, confirmed identity and put the thing into gear. The engine coughed and died.

'No,' cried Rex, 'not now.' Two fearful figures climbed out through the roof hatch. A sheet of flame billowed up behind them. 'Please,' begged Rex. 'Please start.' The spectres loped across the roof towards him. Rex bashed at the dashboard with his fist. The engine chugged, the air car stalled again. Rambo snatched up a length of metal piping and swung it at the windscreen. The plexiglass shattered, Rex covered his eyes, Rambo and Eric clawed at him. The motor engaged. The car lifted. The two Devianti fell away howling bitterly. Rex took to the sky.

Gloria Mundi never paced, she rode upon friction-free bearings housed within her hips. This she did now in the Dalai's sanctum sanctorum. Dan watched her at it. He studied every fold of yielding poli-synthicate as it creased about the exquisite contours of her body. What a waste, thought Dalai Dan.

Gloria turned upon him. 'You should be so lucky.'

Dan cast her an upward gaze, levelling out at the piercing green eyes. 'Your brother intrigues me,' he said.

'It might have been polite of you to mention that he was still in one piece as soon as you knew.'

'So sorry,' Dan replied. 'An intriguing young man.'

'His idea of feeding the iris patterns of your Mr SUN into MOTHER to seek his location does display a certain animal cunning, I suppose.'

'I consider it most enterprising. Sadly time ran out for him. The scan will of course be maintained. We will track down SUN.'

Gloria threw up her hands. 'But to what end? You catch up with him. You kill him. Can one man really be such a threat to you?'

'This is no ordinary man. Do you know what I represent, Gloria?'

'I'm sure you can read my thoughts on this matter.'

'I represent stability. The status quo. I represent safety. To threaten me is to threaten the very fabric of society.'

'Don't flatter yourself.'

Dan sipped his cocktail. 'You have no idea of what I'm talking about. Your mind, although open to me, is closed to reason.'

'And what plans do you now have for my brother?'

'I will keep him on the SUN case. I like the way he thinks.'

170

'He's an uncouth lout.'

'Please Gloria. We each must play our part. You understand the economics of the thing and also the mechanics. Society is no longer self-perpetuating. The unions run me ragged with their outrageous demands, production is, as ever, down. Soon the synthafood plants will run themselves dry. You know this. I know this. We have maintained the protective cloud cover for a decade to allow the ozone layer to reform. This is science, Gloria. When mankind re-establishes itself once more upon the face of the planet there must be no further mistakes. Each must play his or her part, as now.'

'With you running the show, I suppose.'

'And who better?'

'Perhaps Hubbard or Pope Joan?'

'Only me, Gloria.'

'Ha, dreams of the hashish eater.'

'Not a bit of it.' Dan thumbed a remote control. A hologram of the planet formed before them. He prodded into it. 'Cities all laid waste. But here, here, here, vast tracts of arable land. All over, radiation-free, ripe for cultivation. Countless miles, more than in the middle ages. This time we do it right.'

Gloria gazed at the image and then at the man. Could he actually be sincere?'

'Mr Mundi is here,' purred the intercom.

'Send him in,' said the Dalai Lama. The hologram faded and was gone.

The two Phnaargs returned to the medical centre. Mungo clutching his latest wound, Fergus carrying the amputated ear before him at arm's length. As the medics sutured and stitched, tinkered and bandaged, Jason spoke hurriedly into the unsullied ear of Fergus Shaman. 'We

171

have less than two minutes; he's preparing to go on the air.'

'Just do what he says then,' Fergus replied. 'But get him out of that boardroom, as you value your future.'

'Nuff said.' Jason spoke rapid words into a headset. Garstang's manic face appeared on a nearby bio-screen. 'Will you do it, or should I?' Jason asked.

'Best you do,' Fergus backed away. 'He and I aren't really on the best of terms at present.'

'Well?' Garstang demanded.

'I'm afraid Mr Madoc is unable to speak to you at present. But I now have his full authority. You shall have all that you require.'

Garstang drew the ashen face of Wisten within vision and pressed the hand weapon to his temple.

'That's a special service hand-strobe,' Morgawr whispered to Fergus. 'I worked on those. But he shouldn't have one, they haven't been fully tested yet.'

'Something up design-wise?' Fergus asked hopefully.

'Just a bit. They have an alarming habit of feeding back if you don't let them cool between discharges. Very messy.'

'Oh good,' grinned Fergus. 'Now speak to him, he looks rather anxious.'

Jason did so. 'The captive is being brought up to you, Mr Garstang. Then the floors between you and the research labs will be cleared.' The screen went blank.

'So they feed back, do they?' Fergus asked cheerfully. 'And would Mr Garstang be aware of this, do you think?'

Jason Morgawr winked. 'I can't see how he would.'

Fergus Shaman did a big ear to ear job. 'There are going to be one or two vacancies on the board. If this works out I might just put your name forward.'

'Should I clear the floors then?'

'Why not, and get Mr Presley up to him. Place your men in concealment. Don't forget to inform them about the little gremlin in Garstang's gun.' Jason hurried away, rubbing his hands together in glee.

'What did he say?' asked the heavily swathed Mungo.

'Everything is being taken care of, sir.'

'Pardon? You'll have to speak up a bit.'

'Everything is being taken care of, sir!'

'The last bit again.'

'Oh, never mind, you great buffoon,' muttered Fergus, which was a shame, because skill in lip-reading was amongst Mungo's newer modifications.

Mungo smiled benignly. I'll get you for that, he thought.

'So, Rex,' Dan was all smiles, 'what do you have to say for yourself?'

'Plenty.' Rex eyed a tray of sweetmeats and his stomach made an unmentionable sound. Rex let his thoughts be felt.

'Go on then,' said Dan, 'eat your fill.'

'My thanks, Dan. Morning Gloria. Having another day, I'm pleased to see.'

Gloria made a disgusted face and turned up her nose. 'You need a bath.'

'Just had one as it happens.' Rex began to fill his face.

'So, how goes your search then? Anything to report?'

The eater dragged a sleeve across his mouth. 'I have a lead, yes. And a good one.'

Dan looked puzzled. 'Oh, yes?'

'At considerable risk to myself, I have managed to trap two Devianti upon the roof of Odeon Towers. One is the Rambo Bloodaxe you were so keen to meet. Exactly how he and his crony managed to escape the enemy missile,

173

I've no idea. Perhaps they have charmed lives also. Anyhow, I'm sure Bloodaxe can be persuaded to yield up all he knows about your mystery man. Good, eh?'

Dan nodded dumbly. 'Very good.'

'I would suggest you send over your big lads fast. The flames lick even now about the feet of Rambo Bloodaxe.'

'Quite so.' Dan tapped the intercom and issued instructions. Rex munched on, grinning inwardly. His sister eyed him with open contempt.

'He put up quite a struggle,' munched Rex. 'In fact, I fear that he has totally destroyed my apartment, if not the whole building.'

'Ah,' said Dan. 'That is most regrettable.'

'It is,' Rex agreed. 'Many of my priceless family heirlooms gone up in smoke. But no matter, all in a good cause, I'm sure I will be fully compensated. And with the bonus you offered for Mr Bloodaxe, I shall find superior lodgings and in time forget the sad losses.'

'For it is written,' said Dan, quoting scripture, 'that even should he put his hand down a toilet, it will come up smelling of roses.'

'Perhaps Rex might like to demonstrate this skill upon my bidet,' Gloria suggested.

'Still not fixed, eh?' Dan chuckled. 'The service engineers are in dispute, I believe. I will have a word with them when I have a spare moment.'

Rex allowed Gloria the full benefit of his undisguised smirk.

'I have to go now,' she announced. 'The show must go on, you know.'

'Oh, indeed you must. Leave us to it, men's talk, you know.' Gloria stormed from the room, a sensual hurricane. Such abominable disrespect for the living God King, thought Rex, as loudly as he could, surely the Inmost One must demote her on the spot.

'Don't push your luck, Rex,' said Dan, giving the thinker the old third eye. 'You know what I mean?'

Two of Vance City's finest encouraged Elvis along the corridor with the business ends of their truncheons. It's always comforting to know that no matter where one travels to in this universe, there will always be a policeman with a truncheon. Funny that there's still never one around when you need him, though.

'You know what I think, fella?' The boy adventurer turned upon one of his persecutors. 'I think your whole Goddamn planet sucks. That's what.'

The uniformed duo glanced at one another and came to the unspoken agreement that a short sharp shock was the order of the day. They were raising their truncheons just as Fergus Shaman appeared on the scene.

'Thank you, gents,' said he. 'I will take our guest from here.' He noted well the twin looks of disappointment. 'That will be all, thank you.' The two policemen shambled away, grumbling loudly.

'And who the fuck are you?' Elvis asked.

Fergus extended his hand. 'Fergus Shaman, pleased to meet you.'

'Where's my little green buddy?'

'Ah,' Fergus returned his unshaken hand to its pocket. 'Your little green buddy. Now that is what I wanted to talk to you about. You see I have this theory.'

'That to your theory,' Elvis made a gesture which Fergus Shaman didn't know the meaning of. It involved a thrusting movement with the middle finger.

'Quite so. But it's of great significance, nonetheless. Have they been treating you all right?'

175

'Are you for real? One of those bozos stuck his night-stick up my . . .'

Fergus made a pained face. 'I'm terribly sorry. A slight misunderstanding. Now if you will kindly follow me.' He turned to lead Elvis up the corridor. Now it wasn't the American Way, striking a man from behind, this Elvis knew. But he'd had a rough day. And after all Fergus Shaman was an alien.

Fergus Shaman turned in mid stride. Alien perhaps, but no fool. 'If you want to get back to 1958 then I suggest you come with me.'

The moment was lost. Elvis went quietly.

Odeon Towers was well ablaze. News teams from the Big Three were covering the event, jockeying for the key positions. Fire-fighting squads stood at the ready awaiting their cues to make with the deeds of heroism. Their union representatives discussed repeat fees and residuals with the media men. Location directors shouted into handsets and prayed for the rain to keep off. Someone on fire leapt from an upper window.

'Zoom in on the corpse. Hold and cut.'

Rambo Bloodaxe peered over the parapet and sighed sadly. Eric was trying to count his fingers and failing miserably. 'Hot for the time of year,' he observed. Amidst the smoke and confusion a black Buddhavision security craft flopped down on to the roof. Several heavily-armed henchmen stepped from it.

'Botheration,' Rambo exclaimed. 'The old Bill. Eric, me old mucker, it looks as if we are going to be next week's special guests on the *Nemesis* show.'

'Goody.' Eric gave up the unequal struggle with his fingers. 'I've always wanted to be on the telly.'

18

. . . *always whistling. Didn't I mention that? Maybe I forgot, it all gets a bit jumbled some times. Like everything happened at once, not like it was spread out. Always whistling. He'd have this tune, whistle it for days and if, say, I left him on a street corner and he was whistling it, next time I'd bump into him he'd be continuing it right from where he left off. Just like there had been no in between. Used to give me the creeps. It was like I didn't exist between the times I was with him.*

But the tunes, see. They'd get stuck in your head. Real catchy. Popular music tunes. Pop it was called back then, or rock. And then, maybe a week or a month later the same tunes would turn up on the radio. And every one went to the number one slot. Worldwide some of them. So, I know what you're thinking. He wrote them, right? Me too. I bought the records, but they were all big guys and well known. He couldn't have been all of them, could he?

Although, I mean, he was a God. Still is a God for all I know.

The Suburban Book of the Dead

When you wanna move, its what's in the groove that counts.
James Brown

Soul is when the only way you can express yourself is to go Weeeeeeeeeeeeeeeeeeeeeeeeeeeell awwwwwwwwwwwwwwl right.
Same fella

'So,' said Fergus, as they reached the perforated board-room door 'That is my theory and that is my plan. Tell me, what do you think?'

Elvis checked out the alien son-of-a-bitch. 'No shit?' he asked.

'None whatever. I have checked out my figures again and again. Monitored your life readings and I'm certain that I'm correct.'

'Well then,' Elvis straightened his shoulders, turned up his collar and finger-combed his jet-black locks. 'Let's kick ass.'

Fergus gazed along the empty corridor, thinking to glimpse the comforting glint of a multi-function riot gun as it dipped back into a far doorway. 'I'll leave you to it. Just call out for Mr Garstang.'

'No sweat. And fella . . .' Fergus turned. 'Yes?'

'Thanks.'

'You might have the decency to put a fellow's coat upon a hanger.' The torturers ignored Rambo and continued to strap his unclad body into the steel chair. 'No chance of a cushion I suppose?' An anonymous thug, who had just come on shift, dealt Rambo a specific blow to the solar plexus. Ill-mannered oik, thought Rambo. 'Ouch,' he said.

The anonymous thug's equally anonymous compatriot pressed the self-adhesive discs to the appropriate quarters. 'This is going to hurt really bad,' he said with relish.

'First prepared is best prepared, old todger. Don't crease the strides, there's an angel.' The thugs gave Rambo a perfunctory thump or two and left the room. 'So this is Christmas . . .' sang Rambo, although he didn't know quite why.

178

'Rambo Bloodaxe?' The voice crackled into the tiled room.

'Present,' said the man in the chair.

'Mr Bloodaxe, we have some questions to ask you.'

'Then ask away, my dear fellow. I have pressing engagements elsewhere.' The first minor tremor loosened some teeth and scrambled his goolies.

'Leave off there.' Rambo howled. 'No need for that surely?'

'What do you know about SUN?' Rambo hesitated. Up in the control room:

First anonymous torturer: 'Don't be so mean, the power isn't on ration.'

Second anonymous torturer: 'I'm sure Mr Bloodaxe wants to tell us all.'

First anonymous torturer: 'Burn it out of him.'

Second anonymous torturer: 'But he seems like a nice chap. Oh well . . .'

Rambo Bloodaxe: 'Aaaaaaaaaaaaaaaaaagh!'

Rex turned his face away from the viewing panel. 'If you will pardon me,' he said, turning to leave. 'I find this quite upsetting.'

Dan offered Rex the sweetest of smiles. 'No taste for revenge then, Rex? Don't you want to twiddle the dials a bit?'

'No, I don't. I know what it feels like.'

Dan laughed. 'Yeah, you certainly squirmed.' He looked sharply at Rex. 'No hard feelings I trust?'

'You'll kill him, I suppose?'

Dan shrugged. 'Maybe yes, maybe no. I will see how the spirit moves me.'

Rex chewed upon his lip. 'Just another non-person.'

'That's right, Rex. Rubbish, detritus. Millions more

179

where he came from. He is merely a means to an end. My end. You would do well to bear this in mind.'

Rex stared into the narrow face of the Dalai Lama and for a moment his thoughts were unguarded. It didn't matter how much credit he built up for himself, there was very little chance of him staying around for long enough to enjoy it. Dan would simply use him up and then throw him away. So much detritus. And it all just came to him in that single moment. He was going nowhere. Absolutely nowhere.

'I am handing in my resignation,' said Rex. 'I quit.'

Dan laughed, but there was no humour in it. 'No-one quits, Rex. You don't quit on the Dalai Lama.'

'Well I do, and I have.' Rex turned to leave.

'Stop him.' An anonymous torturer sprang from his chair and drew a handgun. Rex turned, kicked the weapon from his grip, punched him hard across the chin. He stooped and snatched up the fallen gun. He turned it upon Dalai Dan. 'I'm a dead man, aren't I?'

Dan shrugged. 'You could always reconsider. Put it down now, there's a good boy.'

Rex swallowed. With a shaking hand he levelled the gun towards the Dalai's face. This had all got suddenly out of control. He no longer understood what he was doing.

'Put down the gun Rex.'

'I think not.' Rex squeezed the trigger. A shot rang out.

Rex Mundi sank to the floor. A gaping wound in the back of his head. The second anonymous torturer blew into the smoking barrel of his gun. Dan gazed down at the corpse of Rex Mundi. 'Stupid waste,' said he. 'Get someone to clear the mess up and get whatever you can from Bloodaxe. I shall be in my apartments. Let me know what you find out.'

'Yes sir.' The anonymous torturer turned the body over with his foot and began to root through Rex's pockets.

An uncomfortable trio edged along the executive corridor at Earthers Inc. Lavinius Wisten, his hands tied securely, was strapped behind Gryphus Garstang. Elvis Presley, his face wearing a nonchalant smile, strolled ahead, popping his fingers. The nose of a certain gremlin-ridden gun prodded his back. 'Move on,' ordered Garstang.

'Can't get a clear shot yet,' came a voice over Jason Morgawr's headset. 'He's got Wisten tied on behind.'

'Stay in touch.' Morgawr turned to Fergus Shaman. Fergus shrugged, 'You know my feelings, it's in your hands now.'

'We could just open up on him and see what happens.'

'You will not,' barked the lip-reader. 'You can do what you like with Garstang, but I don't want to lose any more members of my board. Is that clear?'

'Yes sir,' said Jason Morgawr.

God's nose, thought Fergus Shaman.

'They've taken the lift, sir.'

'Are your teams in place in the research labs?'

'Yes sir. But if we can't get a clear shot at him?' Morgawr glanced at Mungo Madoc. Mungo's look was intense.

'Play it by ear,' said Jason. Mungo looked him daggers. 'Er, sorry sir, no offence taken, I hope.'

'Down the hyper-ponic bench,' ordered Garstang. 'Stop at the tank at the end.' Garstang swung around, dragging Lavinius with him. He raised his gun, Hollywood fashion. 'Stay back,' he shouted. 'Anyone messes with me, they both get it.'

'Dead exciting all this.' Elvis stifled a yawn.

181

'Down to the end of the bench, wasn't it chief?'

'Down to the end, and don't try anything.'

'Sure thing, chief.' The threesome reached the end of the bench. 'Just here, chief?'

Garstang turned his gun upon Presley. 'What's all this "chief" business?'

'Bio-emontic integration, chief. Failing organism maintaining stasis through neuro-enzine shift. Nowhere else to go. Came in here.'

Elvis thrust his hand into the tank. 'Fergus Shaman copped on, sorry you missed it.'

Garstang's face expressed a good many things. Surprise, shock, horror, anger. There's a lot you can do with a Phnaargian face. 'Treachery!' He thrust the nose of his gun up that belonging to Elvis and pressed the button. But the electric pulse struck only empty air before fading into space many metres away. Then the Phnaargian special services opened up and there wasn't much time left for Garstang's face to display emotion. So he fired off his weapon again and again and again. Until it fed back and blew up.

'Oh, help,' wailed a charred and sorry Wisten. 'A change of underlinen required here.'

It was suddenly 3.35 on the afternoon of 7 June 2050 again. The sun still wasn't shining.

Rex took to pacing the floor. It had never been a habit which found great favour with him. Firstly, because it was a waste of valuable viewing time and secondly because it involved a good deal of ducking and diving, if it was to be achieved without cracking one's head open upon the gilded cherub. Now seemed a good time for it though. Twenty-three hours had passed and MOTHER had told him precisely nothing. Surely no-one could go a full twenty-four hours without watching television? It was unthinkable. Rex checked his chronometer. Still two-thirty, he'd have to get that fixed. Rex paced and cursed, cursed and paced. He turned imploringly to the terminal. 'Come on,' he waved his hands frantically. 'Come on.'

'Holy shit,' said Elvis Presley. 'Where the hell are you, green buddy?'

'Inside, chief. I'm inside your head.'

'My head? But how?'

'Told you, nowhere else to run. That Garstang was about to put his foot on me. I had to transfer my consciousness into the nearest living thing if I was going to survive. I didn't fancy his foot, so as your head was the second nearest, once he'd knocked you out, I came in here. Somewhat fortuitous all round, I'd say, chief.'

'Good to have you back, buddy.'

'Cheers. So, when Fergus learned that you were at Earthers Inc., he wanted to check you out, see how come you had survived the time travel and all. So while you were out cold he ran a brain scan on you and saw me in there hiding. He knew that all you needed to do was stick your hand in the top-up tank for me to fully revive. Clever stuff, eh?'

'But that Garstang could have done for me.'

'No chance chief, you're a key figure. No-one wants to do for you. Well, almost no-one.'

'You mean that Dalai?'

'Sure do.'

'Well, as it happens, I've been doing a lot of thinking about him. I worked it all out in my head. If all this mess in the world is because I screwed up in fifty-eight, then I gotta do something about it, right?'

'Right, so back to fifty-eight then, is it?'

'No chance, not yet anyhow. I gotta sort stuff out here first. We gonna have us a revolution here, little green buddy. Shit, what are you groaning for? And, hey, exactly where are we now anyhow?'

They were suddenly inside a bunker. A funny-looking woman in a red gingham dress, her neck hung with medals, each of which displayed the grinning face of the Dalai, regarded Elvis with considerable awe.

'Would you like a cup of tea?' Aunty Norma did a little curtsy.

'No tea, thanks ma'am. But I could use a beer.' Beside Aunty Norma stood a pair of charred boots and a neat pile of ash. These didn't offer Elvis a drink.

'You have come unto me,' crowed the crone. 'You the born again.'

'People keep telling me that.' Elvis spied out the TV terminal.

'Say,' said he, seating himself in Uncle Tony's chair. 'No chance of one of my movies being on, I guess?'

In Odeon Towers Rex's terminal lit up like the fourth of July he knew nothing about.

IDENTIFICATION OF SUSPECT CONFIRMED. LOCATION FOLLOWS: LATITUDE 51° 29', LONGITUDE 0° 18'. HAVE ANOTHER DAY, MR MUNDI.

'I certainly will.' Rex bounced up and down, cracking his head on the gilded cherub. 'Gotcha,' he chirruped. 'Oh, ouch.' Rubbing his skull he danced over to the terminal and bashed through a direct line to Dalai Dan. The Inmost One's face filled the screen.

'Nice work,' he said, before Rex had even had time to speak. 'Very ingenious, we will take it from here.' The screen went blank. Rex's jaw fell. 'What the . . .'

A sudden commotion upon the landing below drew Rex's attention. And a sudden sense of approaching danger that he was unable to explain.

Something told him that big trouble was coming his way.

'There,' said a company medic. 'As good as new.' Mungo Madoc examined his ears. You could hardly see the joins. 'Very good, a quick clean job, expertly performed. We can all learn something from this, can't we, Fergus?'

'I pride myself on a job well done,' he replied.

'And Mr Presley. Back in the right place and the right time, I trust?'

'Have no fear of that, sir. We've seen the last of him.'

Jason Morgawr burst into the room. 'It's Presley,' he gasped. 'He's back on Earth.'

'Yes thank you, Morgawr. We all know that, he's back in 1958, about to take the draft.'

'Oh no he's not, sir. He's sitting down there right now, plotting to overthrow the Dalai Lama. Mr Madoc? Could someone help me pick Mr Madoc up? Are you all right, sir?'

Rex peeped down through the roof hatch on to the landing below. He saw Deathblade Eric and Rambo Bloodaxe creep up the stairs and approach his doorway. Rex had left the door ajar. Rambo put his finger to his lips and nudged Eric, who was carrying an enormous handgun. Half of Eric's head appeared to be missing. At a signal from Rambo, Eric burst into Rex's apartment. Rambo followed him in. Rex gave them a moment before shinning down the metal ladder, slamming shut the door and engaging the anti-theft devices. 'Like rats in a trap,' he observed. Much shouting and beating issued from within, but once locked and bolted the door wouldn't be bothering about that. Rex gave it a little pat.

'Two in the can for later.' He upped the ladder once more and climbed into the air car. Canopy down, straps on, identification confirmed.

'Latitude fifty-one degrees, twenty-nine minutes. Longitude, zero degrees, eighteen minutes. And fast please.' The car dragged itself clear of the roof and swung away into the gloom. Rex belled through to the Dalai. Old Inmost One's face appeared on the dash screen.

'Rex, my dear boy. Something I can do for you?'

'I have further good news to report.'

'You never cease to amaze me.'

'The bounty on Rambo Bloodaxe.' Bounty was a poorly chosen word. 'The bonus I mean.' Rex wondered just how far Dan's telepathic powers extended.

'The bonus, yes,' said Dan.

'Does it still hold good?'

'My word is my bond, Rex. But Bloodaxe and his flesheaters died during the Fundamentalist missile attack, surely.'

'Happily not. Although I have no idea how they escaped. There's another one with him. I have them held prisoner in my apartment. You have only to have them collected.'

'Most enterprising, Rex. My congratulations.'

'You'll have my account credited then?'

'Most certainly. Where exactly are you now, Rex?'

Rex made crackling sounds with his mouth. 'Sorry, getting a lot of static. I'll have to call you back.' He switched off the dash screen. The air car flew on, its engines coughing fitfully.

Rex was left alone, or so he hoped, with his thoughts.

Something strange had happened. Somehow he had known that Rambo and Eric were on their way up to kill him. But how? ESP? The Dalai's gifts couldn't be rubbing off on him, could they? He wasn't altogether sure that the Dalai's gifts were all that reliable anyway. The Living God King seemed somewhat fallible, to say the least. But something strange was going on and somehow the mystery man in the photograph was at the heart of it. A word or two with him, in private, might yield up all manner of interesting information. The air car informed him that it was about to land and ran through its programmed routine of solace . . . should any accident occur . . .

'Om-mani-padme-hum,' sang Rex Mundi. It was a catchy little number after all. The air car whacked down on to familiar territory. Rex screwed on his weatherdome and lifted the canopy. He climbed out.

'Aunty Norma's,' he whistled. 'Now there's a thing.'

A Nemesis security craft was parked near at hand and two heavily-armed thugs swung round to face his arrival. Rex recognized them as his former torturers. 'Hello Rex,' Mickey Malkuth addressed him on the open channel. 'How's your luck?'

'It varies,' he cautiously approached the stun-suited duo. 'Have you made any arrests then?'

'Arrests? Naughty, naughty. Wanted for questioning is all.'

'Questioning? Yes, I see. And you have apprehended your suspect?' Rex stepped warily across the rubble-strewn landscape surrounding his former home. It was grim and somehow it now seemed even grimmer than he remembered.

'Flown the coop,' said Malkuth. He indicated the open bunker door. 'There was an old girl down there. But we couldn't get any sense out of her.' Rex's stomach dropped. He stumbled towards the bunker.

'I shouldn't go in, if I were you, Rex. It's a bit messy, if you know what I mean.' Malkuth's laughter rang in Rex's ears. He fell through the bunker door and tore off his weatherdome. And he remembered that smell. That stale rancid smell. The smell of hopeless doomed poverty.

The bunker was as it always had been. Candles burned in the tiny wall shrine, where an out-of-register photo of Dan grinned at nothing. Next to it was a sketch of Uncle Tony scrawled on a can label in Rex's childhood hand. The two chairs faced the terminal screen.

Aunty Norma lay face down before them. Her face discoloured and hardly recognizable. One hand was twisted unnaturally into the pile of ash which had once been Uncle Tony. Into this her dying fingers had clawed a single name. Dan. Tears ran from Rex's eyes. He gazed down at the broken body. Up at the terminal screen. It blazed colourfully, eternally. Dan's face was there, grinning like a wolf.

Rex ran his fingers lightly over his aunt's hair, rose to his feet and put his boot through the terminal screen.

19

. . . I was with the foundation from sixty-three until sixty-eight, when it went completely underground. If it's still in existence then I don't know where. But he's still around, I can tell you that. Once you've seen how he works, you don't forget. I see stuff in the papers and I say, that's him. That's the God. As I say, I joined in sixty-three, approached in the street, the usual thing. Their technique never altered. Never had to. Why improve on perfection? I was just one more disillusioned kid. Bummed out of high school. These guys just homed right in. All smiles, handshakes, first-name terms. Like they'd known me all of their lives. Invited me up to one of those weekend retreats and I never left. Not for five years. We were changing the world. Or thought we were. And we did it all for him. He was always ahead of everybody else. Knew exactly what was coming, when and where. So we were always one jump ahead. Fashion, music. Music. He was responsible for it all, you know. All that sixty-seven thing. Haight Ashbury, Woodstock, Owsley's acid. You name it. Hendrix, The Doors, The Grateful Dead . . . Shit, The Beatles, man, someone told me that he'd set all that up. Tipped off Brian Epstein, lent him the money, everything. Engineered it all. And he never wrote a single word down. Kept it all in his head. We were laying the stones, that's what he said. Some times back then I can tell you. Yeah, the foundation, what don't I remember about the foundation.

The Suburban Book of the Dead

That which can be thought is not true.
Hindoo proverb

I think therefore I am.
French proverb.

The acid rain began to fall. The Nemesis security craft had long since departed. Rex sat alone upon the rubble before his late aunt's bunker. Hissing droplets smeared over his weatherdome. He sighed long and hard. Fifty years in a hole in the ground, and for what? Rex climbed to his feet. For nothing. Just another non-person. He needed a drink. He needed a big drink. With a very final look toward his former home he returned to the air car and called up the co-ordinates of the Tomorrowman Tavern. 'And fast,' he said.

'Fergus, why do you think it is that I'm losing all confidence in you?' Mungo was propped up in his boardroom chair. Tubes, dangling from an assortment of coloured bottles strung above him, vanished into various parts of his anatomy. He didn't look the picture of health.

Fergus could only shrug helplessly. He thought he probably knew the reasons.

Jason Morgawr was grinning behind his hands. At length he rose to speak. 'If I might just say a word or two,' he ventured.

'Oh yes, Jason.' Fergus winced. 'What would you like to say?'

'Well, sir. The fact that Mr Presley is still here in the present, need not necessarily be such a terrible thing.' Fergus brightened, Jason was back on his side, surely. What a decent fellow.

190

'Although Mr Shaman has clearly made a grave error in judgement—' and none more so than just then, thought Fergus '—the situation can still be turned to our ultimate advantage.'

'I like what I'm hearing, Jason. Please continue.'

'Certainly sir, thank you. I just wondered if I might sound you out upon the subject of Armageddon.'

Mungo clutched at his heart. The dangling bottles gurgled. Mungo gurgled. 'Armageddon?'

'Well, not so much the real thing. None of us want the series to end, do we?'

Mungo shook his head gravely. 'We do not.'

'Well, it occurs to me that it might not be altogether a bad thing if we just let this Presley get on with whatever he has in mind. It's bound to go down well with the viewers. I understand from a recent poll that his antics on the *Nemesis* show were extremely well received. Now if we could just jolly things along a bit. I have a certain scenario in mind which might just do the business.'

'To do with Armageddon?'

'Well, in a way. I'll work out all the figures and get it costed. Then I'll get back to you.'

'And you are suggesting that in the meanwhile we do nothing at all?'

'Absolutely nothing. Just trust me.'

'Do absolutely nothing,' Mungo sank into his chair and began to suck his thumb. 'Absolutely nothing. I like the sound of that.'

The lounge boy dowsed Rex down with decontaminant as he passed through the plastic flaps. Rex entered the uncrowded bar. The one-eyed barman met his approach with an unfaltering stare. 'What do you want?' he said, without charm.

Rex cradled his weatherdome. 'Tomorrowman Brew, mega-large.'

'Eyeball the screen.' Rex hesitated. 'Eyeball or butt out. It's all the same to me.'

Rex eyeballed. 'My, my,' the proprietor raised a matted eyebrow, 'you've come into some scratch lately. The wages of sin, eh?' He glanced at Rex and decanted a triple measure. 'Still it's of no consequence to me. But the pox on you, nonetheless, for it.'

'Your very good health.' Rex drained the fetid cup in three short gulps. 'Another of similar.'

'And have one yourself landlord?'

Rex didn't dignify the remark with a reply. Mine host splashed short measure. 'To the line,' said Rex.

'Company man then, are you?' The barman passed the cup across the unspeakable bartop. 'Station boy?'

'I just quit.'

'Buddhavision car though. Saw you come down.'

'I haven't quit officially as yet.' Rex stared dispiritedly into his spirits.

'No-one quits, asshole. No-one.' With this said the barman took himself off to business elsewhere. Rex ferried his drink to as distant a corner as he could find. Here he sank into a plastique scoop-chair of near antique construction.

Delving into one of his numerous pockets he fought free a pack of Kharma Cools and flipped one inexpertly toward his mouth. He drew deeply on it, chemicals flared and Rex filled his lungs with toxic relaxant. He held the smoke a full five seconds before releasing it in a turquoise plume through his currently serviceable left nostril. Rex turned the packet between his fingers. The Dalai's face grinned up at him above the motto 'You're never alone with a Kharma Cool'. Rex tipped out the two remaining cigarettes before crushing the packet to oblivion. He wasn't a happy man.

Something gnawed away at his insides and it wasn't simply hunger or the senseless killing of his aunt. Nor the Dalai's coldbloodedness nor his sister's contempt.

It was something much more. He was up to his neck in something, but he had no idea what. Perhaps that was it. The helplessness. Lack of control. Rex struggled to put it into words, but his lack of vocabulary proscribed it. H. G. Wells once said that every word of which a man is ignorant represents an idea of which he is ignorant. That Rex was walking proof of the great man's hypothesis would doubtless come as little consolation to either of them. Rex fumed. He sucked upon his cigarette, downed his second triple, rose gloomily and hunched back to the bar counter for a refill.

The one-eyed barman was squeezing his spots. Rex rattled his cup meaningfully upon the bartop. 'Shop,' said he.

The barkeep examined a pus-bespattered fingertip. 'Another? You are a prodigious bibber, and there's a fact for you.'

'Eyeball the screen is it?'

Barkeep angled a cracked bottle toward Rex's cup. 'Conscience pricking?'

'Fuck you,' Rex replied.

'Articulate fellow, aren't you,' the barman observed. 'Man of action.'

Rex eyed the barman. History records that when lost for words many prefer the use of violence to enforce a point. This well-attested truism was not unknown to the professional behind the bar, who now took a deliberate step back. 'You'd love to, wouldn't you?'

Rex shook his head. 'It's not you. You just happen to be here.' He accepted his drink. 'Have one yourself.'

The barman grinned and decanted a large libation of the demon brew into an unnaturally clean glass of his own. 'What's on your mind?'

Rex shook his head. 'I only wish I knew.'

'Not a lot of time nowadays for too much self examination. Look at them . . .' He gestured with his drink-clutching hand towards his patrons. These sat, a row of dummies lined up along the bar counter. Drinks in hands, eyes fixed upon the screens, earning credits. 'No-one thinks any more. Free thought is tantamount to heresy. Thought implies doubt. Doubt equals subversion. Subversion leads to anarchy. Anarchy is heresy. Round in a circle. Like some unholy mandala. I'd not go troubling yourself with too much thought, if I were you.'

'If you were me?'

'Company car. Rooms above ground, I'll wager. Big credits with MOTHER. You're a whizzkid boy. You're the business.'

'So I should say thank you, I suppose?'

'That's the system; you're a part of it. What else do you expect? What else do you want?'

'Integrity?' Rex suggested.

The barman fell about in mirth. 'Excuse me,' he wiped tears from his cheek, 'It's a long time since I heard that word. Are you sure you know what it means?'

'And what of you, then? Running this plague pit, you are above it all, I suppose?'

'Oh no, pal.' The barman shook his head violently, causing his false eye to turn it's pupil into his skull. 'I'm just like you. A victim. We're all victims. There is them and there is us. We're never going to be them, no matter what we do. We're us. You're us. A victim, a non-person,

194

cog in the great wheel, number on the screen. The only difference between you and me is that you haven't come to terms with it yet.'

Rex glowered into his cup. 'But it doesn't have to be like that. It shouldn't be like that.'

'Maybe it shouldn't. How should I know? But it is and possibly it always has been. So what are you going to do? Change the world?'

'I might just do that.'

'No. Please, please.' The barman clutched at his sides, laughing hideously. 'Too much fine humour in one day. Change the world indeed! A crapulous comic, so you are.' He topped Rex's cup without charge, and sauntered away chuckling immoderately. Rex stubbed out his cigarette upon a leg of his radiation suit and thought grim thoughts.

A sudden altercation now occurred which sent Rex ducking for cover. Between the plastic flaps voices were being raised, blows exchanged. The barman made haste along the counter and brought a knobkerrie into play. Rex peeped over a tabletop. Just don't let it be Rambo Bloodaxe, he prayed without shame.

'I'm only doing my job,' wailed a small voice.

'Look at my Goddamn suit,' came a larger voice. A small head was soundly cuffed, and its owner, the pail-toting lounge boy, entered the inner flap with a kind of awkward cartwheel which terminated in concussion against the bar counter. The owner of the head-cuffing hand now followed the inadequate acrobat into the bar. He was a tall, handsome young man, wearing a magnificent, if now slightly sodden, gold lamé suit. And Rex knew that face immediately. It was the face of the mystery man himself. The face of the photograph. Killer sideburns, thought Rex.

195

'What's your game then?' The barman shinned over the bar counter and bore down upon the lounge boy's attacker, knobkerrie raised.

'Take a hike buddy.' The mystery man threw an unusual punch, which came with as much surprise to the barman as it did to Rex. Only more painfully so. He then brought a blue suede foot into action. Rex watched in fascination. Old Adam Earth favoured the ancient Tibetan fighting technique known as Dimac, when disposing of the Dalai's would-be assassins, but this was something far more convincing.

'Goes with the sickle,' said the mystery man, enigmatically. Rex pondered upon a course of action. However the large amount of Tomorrowman Brew now burning its way through his stomach lining made cogitation difficult.

'That's him, chief.' Rex heard the curious voice, although he couldn't see its owner.

'You certain?' The mystery man addressed this question to the air.

'Sure thing chief. The old dame in the bunker showed us the picture, remember?'

'He looks like shit.'

'Hardly surprising. Best tackle him now, eh?'

'No sweat.' Elvis approached Rex Mundi. Rex sought invisibility without success. 'Hey fella, I'd like a word with you.' Rex weighed up his chances. The barman was down and out, the punters, momentarily interrupted from their viewing, had now returned to it. This was what was once called a one-to-one situation. Rex raised an unconvincing fist.

'Have a care,' he said. 'I know Dimac.'

Elvis raised calming palms. 'I ain't looking to fight. I just want to move mouth with you, is all.'

196

'Eh?'

'Talk. Sit down, no problem.' Rex sat down. He almost made the chair. Elvis helped him up on to it. 'There. You OK?'

'I don't feel all that clever as it happens.'

'You'll be OK. The name's Rex, right?'

Rex nodded carefully. 'I don't think we've been formally introduced.'

'The King, just call me the King.'

Why? wondered Rex. 'As you please,' he said. 'So what do you have on your mind, your majesty?'

'Revolution,' said Elvis Presley.

20

. . . the records? You mean the albums, right? Everybody
always asks about the albums. A quarter, maybe half a
million of them, I guess, and growing all the time. And he
kept them moving around, never in the same place for long.
They were stored at the foundation at the first off, he had
them guarded day and night. Then he said that they should
be moved out. They went into containers, we worked on
shifts, took us nearly three weeks to load them up. Then
they travelled. All over the country. All new, all mint
condition, still in the cellophane wraps, never played.
Imagine a collection like that and he never played them.
This would be late in sixty-eight and he was getting real
reclusive by then. We'd get phonecalls and stuff, nothing
in writing of course. Some times we wouldn't hear from
him for weeks. And there were a lot of hassles. A lot of
people asking awkward questions, and none of us had any
answers. Things got real bad about then. People stopped
smiling, do you know what I mean?

The Suburban Book of the Dead

'Kidnap the Dalai Lama?' Rex clutched at his narcotized head. 'That is what you are saying?' He examined his fingers; between them were small knots of
dead hair.

'Sure thing, buddy.'

'I would suggest that it was anything but. But why

him, why not Pope Joan or L. Ron Hubbard the twenty-third?'

'All in good time. I gotta personal score to settle.'

Rex could feel the room circling. 'Let me get this straight. You are telling me that the Dalai Lama is the what?'

The enlightened look we have come to know, if not perhaps to love, was once more upon the face of Elvis Presley. 'Ant-eye-Christ.' (Well, that's how he pronounced it.) 'Ant-eye-Christ.'

'Antichrist. Sorry, this is all somewhat unexpected.'

'I have seen the future. It's much like the past, only worse.'

'I never expected much else. Who are you?'

'I told you. Are you sure we got the right guy?' The question wasn't directed toward Rex.

'Sure thing, chief. He's your man.'

'Who said that?

'I have a sprout in my head,' Presley explained.

'Ah,' said Rex. It was a very meaningful 'ah'. 'I have to take a spray now and very probably throw up. If you will excuse me?'

'I'll bust your head if you try to leave.'

'Yes, indeed. Now let me just recap. Revolution, kidnap, the Antichrist, and a sprout in your head.'

'That's about the size of it.'

'Friend,' said Rex. 'I don't know what you are on. But it certainly is not what I'm on.' With no further comments to make, Rex fell forward across the table and from there to the floor.

'He's out of it for now, chief,' came a voice from the rear of Presley's skull. 'Best away to a place of safety with him until he sobers up.'

'We could have a drink before we go.'

The Time Sprout drew Presley's attention to Rex, who was now puking silently in his narcotic slumbers. 'Best not, eh?'

'So then what?'

'So then he helped Rex up and they went off screen, sir.' Fergus smiled, a little too complacently for Mungo's liking. 'We can't be everywhere. Most places, yes, but not everywhere.'

Mungo sniffed pollen. 'We refoliated that planet, every leaf, flower, mould and fungus all broadcasting back to us. There can't be any blank spots, surely?'

'Well, we've lost Rex before. There are dead areas all over, we never needed to pay them much attention before now.'

'So we can't see what they are up to?'

'Not until they break cover again. But I might suggest the suspense angle. Both of them are geared up to take some sort of revenge, don't you think?'

'Kindly expound further.'

'Rex Mundi must be pretty put out over his aunt, and Elvi . . .'

'Yes Fergus, the mercurial and inspired Mr Presley?'

'Bit of an unknown quantity, I agree. But I'm sure he can be chivvied along in the right direction.'

'I can't imagine upon what evidence you can possibly base that supposition.'

'Oh, wheels are in motion,' lied Fergus Shaman. 'Any more memos from Jason Morgawr?'

'Hourly,' Mungo replied. 'Although none telling me the all important news that he has stopped the spread of the virus. Most read like the outpourings of some crazed evangelist. If I were an uncharitable chap I might be led to the conclusion that Mr Morgawr

201

was pulling some kind of fast one. Your thoughts on this, Fergus.'

'Mine, as ever, mirror your own, sir. A shady customer and no mistake. One of the late Mr Garstang's confidants, or so I understand.'

'Well, you just keep a close eye on him. Let me know exactly what he's up to, there's a good fellow.'

'I certainly will, sir. Something of an upstart, our Mr Morgawr. Not of the old school, like us.'

'Maybe so, just keep me informed.'

Fergus smiled his friendly smile. Mungo Madoc was clearly in a full-time state of confusion. If he played his cards right all kinds of possibility might present themselves.

I'm off the hook here, thought Fergus Shaman.

Oh no, you're not, thought Mungo Madoc. He might not actually be able to read minds. But he hadn't got where he had got by being a complete pillock.

'Aaaaaaaaaaaaagh, ow and ouch.' A good many hours had passed away, but these did nothing to spare Rex Mundi from a hangover of massive proportions. Rex tore at his skull, uprooting further discouraging clumps of hair. 'Where am I?'

Elvis stirred life into the fire. Above it hung a blackening coffee pot. 'How are you doing?'

'Not well,' Rex did some futile eye focusing. 'Where am I, or did I ask that already?'

'You did. You are down below.' Elvis managed to get the sufficiently sombre tone into that. 'Down in the depths. You've been here before, haven't you?'

Rex nodded, he'd been here before, although he couldn't recall exactly how. 'Is it safe?'

'Free from the bio-scan.'

'The bio-what? No, don't tell me.'

'Have some coffee. There's a whole mess of things I gotta tell you.'

Mess is probably right, thought Rex, which was absolutely right.

Dan fed the slim beads into his ears and jacked into the holophon . . . Well since my baby left me . . . It felt even worse than before. Closer somehow and more threatening. The words approached him at great speed, as if wishing to physically assault him. Where once they had been haunting and melancholy, now they were downright offensive. They buffeted him in the face, probed through the pores of his skin. Invaded him. They lay in his stomach like leaden weights. Dan jerked and twitched. It hurt. And the face of SUN leered at him. Put the blue suede boot in and kicked him again and again and again.

'And that,' said Rex, when Elvis had finally run himself dry of exposition, 'is a mindbender to end all mindbenders.'

'How do you think I feel?' Elvis sipped cold coffee. Rex turned his chipped cup between his unwashed fingers. Another nail was coming loose.

'And so to cut a long story short,' said he, 'you were kidnapped in 1958 by a visitor from outer space, who travelled back through time by means of a sprout, which you now have in your head.' Elvis nodded. 'And this visitor from space and his chums have manipulated the entirety of human history so they can broadcast it as a television show on their planet.' Elvis nodded yet again. Rex shook his head. 'And the present situation on Earth is somehow all your fault because you joined the Army.'

Elvis hung his head. 'Joined up. Led an entire genera-tion to disaster.'

'So what are you doing here? Surely you should be back in nineteen-whatever, not joining the Army.'

'Oh and I will. But I gotta sort things out here first, just to be on the safe side.'

'And this sorting out of things includes the over-throw of the Dalai Lama, whom you claim to be the Antichrist?'

Elvis grinned. 'That's it. I had a revelation see. The Presleys belong to the First Assembly of God. My family have revelations all the time.'

'Yes,' Rex agreed, 'although this is something of a revolutionary revelation.'

'Revolutionary revelation.' Elvis chewed it over. 'I like the way you think, brother.'

'Dan is a shit,' said Rex, in all candour, 'but the Antichrist, I think you are on a wrong'n there. He's a buddhist for one thing.' Elvis didn't appear to be listen-ing. He was whistling 'Dixie'. Rex put aside his cup and climbed carefully to his feet. Patting down the knees of his radiation suit. 'Well it's all most interesting and I really do wish you the best of luck. You must let me know how you get on.'

The whistler ceased his whistling. 'Going somewhere?' he asked.

'Thought I'd take a bit of a stroll. Thanks for the coffee.'

'He's going to make a run for it, chief,' came a small green voice.

'How do you do that?'

'He thinks you are a stone-bonker, chief.'

'Should I give him a little smack?' Elvis asked.

'I'd give him a large one, if I were you.'

'Easy now,' Rex put up his hands. 'No need for any

violence. We're both on the same side really. As it happens,'

'Show him your doodad, chief.' Rex flinched. A homosexual rapist, that was all he needed.

'The doodad, sure thing.' Elvis delved into a golden pocket and brought out the small black contrivance which he had lifted whilst on Phnaargos.

'Figured no-one would ever believe a Goddamn word I said,' said the King, 'so I took me a souvenir. Cop your whack for this, our kid.'

'Excuse me?'

'Sorry Buddy. It's the time travel, I've picked up all sorts of weird stuff.'

Rex drew back. 'Diseases and such like?'

'No. Figures of speech. And other figures. Equations and stuff.'

Elvis passed the doodad to Rex, who took it gingerly. 'What does it do?'

'It's a pocket transceiver. Milti-band. Bio-plasmic, of course. Utilising a cross polarization of beta-particles with minimal doppler shift, due to its advanced pseudopodia,' said the Time Sprout, informatively. 'Phnaargian state-of-the-art stuff, chief.'

Rex nodded thoughtfully. 'Has it macro-equalisation through quasi-spectrum nexus bicordials?'

'Er, um?'

'Does the rheostat impede throughout the red-diactinic field variables?'

'Er, um?'

'You looking for a fat lip, buddy?' Elvis asked.

'Sorry,' Rex replied. 'But I draw the line at being talked down to by a vegetable.'

'He's a great little guy when you get to know him.'

Rex let that one slide by. 'So, what does this do then?'

'Just press the red button and adjust the distance control,' Elvis told him. Rex held the thing at arm's length and did so. Light emanated from the slim black box and formed into a fuzzy but self-contained hologram of the outside world. Rex was entranced. Holographics were hardly new to him, but this was something more. Live holographics? That couldn't be done, could it? He twiddled the distance knob and brought the image to clarity. It focused and then passed on. Through walls, across broken streets, into dank homesteads, through further walls. On and on. Rex turned it in a circle. The image remained before him, but the outside world span through it. The Nemesis Bunker appeared upon the horizon. A great concrete pyramid, its peak piercing the cloud cover. Rex angled up the doodad and zoomed in upon it. The roving eye, drawing its information from the mould and lichen, shrubs and mosses, penetrated the bunker's outer defences. Pierced the heating ducts and inner partitions, crossed the studio floor. Entered the sanctum of the Dalai Lama.

'There's a sound button,' Elvis indicated, Rex pressed.

'It's down at the end of lonely street at Heartbreak Hotel.'

'Holy shit,' cried Presley. 'That's one of mine. That son-of-a-bitch is playing my music. Hear that, fella. Am I the King or am I the King? Or what?'

'But that's classical music. I've heard that stuff on the *Educational* when I was a child. Uncle Tony loved all that. But it must be . . .'

'Must be?'

'Must be a hundred years old.'

'Very nearly. Ninety-four to be exact. Recorded in Nashville, Scotty Moore on guitar, Bill Black on slapback bass. First number one single, first gold record.' Elvis sang along with himself. Rex's jaw fell. Only one man in history ever had a voice like that. And Rex was now staring at that very fellow. The goalposts had just been shifted. As the saying of the day went; this man was the real Lieutenant McCoy.

'Then you really are . . .' Rex's voice did all the appropriate quivering and quavering. 'Really are . . .'

'Really am, buddy.'

'Ian Paisley,' gasped Rex, wringing the final bit of life from that particular joke.

21

... sure, I heard about the records. Because it's my business, a collection like that. Muso's dream. The word was that he had the lot. And all the bootlegs. Out-takes. Gash over-dubs, backing tapes. Ten years worth, or so it was said. I'm talking 1970 now, you know, when the place went up. Well, a guy I know said that He was in there, The God. It was a major explosion. Blew in the bar windows. I got cut with the flying glass. See this scar. And this. They say it was the CIA or the FBI but who can say? Anyhow, there's a lot of theories, you can believe what you like. The God got killed, the God didn't get killed, the records went up in the blast or they didn't. Strangest one I heard was that the entire collection was some kind of computer program, right? Sounds off the wall, I know, but consider this. If you take the complete musical output of an entire generation, the whole damn lot, then don't you have something? A kind of a soul, perhaps. The soul of a generation. I mean it's there in the music. We all know it's in the music, somewhere, right. Anybody who's ever really listened knows it's there. Somewhere.

The Suburban Book of the Dead

Rex zoomed in upon the bed chamber of his sister. She was indulging in her second favourite pastime. Her first Rex considered to be the persecution of himself.

'Focus that up, boy,' choked Elvis. 'Lord alive, look at that baby.'

'You see, I actually did you in history,' Rex explained. 'My aunty,' he paused a moment in sad reflection. 'My aunty was a fundamentalist for a while, one of Hubbard's. When L. Ron the third amalgamated with the Gospel Church of America, wherever that was, back in the nineties, they were very big on the musical message.'

'Oh yeah.' The time traveller seemed somewhat distracted. 'Can you bring up the sound? I want to hear the moaning.'

'Yes,' Rex continued. 'As I remember it, there was the Reverend Al Green, Aretha Franklin, this guy called Cliff somebody, who never grew old. And a Michael Jackson, although he would be after your period. His big evangelical crusades were in the late nineties. But you, I did you of course. All the mystical stuff.'

'Mystical?' Elvis turned him a fleeting glance.

'The hard-to-understand stuff. "Wooden Heart", I did that. I passed through with an A grade for my "Metaphysical exposition on the socio-political ramifications of the Latin prayer sequence in 'Wooden Heart' ".'

'Latin prayers, are you crazy?' Elvis dragged himself momentarily from the erotic hologram. 'That was German, I sang one verse in German.'

Rex made a puzzled face, 'German, is that another dead language?'

'Wasn't when I sang it. Say fella, what is that the fat woman has strapped to her nose? It looks like a false . . .'

'It is,' sighed Rex.

'Glory be,' said Elvis.

Rambo Bloodaxe was lodged in a small cell of no

particular charm, somewhere in the sub-basement of the Nemesis Bunker. He was sore.

'Eric,' said Rambo.

'I think so,' came the honest reply.

'Eric, is this what we have come to?'

'It does have the appearance of being that very thing.'

'A sad and sorry circumstance, old chap friend of mine.'

'How are the nuts, Rambo?'

'Smarting, my dear fellow, still smarting.'

'You told a jolly fine tale though.'

Rambo sighed and delicately stroked his singed pudendum. 'All done to save us a further whacking.'

'My memory is sadly deficient, but you appeared to me to be telling a most shameful quantity of untruths, for the most part.'

'Merely giving them food for thought and us a chance of survival.'

'I felt your confession that we were in the pay of the Hubbard organization to be quite inspired. And all that folderol about the Nemesis security network having been infiltrated, spiffing stuff.'

'I think it was the revelation that the Dalai planned to replace the station's union representation with blackleg labour that really swung it. They switched off the power and downed tools around that time.'

'I do fear that there is a good chance of us shortly being rumbled, nonetheless.'

'The thought is in the very forefront of my mind, Eric. We must put escape at the very top of our priority list.'

'Rambo?' said Eric.

'Eric?'

'Rambo, should we succeed in escape, do you feel it possible that some surgery might be made available to me in the head department? Bits of my brain are still coming away between my fingers and I feel certain that my reason is likely to become severely impaired as a result.'

'Perhaps if you ceased to stand upon your head it would help,' Rambo suggested.

'Oh,' said Eric. 'I thought it was you doing that.'

'Killer,' Elvis made pelvic thrusts. 'Now I have seen everything. I wonder who she is.'

'She's my sister.'

'Your sister? Shit man, anyone on this planet not in your family? I mean, no offence meant.'

'None taken, I assure you, but between us both, don't you think that we should get down to the nitty gritty as it were?'

'Then you believe, right?'

Rex put up his hands, they still needed a wash. 'I'm not saying I believe everything, but that,' he indicated the doodad Elvis had snatched from him, 'that I do believe. With a thing like that, you could pull off all manner of things.' Rex thought on, the possibilities were, to him, endless.

Elvis looked severely put out. 'You believe in this gizmo but you don't believe in me.'

For one terrible moment Rex thought he was going to smash the doodad to smithereens.

'No, wait,' cried Rex. 'Wait, I want to show you something.' He delved into his radiation suit and produced the photograph the Dalai had given him. 'See this, am I or am I not one of your followers?'

Elvis stared at it in amazement. He stared at Rex in amazement.

'Goddamn,' he swore, and that look of enlightenment

212

(yes, that one) shone upon his flawless face. 'I see it all now. One of my followers, you were just checking me out to see if I was the genuine article. But you knew it all the time, didn't you?'

'Of course I did.' Rex relieved Elvis of the precious doodad. 'There can only be one King,' said he. 'I had to be sure.'

'Then you're with me?'

'Put your trust in me,' said Rex Mundi.

'Assassinate me?' Dan made wild gesticulations to man and God alike. 'Assassinate little me?' Rex nodded gravely. They were in the sanctum of the Inmost One, all swathes of silk and soaring erotically-painted columns. Blue sky to every side.

'That's about the shape of it, Dan.'

'No, no, no. Madness, madness.' Dan paced the floor with gusto.

'Oh, it's certainly that, Dan.' Rex lazed upon the Dalai's settee, drink in hand.

'Why me? Why me? Yog-Sothoth, why me?'

'The guy reckons that you are the Antichrist.' Rex gazed into his glass.

'The what???'

'Ant-eye-Christ. He considers himself to be upon some kind of Divine Mission.'

'I knew it. I just knew it. I felt this coming. How did you get out of there anyway?'

'It wasn't easy. Between you and me, I told the fellow lies.'

'Good boy. And where is he now?'

'Down in the caverns, I suppose. But you'll never find him down there.'

'Rex,' said Dan. 'My dear boy. My own dear boy. I am

surrounded by traitors, ne'er-do-wells, heretics and bloody unions. The Antichrist! I'm a Buddhist, for fuck's sake.'

'Such would seem to be the case. I did broach the matter of the theological inconsistency, but he remained adamant.'

'What am I to do?'

'You are asking me, Inmost One?'

'Ah,' Dan shrugged his shoulders, without conviction. 'Of course not, dear boy. No, no.'

'Of course not, Inmost One. You were speaking rhetorically, I understand. The Divinely Inspired One wouldn't seek advice from lesser mortals. You were, I believe, merely enquiring my opinion of the current dilemma and suppositions based upon my personal experience of this heretic.'

'Exactly. Got it in one.'

'I'm honoured that you should spare valuable moments to hear the words of your humble and devoted servant.' Rex was really warming to the situation. He could never have previously hoped to get away with such blatant sarcasm. But now, the previously alluded to goalposts had been moved. The pitch queered.

'And you are sure it's this man, the same man?'

Rex pulled out the now autographed photograph and laid it upon the black marble desk. 'Him.'

'SUN,' said the Dalai Lama.

'Father?' said Rex.

'SUN. And you think you can get to him, Rex?'

'I have his confidence, it shouldn't be impossible to . . .' Rex's eyes wandered toward the cocktail cabinet. It resembled the prow of an antique galleon. Rex took it to be a stylized privy.

'Help yourself Rex.' Rex did so.

'Dangerous though . . .' Rex clinked a chunky-looking decanter into the largest glass he could find. 'A very tricky and dangerous business.'

'Which means, I expect, a very costly business.'

'I suppose it does. But then cost hardly enters into it. To preserve the life force of the Living God King, should it take the wealth of the entire company, would come cheap.' Rex kept his eyes down.

'Indeed it would.' Dan's face was by no means cheery to behold.

'Thus, in all humility, I shall ask for but a trifle. An early retirement, an apartment fitting to my needs and the services of an all-female staff to attend upon my wants. Should I live through the perils ahead, of course.'

'You are a true soldier of God.' Dan rolled all three of his eyes toward the ceiling. Rex felt that it might be wise to elaborate.

'I do understand that you might consider my request over-presumptuous. But the circumstances are somewhat unique. Your security people can't contain this man. When he makes his move he will be unstoppable.'

Dan laughed. 'No man is unstoppable. Other than myself, of course.'

'A man who can travel through time, as this man can? He is unstoppable.'

'Through time?' Dan's jaw dropped. Further confirmation of what he already feared. 'Rot, no man can travel through time.'

'This man can. He has some kind of implant in his head. It enables him to void time. But you know all this. You have seen him in the flesh and you have his vinyl on your machine there.' Rex indicated the holophon.

Dan's eyes did a triple flash. 'How could you know this?'

'Surely it is enough to know that I do. If I can breach your security . . . then this man—'

'Yes, yes. So, say that I agree to your demands?'

'Demands? A fair day's pay for a fair day's job is all I ask.'

'Please, please, Rex, I hear that from morning to night. Suppose I was to agree to your most reasonable request. Then you would deliver this monomaniac into my hands,' Dan paused. 'Or better still . . .' He turned his gaze full upon Rex. Rex felt the hideous strength. The malevolence. Dan's lips never moved but his voice howled in Rex's ears.

'No,' Rex turned his face away, but couldn't escape the voice. 'No, not that. I'm no assassin.'

Dan's lips moved. 'Hardly assassination, Rex. More extermination. As in vermin. You shall have your penthouse in the sky and your early retirement. I will throw in the services of the two saffron nymphettes and even a chef. How does that sound?'

'All very nice. But . . .'

'But me no buts Rex, only bring me his head.' Dan's voice was death itself.

Rex felt his drink rising in his throat. 'His head . . .'

'His very valuable head.' Dan smiled a terrible smile and laughed a long and equally terrible laugh. Rex Mundi was violently sick.

22

. . . and then the CIA busted us. That would be in the summer of ninety-six. I'd been on the project for more than a year and had fooled myself into thinking it was safe. Probably would have been, but someone had to get greedy. Always happens. The country was election crazy. But no-one had any doubts about Wormwood. No-one could bust a hole in his campaign. If there were any skeletons in his closet, he'd bought them all off and sent them to Miami. The CIA were already in Wormwood's pocket. Someone had tipped him off about the project. He wanted it killed.

We'd been feeding the stuff into a COTEXT TEN computer, then selling it off. Perfect situation, mint copies. We could process them without even taking them out of the cellophane wraps. The records went out into circulation still brand new, but we'd got them into the processor in analogue. With the revenue from selling the mint copies we could constantly update our equipment. Some of those records were worth $10,000 apiece. We are talking collectors' items. So, as I say, someone got greedy. And we got busted.

We should have covered our tracks better. Kept on the move, like in the old days. But with the gasolene rationed and stuff you couldn't move about much. And the equipment was that delicate and we were all far too obsessed with the project. Because, you see, stuff was beginning to show up. Abstract most of it. Patterns, visual, audio. We were running it through a 409 CS deck overcut with a sequence analyser. We could pick up frequency levels that would

217

never have registered on ordinary equipment. And it was
there in every single one of those records. And it was all
coming together.

The Suburban Book of the Dead

The lads at the motorpool gave the pale-faced Rex a rowdy sendoff. He had become quite a celebrity thereabouts, having now outlived any previous Religious Affairs Correspondent by two full days. The chief mechanic addressed him as Captain Mundi, shook him vigorously by the hand and wished him 'another day'. 'We're all rooting for you "Ace",' he said, adding confidentially, 'If you could just see your way clear to surviving until Friday, it would be very much appreciated.' He showed Rex his sweepstake ticket. 'Thought I was on to a definite bummer with Friday afternoon. Backing a rank outsider, know what I mean?'

Rex applied his knee to the chief mechanic's groin. 'Be lucky,' he smiled as he tore away the bunting which gift-wrapped his air car and climbed into the cab.

He punched in a series of co-ordinates and eyeballed the small screen on the dashboard. 'You again, Mr Mundi?' came the silicone voice.

Rex made a sour face. 'Up and away,' said he. The car took grudgingly to the air, the Nemesis Bunker diminished in the rear-view mirror and was gone. Rex addressed the computer.

'Have my security team left the landing strip yet?'

'Security team?' The voice had no tone to it.

'Certainly, the Dalai assured me that a security team would follow this vehicle. Could you confirm, please?'

There was a short pause. The screen then flashed INFORMATION CLASSIFIED. Rex managed a wan grin, suspicions confirmed. He had been pretty certain that Dan would have him followed.

'Heat-seeking missile approaching,' cried Rex. 'Red alert.'

'I'm receiving no such radar warning,' the computer complained.

'Evidently, a new strain with advanced camouflage, no time to argue about it, surely?' The air car's computer chose not to make a fuss. It flung itself about, nearly dislodging Rex through the canopy, performed a number of stomach-loosening manoeuvres, switched off its engine and tumbled down to land in a cloud of smoke and sparks.

Rex's head appeared above the dashboard. His nose was bleeding. Two black-bodied Buddhavision security craft cruised by and vanished into the distance.

'Beautifully done,' said the dishevelled Rex. 'You are a credit to your series.' The computer kept its own counsel. It was sure that it had been had.

'I don't like this, Fergus, and that's a fact.' Mungo paced his private quarters, savouring the exquisite perfumes of his rare orchid collection. 'He's got that thing in his head. And that thing itself told us that time travel unhinges the traveller. Delusions of Godhood and whatnot.'

'He seems sane enough.' Fergus put his nose forward for a sniff. Mungo pushed it aside.

'From what we have been able to salvage from the storage beds, it appears that this Presley was of a singularly religious bent anyway. Gospel music or such-like.'

'All keys together rather well, sir.'

'All too messy,' Mungo complained. 'Too many loose ends. All this end-times twaddle from Morgawr. We can't have Armageddon on Earth, it's quite out of the question. We'd all be out of work.'

'Well, it's not real Armageddon, is it?' Fergus Shaman's nose crept forward again. 'And the revenues we can take from the advertisers can buy an awful lot of orchid bulbs.'

'Yes, but what when the advertisers discover that Armageddon has all come to nothing?'

'The series continues, we keep our jobs.'

'All too iffy. And the virus, Fergus, what of the virus?'

'The news isn't good sir, the virus has now reached the 1990s, and is still moving forward. Geneticists have been working around the clock, but nothing seems to stop it.'

Mungo sighed wearily. 'Truly, truly do I weep for the errant sons of Phnaargos.' He sniffed. So did Fergus Shaman. Mungo cuffed him about the head. 'Keep your bleeding hooter out of my *Lilium auratum rubro-vittatums*,' he advised.

Rex parked the air car within the ragged crater which had once been the Hotel California and scuttled from it to the concealed entrance of the underground cavern. Here was currently domiciled the man with the sprout in his head.

The caverns had undergone considerable refurbishment. Elvis lounged on an atrocious banana-shaped settee, his feet upon a thick-pile 'explosion' carpet. A cocktail cabinet, which in 1980 had vanished improbably from a Bayswater bawdy house, reflected candelabra glow within its mirrored front.

'Very nice,' said Rex. 'Very homely.'

'Thought I'd just pop back and pick up a bit of dee-cor.' Elvis sipped at something tall and blue, which had a small umbrella sticking out of it. 'So, what's happening?' Rex shrugged.

Elvis stretched out on the settee. 'Did you see the Lama?'

'We exchanged a few pleasantries.'

'Did you tell him I was going to kick his ass?'

'That's what you wanted me to tell him, wasn't it?'

'And how did he take it? Real bad, I hope.' Elvis laid aside his drink.

'He wasn't pleased. He said I was to cut your head off.'

Elvis clapped his hands together and bounced up and down. 'Son-of-a-bitch.'

'Easy on the bouncing, chief.' Rex bade the sprout the time of day and dropped on to a purple bean-bag which had escaped previous mention.

'Are you still completely serious about this revolution stuff? I mean, you do know what you're taking on? The Dalai Lama is worshipped by half the folk on this world. You give him the chop and you aren't going to be Mr Popular.'

'That is why we gotta expose him for the thing that he is. You are still with me on this?'

Rex shrugged. 'I have been giving the matter some thought. And what I don't understand is why you need me at all. Why don't you just breeze down some time channel or other and do the dirty on him?'

'Good point,' Elvis tousled his quiff. 'Why don't I do that?'

'Not in the plot, chief. Got to be done according to the plot.'

'Why?' Rex asked.

'Yeah, why?'

'Because,' intoned the squeaky green voice. 'We are

already messing about with the past and the present. If we start messing with the future there is no telling where it will all end.'

'There,' Elvis patted the back of his head. 'That's why.'

'That's no why at all,' Rex protested.

'Well, let me put it another way, chief. We are doing it this way because I know what is going to happen. And because if you do it this way, you are going to come out of it very well indeed.'

'I do? I mean, I will?'

'I been there chief, I know. And anyway you want to see justice done, the Dalai killed a member of your family.'

'My aunt.'

'Oh no, Rex, he killed your uncle. And he did it personally.'

An hour later Rex left the caverns, he screwed on his weatherdome, slipped through the concealed entrance and gazed across the blasted landscape. The amazing revelations conveyed to him by the Time Sprout had snapped the few last worn threads which held together the tattered trouser-seat of his world. It was a very heavy-duty number indeed. And one so heavy that it must at all costs remain concealed from the reader for fear of spoiling the superb and totally unexpected trick ending of the book.

Let it only be said, then, that Rex Mundi was now a man with a mission. A mission which, barring certain horrid obstacles that for the life of him he could see no way around, might ultimately lead to him, Rex Mundi, scabby, unwashed, pock-marked and now half-gone with the mange, becoming the very saviour of all mankind.

No, don't flick forward, you'll spoil it!

*

Dan left the two aspiring Lamarettes in his bed with something to meditate on. Specifically, how a single individual could possess the power to ravish them both simultaneously. Reincorporating before the bathroom mirror, Dan stuck his tongue out at himself and made a prial of winks. Being the Living God King did have its advantages, although sadly his metaphysical repertoire didn't stretch to invulnerability. And although he had tripled his personal guard and cast a psychic net about his quarters, he couldn't help but feel that things boded no good for his immediate future. It was so damnably unfair. Here was he, a man who had brought joy to millions, well, thousands anyway, and here too was this loonie, with powers apparently outstripping his own, out to kill him. Dan did a big shuddering number. This loonie? This was The Loonie. The one he had dreaded. SUN, the born again. SUN, whom the underground press worshipped, whom, their scriptures foretold, would be 'welcomed by the many and feared by the few'.

'Welcomed by the many,' muttered Dan. 'He's about as welcome as a jobby in a swimming pool.' With no further ado he girded up his loins with saffron girders and declared in a voice of gilded splinters, 'The show must go on.'

'The show must go on,' said Mungo Madoc. Twelve whole hours had actually passed since the Dalai said it. But you could hardly tell that just by looking at it, could you?

'Now, about this Armageddon,' Madoc arranged the unruly stack of Morgawr's memos before him on the desk, 'exactly how much will it cost?'

Jason Morgawr sprang to his feet. 'I have all the

223

projected figures, I think you will find them most favourable.' Fergus Shaman composed his long fingers into a Gothic arch and kept himself to himself.

'We don't have an inexhaustible budget.' Mungo did piercing eye-stares at the board's newest member. 'In fact, anything but.'

'All taken into consideration sir. FX, if you understand me.'

'I don't, Morgawr.'

'Special effects, sir.'

Mungo sighed deeply. 'Continue for now, Morgawr. I will stop you when I'm fed up with it.'

'Indeed, sir,' Morgawr paced about the boardroom, like a Hollywood lawyer of old. Placing his hands upon leafy chairbacks, punching the air, turning to face the window, flexing his shoulders. It was all too excruciating. 'What we have here is a situation,' he said at great length.

'Is that it?' Mungo asked.

Fergus, to whom Mungo's glance momentarily turned, twirled his forefinger against his forehead and said, 'Stone bonkers.'

'A situation which offers the series an opportunity to rise to heights as yet undreamed of. To scale summits, hitherto considered unscalable. To venture into territories . . .'

'Warily avoided by the sane of mind?' Fergus suggested.

'Cosmic cataclysm,' crowed Morgawr. 'And all live on screen.'

'Did you have anything specific in mind?' Mungo asked.

'Apocalypse.' Jason Morgawr made extravagant gestures with his arms. 'Picture this in your minds. Earth's final hour, battle rages, bombs go bang and boom and whoosh and . . .' ('We have a picture of the bombs, yes,' said Mungo.) '. . . the final showdown between good and evil. Will good succeed? Evil has the upper hand, missiles are flying, bombs going . . .' ('Yes.') '. . . fire and brimstone. And what is this? The heavens are opening, a trumpet speaks, and across the clouds the riders come. Angels with swords of fire. Michael and all the saints. Celestial chariots bearing down and at what? Up from the bottomless pit come the hordes of hell, led by the angel of death himself. With the skull face and the horrible claws.' Jason mimed that bit. (Lavinius Wisten said, 'Oh, my.') 'The battle rages across the sky, the armies of God and the legions of the Devil. And are the baddies winning? Surely not. But they are, the terrible cutting and hewing and chopping.' Jason paused a moment to draw breath. The board members watched him, uniformly dumbstruck and open-mouthed. Jason plunged on, 'And hacking. The saints are losing, evil crushes them. It's terrible, terrible.' Heads began to nod, it *was* terrible. 'Then look up, what is this? The sky parts, bursts of golden rays, more angels and a great light streaming down. Can it be? Yes, yes . . . it is He, upon the beryl throne, shining like a thousand suns . . . the second come . . . the second come . . .'

'Morgawr!' The voice was all Mungo's. The board members all went aaaaaaaaaaaaaaaw. 'Morgawr. The second coming, fire and brimstone, angels and devils and bombs that go crash bang wallop. All these things are included in your projected budget? Your projected modest little budget? Your projected strike-me-down-I-don't-know-how-they-could-do-that-on-the-money little budget? Your . . .'

'Already been taped, sir.' All eyes turned upon Jason Morgawr.

Mungo said, 'What did you say?'

'Already been taped.'

Fergus Shaman waggled his hand in the air. 'I think what Mr Morgawr is trying to tell us is that he had already recorded the entire caboodle with some enthusiastic and religiously minded members of the Earthers Inc. Amateur Dramatic Society.'

'Indeed,' said Mungo. 'Just as I thought.' He turned toward Morgawr. 'You can't be serious!' he screamed.

'No, truly sir, it will hardly cost the station a bean. You see we recorded it weeks ago. It was going to be the *Big-nose-mass Show. Armageddon, the Musical* we call it.' Mungo was beginning to make small grunting sounds.

'And sir, we can holographically project it over Earth. Even the Earthers themselves won't be able to tell it from the real thing. It's all Holy Writ stuff, and I've cut in lots of old stock footage to beef it up. All it costs is time to mix it with the real events on Earth.'

'These actors . . .' Fergus put in.

'Solid, dedicated, true in word and deed to the Holy Writ.'

Mungo turned the tip of a high-flying moustachio. 'Hm,' said he. 'Morgawr.'

'Yes sir?'

'Morgawr . . . Jason, I like this. I like this very much indeed.'

'Oh, thank you sir.' Morgawr preened his collars. 'Oh, thank you.'

Fergus raised a very tentative finger. 'If I might just ask one small question.'

Mungo nodded. 'Make it small.'

'Regarding the Second Coming. In fact, shall I say, regarding the Second Come. The actor playing this somewhat crucial, nay extremely crucial role. How might we be absolutely sure that he could be trusted?'

Jason Morgawr pinched reverently at his nose. 'Because,' said he, 'You have my word upon it. *I* would never let you down.'

23

Whether you're rich, or whether you're poor, it's nice to be rich.
Max Miller

Rex Mundi crept along a plushly carpeted corridor, seeking his destiny. Rex, whose character must now be well known to the reader. His failings, few as they are, forgivable considering the circumstances. His valour tried and tested. His integrity absolute. His complexion, although scabious, leaving his good looks romantically untarnished. His underpants unchanged from page one. Rex continued to creep along.

In the changing distances, station employees came and went about their particular businesses. Well dressed, clear skinned, keen, dedicated, enthusiastic. 'Bastards,' muttered Rex. He checked his chronometer. It was still on his wrist. Apart from that not much was doing. The sign on the door ahead said DO NOT ENTER, but Rex didn't hear it. The carpet spoke fluently of a more glorious age and the walls told the informed observer that rag-rolling was back in fashion. They really needn't have bothered. Rex was deaf to the whole damn works. For, as it has been said, Rex Mundi was a man with a mission.

Elvis Aron Presley (it really is a matter for great debate whether it was actually Aron or Aaron) gazed lovingly into a mirror which had once belonged to an Arab prince.

A forty-minute walkabout through the splendours which now adorned the caverns, would have had Lucinda Lambton delving into her wardrobe for inspiration. Which possibly dates things a bit. Elvis looked good. Spotless. Although a Rock 'n' Roller far from home, the golden one, now sprout-invested and wised up to a degree previously considered unthinkable by the likes of Albert Goldman, was squaring up for the big showdown.

'Shall we go for it?' he asked his integral veg.

'All tooled up, chief?'

The literary camera pulled out to reveal Elvis's duds. White and sequined and for the most part bullet-proof. The shoes were somewhat special, the Time Sprout having permitted Elvis a brief swish into an alternative future where a wasted mannish race was unable to get about without the aid of pneumatic footware of a self-propellant nature. Elvis zipped aside flap pockets revealing an arsenal of super-weapons, mostly of Phnaargian construction.

'Hot to trot,' said he, springing about in his ten-league boots.

'Then let's make tracks and go for the Big One.'

'I can dig it,' said the once and future King.

Rex pushed open the door to the control room. The assistant controller looked up momentarily from his desk. 'Restricted area. Sorry friend, try down the hall.'

Rex flashed his security tag. 'Rex Mundi, brother of Gloria. On special assignment for the Dalai.'

'Sorry friend. Stay quiet then, rehearsals you know.'

'Yes I know. I'll just sit down here then.' Rex indicated a vacant chair. The AC, being aware of its vacancy, didn't give it a glance. 'Big show tonight?' Rex asked, when comfy.

'Ssssh.'

'Sorry.'

'Big isn't the word.' The AC touched lighted panels, did pannings ups and fadings outs and all manner of other technical things.

'How big is big, currently?'

'Not all that big when considered in universal terms, I suppose. But big for the show.'

'Ah,' Rex almost scratched his head, but thought better of it. 'That big or small, as you choose to consider it.'

'About the same. Routine for some, outstanding for others, a right bastard for couple of Devianti, and as usual, a huge ego-trip for one in particular. Hold on for just a moment,' the AC made several self-assured button pushes. One plunged the studio into darkness, another broadcast the sounds of his flatulence to the entrance hall.

'I have to do that every five minutes or so,' he explained. 'The union is in dispute with the management.'

'Why are you always in dispute with the management?' Rex asked. 'I always wondered.'

The AC shrugged. 'Never given it a lot of thought. The way I see it, it's the duty of every working man to be in dispute. It's our legacy. Almost a divine right.'

'But surely you're treated well enough.'

'Certainly. Extended credit. Overtime bonuses. Access to the nympharium. Food's good, too.'

'So why are you always in dispute?'

'A sense of duty?' the AC suggested. 'You're not a scab, are you?'

'Certainly not. Actually I'm a revolutionary.'

'A what?'

'A revolutionary. I'm going to help overthrow the system.'

231

The AC threw up his hands in horror. In doing so he cut off the studio sound and left the rehearsing Lamarettes miming foolishly.

'Overthrow the system.' He retwiddled his dials. 'You can't do that.'

'But I thought you were against the management.'

'Yes, of course. But you can't overthrow the system. Oh, my dear paws. Where would we all be? What would we do?'

'You could go into dispute with the new management.'

'That might take years. The thing requires a great deal of mutual understanding. You have to build up a rapport. No. Revolution just won't do. We can't have any of that. I shall call down to security and have you removed at once. You are obviously in need of treatment.'

'Do you see this?' Rex exhibited a handgun Elvis had thrust upon him. 'I can either shoot you or bop you on the head. Which would you prefer?'

The AC mulled it over. 'Could you not perhaps bind and gag me, or even swear me to silence and pack me off to the canteen?' Rex raised an eyebrow which asked the question, would you? The AC nodded gloomily.

'I think I'll plump for the bop on the head then. But before you do I would just like to stress the extreme folly of revolution. Firstly . . .'

Rex bopped him on the head and seated himself at the controls. He had just completed phase one of Mr Presley's revolutionary masterplan. Where it was all going to lead now was very much in the lap of the Gods.

Mickey Malkuth stuck the business end of his electric truncheon up the left nostril of Rambo Bloodaxe. 'In answer to your question, "old bean", you will put on this suit because I tell you to.'

'I see,' Rambo said, nasally. 'That clarifies things no end. Let's tog up then, Eric. No need to keep the gentlemen waiting.'

Deathblade Eric perused the outfit which had been flung in his direction. 'Khaki. It doesn't suit my colouring. And the cut of the cloth. Inferior.' He shook his head, spraying the onlookers with skull fragments. 'Do you have anything in royal blue?'

'Do you want this up your chocolate speedway, dreamboat?' Malkuth waggled his truncheon toward the doubtful Devianti. 'Them's battle fatigues.'

'We rather gathered that, dear sir.' Rambo held his projected apparel towards his extended nostril and gave it a little sniff. 'Are we joining up then, or what?'

'You're revolutionaries, ain't you? You got to look the part.'

'Revolutionaries?' Rambo chewed upon the word. To him it didn't taste good. 'We are Devianti. Tomorrow belongs to us, as yesterday once did. We are victims of a slight hiccup in the status quo. Once law and order are properly restored, then we—' Rambo sank to the floor clutching his betruncheoned head.

'It hurts even more when it's switched on,' Malkuth informed him. 'Now, get dressed.'

'Might we not be permitted some privacy?'

'You've got nothing I haven't seen and thumped.'

'True.' Rambo slipped out of his soiled, yet spiffing togs and zipped himself into the evil-smelling fatigues.

'Could have been made for you. Now the headband.'

'Oh really. Headbands are so passé.' Malkuth raised his truncheon.

Eric had his trousers over his head. 'The sleeves are a bit long,' he mumbled. 'And I can't seem to find the neckhole.'

233

*

Dan was in the Green Room. A row of empty glasses was before him. Gloria's voice was close at his ear. 'Get a grip of yourself, man.'

'I'm in total control, Gloria, thank you.'

'You are totally out of control. Things are getting beyond your control.'

'Nothing is beyond my control.'

'And your Mr SUN?'

'Rex has that in hand.'

'That little cockroach. My bidet is still not fixed.'

'The engineers are in dispute. Must you go on and on?'

'You're losing it, Dan.'

'I don't recall sanctioning such informality.'

'Dan, listen to me.'

'Gloria. I think it's time you took a holiday.' Gloria made mouths. Dan continued. 'Frankly, Gloria, you are beginning to get on my tits. You nag me. I don't feel that the Living God King should be nagged. In fact, Gloria, I think I will send you on a little sabbatical. A study of waste disposal maintenance in the sub-basements. I'll arrange it all after the show. Go toss a few things into a travelling bag. Whatever you think you might need for a year.'

Gloria's face was ashen. She opened her mouth to speak.

'Best not,' Dan advised. 'Or I might extend it to two years.'

Gloria turned in fury and tore out of the room. Dan whistled a little tune of his own confection and tapped upon the housephone.

'Inmost One?' came the voice of Mickey Malkuth.

'Ah yes, Malkuth. Leave what you are doing and

take yourself off to the control room. Rex Mundi has just bopped the AC on the head. Put a couple of bullets through him for me, would you? So kind, thank you.'

Losing it, thought Dan, that will be the day.

24

. . . I came into this maybe by chance. But having read these documents all through, I'm not sure what chance actually is any more. I opened my little place in ninety-four. Software, hardware, decks, breakers, peeps, intermixers, decoders. Of course you won't find me in the yellow pages. You have to know who to ask and then some. I deal in all the stuff that the mainstreamers deny the very existence of. And I only deal for currency. A kid of twelve can milk a comp-account nowadays with the kind of gear I market. So I'd be some kind of turkey to bank my own ill-gottens. Now, the guy you're talking about. He gets my name from a trusted friend. I, of course, run him through the works to see if he's clean and hit a red-light classified. I dig and delve a little. Skirt around the big security areas and penetrate the police files to check him out. Like I say any twelve-year-old with nous can do this. Turns out that there is an all-points out on this guy. The CIA want him bad. Bad for him, but not so bad for me. In my books this makes him triple safe to deal with.

So I arrange a meet in Fangio's. It's a connection bar, no questions asked. The guy comes in and he's got the craziest eyes I ever saw. And sweat, can this guy sweat. I give him a stiff drink and he tells me what he wants. Seems he has got hold of some million byte carbon and wants it transferred into something innocuous before the agency catches up with him. It's some kind of super-duper program belonging to some project that got busted. I raise my eyebrows to all this intelligence. Million byte carbons, K^2s to those in the know, are about as scarce as the fertilizer which issues from the tail end of the treen pony. Very much the state-of-the-art. I tell this guy that I will require big boodle for this operation, and what variety of thing does he want it compacted into? He says he doesn't care as long as it's no longer recognizable for the thing it is, and will I take the carbon as payment? Yes, I reply. We take a trip across town and I shan't be putting you on if I tell you that I'm cautious in the extreme to assure myself that we aren't tailed.

I also make sure that I carry the carbon, in case we have to split up for any reason. So anyway, we arrive back at my place unmolested and I jack up my deck. Which for those who wish to know such things is a GIBSON 440 with cross-pattern interface and lock-in multi-broads, full spectrum. I don't tell this guy that his is the first K^2 that I have ever laid hands upon and the chances of compacting the incompactible are less than zero. He looks as if he was worried enough. But looking back it was somewhat neither here nor there, because the next thing I know is the terminator which is stuck in my ear. And the guy making mockery of my equipment and using jargon the like of which is perplexing to my ears. I wind up handcuffed to my chair whilst he sets up my linkages and runs the whole program himself, before my very eyes. And all the time he is going, 'crude, crude, crude', some thanks. So once he's run in the program he then looks about my place for something to store it in. And then he sees my collection and he starts to laugh. 'Just the trick,' says he, 'pure irony.' Well, I don't know what irony is, but my collection is something else. For one thing it is complete, was complete. I had everything the Man ever did. And this son-of-a-bitch just dips in at random. And does he take some remix or

238

cover version? Does he king shit. He takes the jewel of my
fucking collection. Laughing like a drain as he does it.
The Suburban Book of the Dead

'He's a friend to the foe
The star of the show
The man we all know
By his king-sized karma
He's a real breath of spring
He's the Living God King
He's the Dalai . . . Dalai . . . Dalai
Dalai . . . La . . . ma'

Dan's suit was electronic jiggery-pokery. Although nothing new had been invented upon Earth during the preceding three decades, the scope of the Dalai's wardrobe, allied with the brief lifespans of his audience, saw to it that he always remained Mr Wonderful. Commerical holographics, sired in the late 1980s and milked for all they were worth after the NHE, were still capable of impressing those conditioned to be impressed. Dan's suit seethed with three-dimensional erotica. A heaving panorama of taut buttocks, pert nipples, milk-white thighs, armpit hair and exposed front bottoms.

Dan took a major bow toward his viewing public. Willies of every colour and hue came and went across his shoulders.

'My dear friends,' said Dan, in a manner much favoured by American Evangelist fornicators of the late eighties, 'my dear, dear friends. I am with you once again.' Dan made a profound and sacred sign. The Pavlovian bunker-bound responded. Ringpulls popped from Buddhabeer cans and the narcotized contents bubbled into waiting throats. Today's delivery had been double-strengthed, just to be on the safe side. Dan filled in the twenty seconds before the beer took hold by performing a little dance amongst The Lamarettes. In the control room Rex began to feel somewhat strange. He found his right hand pulling at a ringpull that wasn't there. Things were becoming clearer and clearer to Rex Mundi. Mickey Malkuth entered a lift many floors beneath. Second anonymous torturer was with him.

'Showtime.' Dan twirled upon his heel. 'And what a show have we got lined up for you tonight. It is going to be big and when I say big, what do I mean?'

The bunker-bound knew exactly what he meant. 'Big,' they went, all together.

'After all, who is it that cares for you? Who clothes you? Who loves you? Yeah, that's right. It's me. And that's why you love me, isn't it? And you do love me? Don't you? Love me. Love me. Love me.'

Rex peered down at the performance. He chewed upon his knuckles, he felt wrong inside. He perused the console deck before him. The show's running time flashed, five minutes gone already, how could that be. He looked out at the Dalai. Dan made another profound gesture. Rex yanked at his trouserleg. 'Gotta get a beer, gotta get a beer.'

'Easy Rex.' She seated herself beside him. 'You're not thirsty.'

Rex couldn't take his eyes from the Dalai. 'Gotta get a beer.' Christeen pulled his face away and gazed into it, she turned down the sound. 'Conditioning. Don't watch him. You're not thirsty.'

'Thirsty?' Rex stared into her eyes. 'Why should I be thirsty?'

'Why indeed? Now if you will kindly place yourself behind the door. Do you have your gun?' Rex proffered the piece, the way one does.

'Now, hold it in your right hand and count to ten.' Rex did so, the door burst in.

'. . . ten.' Rex swung the gun. Mickey Malkuth hit the floor.

'And just to four this time.'

'Two . . . three . . . four.' The second anonymous torturer joined Malkuth in the 'prone position'.

'Thanks again,' Rex pocketed the pistol. 'I owe you.'

'You owe yourself, Rex.' The lad peeped over the console deck and down through the plexiglass toward the studio floor. 'He's on to me, then?'

Christeen nodded, Rex didn't need to see her. 'You just retired without the pension.'

Rex slumped back in the AC's chair. 'I hope I'm doing the right thing. I do appear to be a little short of options right now.'

Christeen drew attention to the liberal distribution of KOed station folk. 'I think that no matter how you might unwish it, you are committed.'

'I hate him.' Rex turned away from the glass.

'So do I,' said Christeen.

'I hope you won't accuse me of fatalism,' whispered the dangling Deathblade. 'But having given my all to the considered assessment of our present situation, I'm forced to conclude that there is no hope left to us.'

'Very well put, old muckamuck, but never say die, eh? The fact that we are currently hanging upside down before the viewing public, with explosive capsules nestling in our privy passages, might on the face of it, I grant you, appear cause for just concern.'

'On the face of it?'

'But,' Rambo rambled on, 'I myself subscribe to the credo of "think positive". Should the worst possible occur and our bums blow us to oblivion, we must look on the bright side. We will be making a political statement.'

'Making a mess of the studio, more like.'

'Eric, in some future time our names may well be writ big upon the wall of martyrdom.'

'The blood is running to what remains of my head.'

'Chin up, think of England.'

'Of where?'

'Never mind, it's just a saying.'

'It's the questions I worry most about, Rambo.'

'Questions, Eric? Do you mean like, what does all this mean? And is there really a divine purpose behind it, and things of that nature?'

'No, Rambo. I was thinking about the questions the Dalai will ask, I hope they are on gardening. Do you think he will let us choose or will we just have to take what comes?'

'We'll just have to play it by ear, Eric. No offence meant.'

'None taken, I assure you.'

'Extremists and heretics,' the Dalai was screaming, 'like really bad people. Like well, you know, how bad can bad be, right? Really bad, yeah, you got it. They hate me, so they hate you, it's the same thing when you think about it, know what I mean, innit? These people just hate, that's all they do. Who needs them, do you need them? I don't need them . . .'

'He's talking gibberish.' Rex had fearfully tweaked up the sound in the control room, but wasn't daring to look.

'He's talking the universal tongue.'

'He is what?'

'The language of the stoned, the blitzed, the smashed and well and truly out of it. The Enlightened.'

'But it's rubbish, it just goes on and on.'

'Enlightenment is like that. Refined knowledge is no knowledge at all. Every question has a million answers and all of them probably wrong. The Dalai now has his followers narcotized, he speaks to them in their language. We've all been stoned at some time or another and felt certain that we knew what was what. When we woke up the next day and couldn't precisely remember, what did we do?'

'We got stoned again.'

'Precisely, the bunker-bound will recall some of it, the bits that are drummed into them and they'll be back for another helping.'

'Then surely I have listened to this, again and again?'

'Rex, you slept through the most part of it with your eyes open.'

'My uncle taught me.'

'And you know now who killed him.'

'Yes, and I know why.'

'So, keep watching the show, carefully of course. There's a very good bit coming up in just a moment.'

'Dear friends, do you have your remote controls at the ready? Yes, I just know that you do. Well, I'm gonna ask you a question and you, the viewers at home, are gonna answer it. You got the two buttons, right, one marked yes and the other marked, you guessed it, no. So I ask you the question and you have the choice. All ready, right. The question is, should we let these vindictive murderers and would-be assassins of my good person live, or should we blast the heretic sons of Satan off to hell, live in colour?'

'One feels the question might have been better phrased,' Rambo observed.

'If the opinion of a man with half a brain is of any interest, I have the feeling that our goose-flavoured food cube is well and truly cooked.'

'Now the choice is all yours. It's a yes if you want them blown to pieces, and a no if you don't think they deserve to live. So what's it going to be then, eh?'

'What about the don't knows?' Rambo protested.

'Ask him if he could kindly repeat the question,' the bewildered Eric put in. 'I don't know which way I should vote.'

'Ask him to stick up his hands and shut his mouth,' said Elvis Presley.

Dan turned in horror to view the materialization. 'SUN,' he gasped.

'Messiah,' went the inverted Rambo.

'Golly,' said Eric. 'And in the nick of time, eh?

'This station is now the property of the people.'

'But the people are stoned. Cut the sound, fade out . . .'

'I think not,' said Rex Mundi.

'Get me Fergus Shaman.'

'I'm sorry Mr Madoc, but Mr Shaman is no longer in the building.'

'Then get him at home.'

'I regret that Mr Shaman isn't at home.'

'Then where is he?'

'Mr Shaman has, and I quote, gone to Earth upon pressing business.'

'Mr Shaman isn't authorized to visit Earth.'

'No, sir.'

'Get me a spaceboat at once.'

'Mr Shaman said that you might require one. It's all prepared on the top landing.'

'Thank you, Mavis.'

'Thank you, Mr Madoc.'

'Cut down those sons of freedom, father-raper,' snarled Elvis, from the trigger end of a four-barrelled Phnaargian peacekeeper. 'And don't get smart.'

Dan made frantic motions towards the lovely Marion, who was making goo-goo eyes at the mystery star guest. 'Marion!'

The bra-busting beauty, whose hobbies included doing voluntary work for the terminally underprivileged, running on the spot and learning a first language, wiggled her unlikely hips and nose-dived a lurex finger towards a row of garish buttons. These were housed beneath the score board, which really should have been mentioned earlier. But there you are.

'To hear you say, is to obey,' she coupleted, most prettily. Rambo and Eric tumbled to the studio floor in khaki confusion. Dan glanced toward Elvis.

'Don't even think about it.' Elvis cocked a second hammer on his piece.

Rambo struggled to free himself from the harness about his ankles. Rising to his feet he straightened his lapels and put his hair in order, before delving into his trouser seat, to remove something singularly distressing. 'I feel we might dispense with further formalities and stick this where it belongs.'

'All in good sweet time.' Elvis opened his jacket, exposing his considerable weaponry. He tossed a hand-gun to Rambo. 'Stay loose.'

'I have every intention of doing so, Lord King.'

'Someone untie my hands,' moaned the Deathblade.

'It's your feet that are tied, close friend of mine.'

'Ah yes. I see my mistake now, thank you Rambo.'

'Don't mention it, Eric.'

'Now just you listen,' said Dan, whose telepathic cry for help now echoed about the building. 'You are making a terrible mistake.'

Elvis shook his head. It was a very definite shake. It said a very definite no.

'End transmission,' said the Dalai Lama. But he didn't say it from the studio floor, where he stood trembling. He said it close by the ear of Rex Mundi.

'Shock horror!' Rex lurched back in his borrowed chair. Dan leaned forward, his wide eyes showing only the whites. 'End transmission.'

'Stay away from me,' Rex lashed out at the holyman, his fist struck empty air. 'A hologram.'

'A holygram,' said Christeen. 'A tulpa, an astral body.' The other Dan turned slowly away from Rex, the pupils returned to his eyes, one from above, the other from beneath. It wasn't a pretty sight.

'He can see you,' croaked Rex.

'Of course he can, in his present state we occupy the same plane.' Christeen walked slowly toward the tulpa, smiling sweetly. Her fingers were cupped demurely before her. She drew back her beautiful face and brutally head-butted him. Back on the studio floor Dalai Dan collapsed in a heap of holy confusion, clutching a bleeding nose. Rambo and Eric went into a big twentieth-century American cop routine over him. Legs akimbo, both hands upon the gun.

'Are we rolling?' Elvis squinted into the lights. Rex gave an invisible thumbs up. Elvis tucked away his weapon. 'People of the World,' said he, addressing the automated camera with the red light on. 'I wonder if you're lonesome tonight.'

Now it might have been a blinder of a speech. A heartfelt heart-string puller, a rowdy rabble rouser, or a wise and witty tickler of ribs. It might have been a Churchillian upper-lip stiffener or even a metaphysical mind-blower. (Well, it might have been.) Or of course it could well have been a load of old pussy-cat poo. But whatever the case, that's as far as it got. Because just then the stage doors opened to reveal the Dalai's special guard, the Orange Agents, as they are unaffectionately known.

They were stunningly clad in this year's look. Heavily-padded shoulders giving that fuller feel. Belts worn at a jaunty angle, rakish high-boots beneath hip-hugging combat trousers, pocketed for convenience at thigh height. The stun guns, grenade launchers, flame throwers and rapid-fire machine pistols were all standard issue, but the straps and fittings had been whimsically toned in bold primaries, which although adding that essential splash of colour, in no way detracted from the bold, macho image.

'Nobody move.'

Rambo and Eric, now both tooled up, turned their inadequate firepower upon the intruders. 'Drop those weapons,' called Eric, whose complete lack of comprehension, regarding the sudden shift in the balance of power, had a certain naive charm. 'Give yourselves up.'

Elvis sighed deeply. Up in the control room, Rex Mundi said, 'Phase Two.' He pulled from his radiation suit a pre-recorded transmission disc Elvis had given him for the occasion. It was entitled ELVIS PRESLEY'S GOLDEN GREATS. Something about going out on a song, the King had said. Rex slotted it into the desk housing and sat back awaiting further events.

On the studio floor a little tableau was now arranged. At its centre knelt Dan, somewhat green about the gills and red about the hooter. About him were ranged Eric, Rambo and Elvis, their guns were angled down towards the kneeler, aimed at points of their respective choosings.

'Back off fellas,' called Elvis. The Orange Agents looked at one another, they looked at Elvis, they looked at the Dalai. 'Now,' encouraged Mr Presley, before all the looking got out of hand. 'And clear the decks, we're leaving.'

Dan looked up bitterly, 'I'm wounded,' he complained. The look on Elvis's face told him all he needed to know. 'Quite so. Kindly move back, gentlemen.'

'Cue it in, Rex,' Elvis called up to the control box.

Rex tipped the switch. The passionate strains of the immortal classic filled the studio air. 'It's now or never,' it went.

Elvis said, 'Let's go.'

Rex turned towards Christeen, she had gone, and once more all memories of her had gone too. The disc was running and now it was his turn.

Four men dashed along the studio corridor. Three held guns, one held his nose. 'Into the lift.'

'They will cut the power,' said Eric.

'Very good, Eric.'

'Thank you, Rambo.'

'They won't,' Elvis bundled Dan into the lift. 'In you.' Dan had nothing to say.

'Up, Lord King?' Rambo enquired.

'Up to the landing platforms.'

Eric was bobbing his half a head about. 'This really is exciting,' said he.

'Never a dull moment, old inseparable bosom friend of mine.'

The lift ground to a shuddering halt and the lights went out. 'What's happened?' Eric asked.

'They have cut the power,' Rambo told him.

'The bounders, who ever would have thought it?' In the darkness, Eric went to scratch his head and missed.

'No sweat,' said Elvis. The lights went on and the lift continued up the shaft.

'There.' Rambo was all smiles. 'Is this man the Second Come, or what?'

'Forward planning is all. I had Rex slot in an automatic over-ride earlier in the day.'

'I shall prostrate myself before you when there is little more room, master. Rex, did you say? That wouldn't be Rex Mundi by any chance, would it?'

Up on the landing platform Rex revved up his air car. It appeared to him extremely doubtful that the battered craft could actually carry five people. It could possibly take three at a push, if one was prepared to travel in the trunk. But five? No way.

The lift doors to the motor pool rattled open and three revolutionaries and a hostage bundled out. The night rain was now falling hard. Rex couldn't see a lot through the rear wind-screen. He heard the trunk open and close, then the canopy swung up and Elvis clambered into the cab. He squeezed himself in beside Rex. 'Take her up.' He waggled his weapon towards the sky. Rex turned his mouth into a bitter line.

'You are leaving those two, then?'

'Fortunes of war, Rex. And the guy with all the

head ain't no fan of yours.' Security lasers cross-meshed the landing platform, the rattle of machine pistols put paid to any further discussion. Rex took the air car hurriedly aloft and made off into the storm-tossed darkness.

25

. . . *you dug for stuff back then. That's all you did.*
There were these schemes, job opportunities and youth
training and the like. For some of us, those who weren't
just stuck in the bunkers with no hope, anyway. We were
picked out to dig. I dug. I never knew what we were
supposed to be digging for. Food, weapons, anything
serviceable. We were never told. We just dug. Three hours
a day was about all you could take. And we did it because
that was what you did. That was 2001 and Arthur C. Clarke
had got it all wrong. Nuclear night, no seasons and some
smart-arse had come up with decimal time. Ten minutes
to the hour, ten hours to the day, ten days to the week, and
so on. Stupidest idea you ever heard of. So we dug and
sorted and handed it in. I reckon now, looking back, that
they had us searching for one specific thing. And I reckon
too that they must have found it. Because one day the
scheme just closed down and we were all sent back to our
bunkers. Just like that. Stupid scheme, stupid time, stupid
world. What a life, eh?
The Suburban Book of the Dead

You're probably wondering why I'm here, well so am I, so am I.
Frank Zappa

'Am I here?' Fergus Shaman addressed the glorious
confusion of tendrils, membranes, pulsating pseudopodia

and bulbous dendro-composites, with digital read-em-outs, which composed the interior of the Phnaargian spaceship. 'It's all somewhat sudden.'

'You are now on Earth,' came a voice of oozy user-friendliness, 'first star on the right and keep on until morning.'

'I must have been asleep.'

'Indeed you must.' It may be of interest to note that the computer voice in the Phnaargian spaceship was identical to that of Rex's air car. Or there again, it may not.

'Will I require a spacesuit or something?'

'No sir, you just step right out there.'

'Could I have a visual then, please?'

A circular screen before him displayed the immediate panorama. Remnants of a building or two, their contours dulled by decades of acid rain, ruin and rubble. A monochrome gloom beneath a dun-coloured sky of sliding cloud. Fergus shivered. 'Where exactly am I?'

'Ten leagues north of the Nemesis Pyramid, as requested.'

'Oh, really, then thank you.'

'Thank you, Mr Shaman, and have another day.'

'Get inside . . . close the door Rex.' Rex swung shut the bunker door. They had flown about blindly for half the night and now they were here. Aunty Norma's. Rex closed his eyes to it. 'Why here?'

Elvis was lashing the Dalai into Uncle Tony's chair. 'Where else could it have been? Stick the TV on Rex, let's see what's to do.'

Rex recalled what he had done to the terminal. 'Can't,' said he.

'Can.' Elvis indicated the reconditioned terminal which

252

now replaced it's defunct precursor. 'All planned for, I told you.' Dalai Dan said nothing. Rex gave the place the once-over. Aunty Norma was no longer to be seen. Uncle Tony had been swept away. Elvis plucked up the remote control and flung it to Rex. 'Viva the revolution,' he said, a little too cheerfully for Rex's liking. Rex sank uncomfortably into his aunt's chair and thumbed the controls.

The TV cranked into action. It jiggled and popped and then the face of Elvis Presley appeared. 'And that,' said the voice of Gloria Mundi, 'is the face of the Devianti terrorist, who just eight hours ago kidnapped our beloved Dalai Lama.'

'Good old Gloria,' Dan piped up. 'Loyal to the end.'

'His demands are as follows,' Gloria continued. 'Close down all TV channels, cease all food and medico production to the population and impose a twenty-four hour curfew.'

'What?' Elvis's eyes popped unpleasantly. 'I never . . .'

'The Devianti terrorists have been tracked on radar to their hideout. They are known to possess a pre-NHE nuclear warhead, which they intend to detonate if their demands aren't met in just one hour.'

'They what?' Elvis's bottom lip became a passable bidet. 'I what?'

An on-screen hand passed Gloria a sheet of paper. She mimed the reading of it. 'Ah,' she said, all smiles. 'We have just received a telepathic message from the Dalai. It reads: "Do not fear for my safety. Refuse all demands. I look forward to seeing you all again in my next incarnation. PS. I would like Gloria Mundi, my loyal and trusted second in command, to take over all my respon- sibilities until I come amongst you once more." Message ends.'

Dan's mouth open and closed, but it didn't say anything. Elvis performed likewise oral perambulations. Rex wondered if they were miming some song.

'The detonation can be seen live only upon this channel, so don't touch that dial. But for now we continue with a programme of silent meditation. *Om-mani-padme-hum.*'

Rex touched the control. The screen fell into darkness, Rex fell into laughter. 'They're going to blow us all up,' he gasped where he could. 'They'll launch a missile.' He turned a momentary glare towards Dan. 'Just like last time.' Then he doubled up again into further convulsions.

'No,' croaked Dan, 'this can't be happening, this is all wrong.'

Elvis looked at him sternly. 'Shut your rap,' said he.

'But they're going to kill us, kill me . . .'

'Well, that's not a problem for you, is it?' Tears rolled down Rex's unwashed cheeks. 'Straight on to your next incarnation, eh?'

'It's not always as simple as that.'

'Simple as that?' Rex clutched at his knees, hysteria was taking over from mirth.

'Shut up buddy and that means you.'

Rex chewed upon his lip and tried to sober up. 'What a waste of time,' he said.

'I'm perplexed,' said Elvis Presley.

'We forgot about Gloria, chief,' came the voice from his head. 'Can't understand how we overlooked her. Thought it was all sewn up.'

'We are all going to die,' moaned Dan. 'We're all doomed, doomed.'

'Yeah,' Rex agreed. 'Really stinks when it's your turn, doesn't it?'

'There's still time. We could fly back to Nemesis. Well, I could and once I was back there . . .' Two men were looking at him. They were both shaking their heads.

'No?'

'Uh uh,' said Elvis.

Dan looked toward Rex. 'My dear boy, I appeal to you.' Rex shunned the snappy rejoinder. Dan continued to speak, but through the medium of mental telepathy. 'Come now, Rex, this is all a big mistake. Why throw away your retirement, those two lovely ladies, all that sweet food and drink, all that luxury? All for this foolhardiness. You don't want to die, do you? Such a stupid waste.'

Rex scratched at his stubble, he didn't want to die, this was true.

'Catch him off guard and off with his head.' Rex turned his gun between his fingers. 'Between the eyes?' he thought.

'No, not that, you would damage the . . .'

'The Time Sprout?'

'Exactly. I deplore waste. I could put that thing to great use.'

'I'll bet you could.'

'Snip, snap,' thought Dan. 'Time is running out.'

'Why don't you simply do your vanishing act, despatch your tulpa back to Nemesis?'

Dan's thoughts turned toward his nose. Rex felt the twinge of pain. 'Fuck you,' thought Rex.

'Bravo, chief,' chortled the Time Sprout, who had been listening in upon the unspoken converse. 'Thought we'd lost you there for a moment.'

'No way,' said Rex Mundi.

*

Fergus Shaman picked his way across the precarious landscape. It smelled about as bad as it looked. He fanned at his nose, but that only seemed to make matters worse. All in all Fergus wasn't a happy Phnaarg. It was more than possible that even now his movements were being observed by the viewers of Phnaargos. All wondering who this new character might be and indeed where the plot was leading. They weren't alone in this latter thought, as it was very much to the fore in Fergus's mind. What had started out as an inspired idea to boost the flagging ratings seemed now to be degenerating into chaos. If only these morons would stick to the plot. If only throughout their history they had done what was required of them they would all be living in Utopia now. But Earthers never seemed to get it right. They had been given the whole planet to play with and the end result was this. It didn't say much for them as a race. But perhaps it wasn't really their fault. Perhaps it was some genetic cock-up, some in-built wish for destruction. But possibly, and here a terrible thought entered Fergus's mind, possibly it was all the fault of Phnaargos. Perhaps if the Earthers had just been left to get on with it, rather than being nudged along for the sake of good television, they might have done very nicely, thank you.

'No,' said Fergus, 'it wasn't our fault, not all this.' But it did seem a terrible shame, nonetheless. But there was still time. There was always still time. In fact time was the key to the whole issue, and Fergus, who for reasons unknown even to himself now felt an awful sense of responsibility, was certain that there was still a chance to sort it all out. The all but altruistic Phnaarg plodded on through the danger zone. And finally, there ahead of him, sighted a little jewel in the bleak and corroded setting. Rex's battered air car, parked close to a bunker door.

Fergus straightened his shoulders, thought positive and tripped flat on his face.

26

. . . *and now the book has come to me. Through coincidence, through chance? Forget about those, through fate. My parents taught me olde English. The archaic written word. They changed all that after the NHE, an entire new alphabet, so no-one could read the truth about the past, I guess. The terminal spoke and showed you the way. We watched and learned and clocked up credits. No other options. Only the lord high terminal. The new god. He who gave or took away, depending how long you spent at your devotions before him. So you worship in your shrine, your home, your tomb. But I had the word. The Logos. I was the last, it had to be passed to me and it was. I could confide in no-one. Hardly Norma. But then Rex was sent to us. I studied and I studied and at last I began to piece it all together. And I began to realize what I should be looking for and ultimately where it was to be found. And in the mean time I played the fool, the mad uncle, until I could teach the boy.*

The Suburban Book of the Dead

Macbeth hath murdered sleep.
Anon

I have done questionable things.
Roy, Nexus 6

Gabba Gabba Hey.
The Ramones

The silver spaceship still stood upon the upper deck, atop the spiral tower of Earthers Inc. In it sat Mungo Madoc; he was picking his nose. Before him screens displayed the current state of things. Three men in a bunker. One Phnaargian struggling to his feet. A beautiful woman in a control room. A curious vortex, which was probably just interference. The doings in his own boardroom. He would have to put a lock on that cigar box. Mungo examined a fingertip, made a face and applied scented drops to a now upturned nostril.

'It won't do, will it?'

Mungo, alone of all Phnaargians, knew the speaker's voice. The series' backers communicated with only the station head. And to him rarely. 'I hardly feel that I can be held directly responsible.'

'Oh, then perhaps you wish to step down from your position of responsibility.'

'I didn't say that exactly.'

'But it amounts to the same thing. The buck stops with you.'

'I would have thought that ultimately it stops with you.'

'Oh, no. It never does that. Non-intervention is our policy. This is the way it has always been. Always will be.'

'Well, I hardly see how I can influence events. We shall just have to see what Fergus Shaman does.'

'It might all prove to be somewhat academic. You are aware, are you not, that the virus has now reached the twenty-first century?'

'Word has reached me, yes.'

'And it's gaining momentum. If you can't halt the process then it will shortly reach the present. And when it does . . .'

'When it does? Yes?'

'Armageddon,' said the voice. 'But not the one you have planned. You are going to need a veritable miracle this time.'

'Hellooooeeee,' called Fergus Shaman. 'Anybody in there?'

'I know that voice.'

'It's Mr Shaman, chief.'

'Who?'

Elvis turned to Rex. 'Fergus Shaman, the man from outer space, I told you about him.'

'And he's just popped by for a chat. How sublimely opportune.'

Dan felt the hand of Christeen tweak his left testicle. He wasn't going anywhere for the moment.

'Open up,' called Fergus. 'It's important, honestly.'

'Best let him in, chief.' Elvis cranked the turncock and swung open the bunker door. Fergus stepped inside, grinning broadly.

'Hope I'm not intruding.'

'Not a bit of it,' Rex helped him through the hatch. 'We have about four minutes to kill before the bomb drops. We've been playing a game called "I spy with with my little eye", except we seem to have run out of expletives to describe Dan.'

'Just four minutes; here in the nick of time, eh?'

'I doubt it,' Rex replied. 'But if you have had any hand in all this, then I will take some pleasure in knowing that you perish along with us.'

261

'You have a ready wit upon you, young man.' Fergus hastily addressed himself to Elvis. 'Mr Presley,' he puffed. 'You really shouldn't be here, you know. It really would be better for all concerned if you just went straight back to 1958 and dodged the draft. As we suggested in the first place.'

'No way,' said the Big E, shaking his head vigorously.

'Easy there, chief,' howled the sprout.

'Can't you reason with him?' Fergus addressed the rear of Presley's head. The sprout for once had nothing to say.

'I screwed up once already. This time I gotta make it right. I got me the Ant-eye-Christ here, for Chrissakes. No offence to the Good Lord intended there.'

Fergus perused the bound lama. 'He's much smaller than he looks on TV,' he observed.

'But I ain't no frigging Antichrist. You tell him.'

'Shut your mouth, fella.'

'Really, this is getting us nowhere. Rex, what do you think?'

'Rex?' said Rex. 'I don't know you, do I?'

'But I know you. All Phnaargos knows you. You're a big star.'

'A big star?'

'A real crowdpleaser. I shouldn't be saying this because we're probably on camera, but it would be a sad day if we were to lose you, Rex.'

'Butt out of here, Shaman.'

'No, hang about. I want to hear more. A big star, did you say?'

'I'll tell you everything, but not here.'

'Yes,' Dan agreed, 'this is all most interesting, we should go somewhere more comfortable and discuss it. My place, perhaps?'

'Button it, schmucko.'

'Well somewhere, and now.'

Elvis chewed upon his curly lip. 'We really should, chief,' his cerebral companion agreed. 'Or at least *we* should.'

Elvis dithered and dathered. 'I just don't know.' He just didn't know.

'Nuke them out,' said Gloria Mundi.

'But your brother, dear.'

Gloria paused. 'Bugger him.'

'But dear, blood is thicker than water and all that. And if we are going to build a better world surely we must do it with compassion. Or we will be no better than . . .'

'Than men.'

'Exactly.'

'But we may never get as good a chance as this again.'

'But he is your brother, dear. Flesh of your flesh.'

Gloria hung her beautiful head. 'You are right. It would be murder.'

'Exactly, we must rule with love, care and feeling.'

'We must, we must.'

'Even if, when all is said, he is just another man.'

'Even if.'

'Representing, in microcosm, all men.'

'Even if.'

'All men with their shallowness, lust, greed and craving for power.'

'Even if.' This 'even if', although looking the same as the previous 'even ifs', had about it a more prolonged and thoughtful quality.

'Even if he did crap in our bidet.'

Gloria gave Ms Vrillium a very knowing look.

'I'll nuke them out then, shall I dear?'

'Best to, eh?' Gloria ran the intro.

Over the hills, but not a great way off, was another vast concrete pyramid. It was the headquarters of number two in the Big Three.

L. Ron Hubbard the twenty-third lounged on the comfy rear-ends of a dozen nubile lady acolytes. As with the previous twenty-two L. Rons, who had gone before him to wherever it is those lads go to, this one was rotund and ruddy and bore a striking resemblance to the late and legendary Andy Divine. Plumping himself upon those who were grateful for it, he nodded towards she whose job it was to work the controller. And then he watched the wall screen with an eagerness which many might just have considered a smidgenet unhealthy.

And way up over on the other side of town, Pope Joan knelt alone in the viewing chapel of Vatican City. Actually it wasn't really a city at all, just another dirty great concrete bunker, but city says something which bunker just can't seem to. For Joan there were never any pleasures of the flesh. Such were strictly proscribed. To fall into such iniquity would be to fall from the true faith. When you fall heir, or in her case heiress, to a legacy of pious turpitude, which includes within its holy ranks such exemplars as Pope Alexander VI and Innocent VIII, you have something to live up to. Mind you, the weekly burnings were, as they had always been, something of a turn-on. And although the Dalai wouldn't actually be broadcasting live from his bunker prison, the mere thought of his forthcoming immolation sent pure frissons of pleasure all around where the rosaries dangled.

She genuflected, whacked herself a couple of times across the naked shoulders with a plastique flagrum and pumped up the volume.

Down in the bunkers, Mr and Mrs Joe Public whacked into today's deliveries and kept on watching that screen. It was a bit early in the day for all this mega-excitement, but they were feeling fine about the whole thing. Today's deliveries had been suitably laced for the occasion.

Gloria's face filled the screen. Gloriously. Her green eyes were red-rimmed and welled with tears. Her exquisite cheeks streaked. Her lipstick smudged, just so. The makeup department had really excelled themselves. 'It's now an hour since the telepathic communication from our beloved Dalai Lama. My dear friends, I'm lost for words. My grief is your grief. For if the loss of one of the world's greatest figures isn't enough in itself to fill our hearts with sorrow, the ghastly news that I have just received, and which I now convey to you, is more terrible yet. It was previously believed that the Devianti was a separatist group acting upon their own insane dictates. But this isn't the case. The terrorists are in the pay of one of the other networks. Even now another kidnapping is in progress. A Devianti death squad is penetrating the security of . . .' Gloria choked back a tear and blew her nose on a handkerchief of crêpe de Chine. Then the screen crackled and went dead.

L. Ron Hubbard collapsed into a turmoil of heaving buttocks.

Pope Joan pulled the plug from her flagrum.

'Joan,' screamed Hubbard. 'The treacherous . . .'

'Bastard.' Pope Joan finished the sentence. 'This means . . .'

'War, I should think.' Gloria pressed the firing button.

'You really are a genius, dear,' sighed Ms Vrillium. 'Do

you think we should take to the shelters just to be on the safe side?'

'Now, why on Earth should we do that? No-one is going to be shooting at us, now are they?'

Mungo Madoc buried his face in his hands, and said, 'Oh, calamity.'

27

. . . the underground. There's always an underground. Tradition nurtured this one. And the Book. Because it had all come so far. It had to be seen through to the end. We all had to know what was on the K^2 carbon, in whatever form it was now hidden. Of course rival factions split, reformed, resplit. But at the core of them all was the certain knowledge that at the core of it all was some fabulous treasure just waiting. So the conviction became obsession and in no time obsession became religion. Some members of the underground became wholly convinced that some kind of cosmic warrior was coming, that he would unlock the secrets of the carbon and set the world to rights. Some said he was here already, some that he would soon be born. Others, and this includes the Devianti, split from the underground in the early years. Developed this cult of the Born Again. A sort of other Christ. We let that one spread, put the wind up the Big Three.

The Suburban Book of the Dead

The missile Gloria despatched was the last of its breed. A Sneaky Reekie. Designed in the late nineties, its brethren had done a thorough job of laying waste to the greater part of the known world. Dan had been saving it for a very special occasion. It hedge-hopped, or it most certainly would have done, had there been any hedges extant for it to hop over. Shall we say that it rubble-hopped? It slunk out of the tradesman's entrance of the Nemesis Bunker, looked both ways to assure itself that it wasn't being observed, ducked into a Metro terminus, soared along a trackway, snook up a ventilation shaft, near the Tomorrowman Tavern, now undergoing extensive renovations. Created a cloak of invisibility, through the adaptation of Einstein's Unified Field Theory, turned up Park Avenue and finally nuzzled its nuclear nose into the front parlour of the late Aunty Norma.

'Gotcha,' it said. Loudly.

The switchboard (for why belabour the reader with a lot of sci-fi-hi-tech-hokum, regarding its multi-cellular, bio-embrionic jiggery-pokery) at Earthers Inc. jammed. Minor employees scurried up and down the membrane tubes. Board members paced the lush and tufted carpetings. One or two of the more highly-strung took the opportunity to fling themselves from upper windows. Mungo Madoc sought divine guidance from He of the Nose Enormous. But as is so often the case with deities, old Holy Hooter was being just a little backward in coming forward. He was keeping out of this one. At length, Mungo knelt, pinched his nostrils and took himself off to the lift. For a man's gotta do what a man's gotta do.

Jason Morgawr met him on the boardroom landing. The intense young Phnaarg had never looked more so. 'No warning,' he shrieked, 'well, not enough at any rate. My team isn't ready. This is really too much. Really too much.'

Mungo brushed him aside. 'Are the other board members within?'

'Those that still remain amongst the living.'

Mungo sighed as only he could sigh and ordered the door aside.

'Gentlemen,' he declared, although the appellation seemed inappropriate to describe the bunch of jibbering ninnies now huddled at the far end of the Goldenwood table. 'Please be seated. There is *no*, and I repeat, *no* need to panic.'

The unmagical mushroom cloud rose above Aunty Norma's bunker. At 500 feet it flattened against the artificial cloud cover, which had been expressly designed to cope with such eventualities. The poisonous residues reflected downwards and outaways. The long-range cameras atop Nemesis which had been recording the great event, retracted into their blast-proof housings.

'We'll meet again, don't know where, don't know when,' sang the Lamarettes, clad soberly in black armbands, although very little else.

'And remember,' Gloria mopped at a tear and smiled bravely, 'if you are in the latter stages of pregnancy or even giving birth at this very moment, give your EYESPI a little wave. Because you could be carrying the next incarnation of the Living God King himself. Here today and here tomorrow, that is the watchword of Buddhavision. Tomorrow belongs to you.'

'For I know we'll meet again, some sunny day . . .' Fade out.

L. Ron Hubbard's glory girls freighted their precious cargo at great speed towards the Chosen One's thinking quarters. Scores of vacuum-eyed young men, with swish black suits, clutching antique filofaxes to their bosoms, followed at the double. 'Arm 'em up!' trilled the portly Thetan. 'Run every son-of-a-bitch through the E meter and send 'em out.' The pale young men shouted into their radio-phones and did what they could to add to the general confusion.

'And get my chef down here,' L. Ron continued, 'I want to discuss lunch.'

Pope Joan stayed put. Popes don't rush about in panic, it simply isn't done. She merely addressed the assembled clergy.

'Consider the guns blessed. Aim them directly at Fundamentalist Foods and discharge them. That is all.'

The lads at the Nemesis motorpool grudgingly paid off the chief mechanic. One bright spark suggested a whip-round to get up a wreath for Rex. But no-one was particularly keen, so they got on with the business in hand. 'Who will give me evens on the Jesuits?' asked the chief mechanic, who was feeling lucky.

'News teams are covering both the rival stations,' said Ms Vrillium. 'We are monitoring all their broadcasts, internal as well as external. We will relay all relevant information to the viewers the moment anything truly significant occurs.'

'You consider that a state of war now exists?'

'Oh yes, dear. No doubt about it.'

Gloria was all smiles. 'Good. And technical are going to run all the appropriate archive footage? Threats, recriminations, cover-ups, scandals, corruption in high places. All the horny stuff?'

'The stuff we have been manufacturing for years, dear? All taken care of. Overkill, is, I believe, the expression.'

'There is, I trust, no chance whatever that Dan might have survived the blast?'

'None. Intelligence informed us that a bomb had been fitted to Rex's air car. We took the liberty of exploding that first. They had nowhere to run to.'

'Shame,' said twenty billion Phnaargs. But they remained glued to their sets, all the same.

'Good.' Gloria stretched languidly and ran her fingers through her hair. 'I am, of course, very sorry about Rex. But, as they say, you can't make a really good lubricant without breaking eggs.'

'You certainly can't,' Ms Vrillium willingly agreed. I wonder what an egg is, and where you can get one at this time of day? she mused.

'Oh, boo and hoo and boo hoo hoo,' sobbed the Sneaky Reckie. 'I'm a dud. A great big dud. The shame, the shame.'

Rex patted the blubbering bomb upon the dented nosecone. 'Never mind,' he said encouragingly. 'It's all for the best, you know.'

'The last of my line,' wailed the missile, 'and how does my world end?'

'Not with a bang but a whimper?'

'Oh cruel, cruel.'

'But let's look on the bright side,' Rex was all for that, 'you could have injured us badly.'

'Injured you badly? I would have atomised you. My destructive capabilities are . . . were . . . should have been . . . oh, the shame . . .'

'Hey, hold on there,' Elvis put in. 'If it wasn't this SOB, something made one hell of a bang out there.'

'I think I might be able to explain,' said Fergus Shaman. 'There was a bomb in Rex's air car. It was detonated by remote control from the Nemesis building. I fear it must have set off the Dilithium Crystals in my spaceship

271

causing the major explosion. Luckily for us the rear end of this loquacious missile absorbed the impact upon the bunker, sparing our lives. There's always a logical explanation if you are prepared to stretch credibility far enough.'

'Hang on there.' The voice belonged to Rex. 'What bomb in my air car?'

'The one *he* placed in it.' Fergus pointed the finger of guilt toward Dalai Dan. 'To destroy the car as soon as you had picked up Mr Presley.'

'Oh I never did,' lied the Living God King. 'As if I would.'

'What about me?' wailed the Sneaky Reekie. 'My reverse gears are buggered also.'

'Talking bomb,' muttered Elvis. 'Pile of horseshit.'

'Oh, I don't know, chief. Logical progression, life always imitates art, you know. Remember that science fiction film, *Dark Star*, on Concorde, when we were on our way to Hong Kong?'

'Shit, yeah. That where this guy swiped the idea from?'

'Bound to be, chief.'

'But in the movie, the bomb finally blew up.'

'Yeah chief, just what I was thinking.'

'You put a bomb in my air car?' Rex was now shaking the Dalai by the throat.

'Rex, no, please, ouch. You can't believe him . . . gag . . . gurgle . . . What about our working relationship, your pension plan? Ow, gulp . . .' Rex took his hands from the holyman's throat and kicked his chair over. He turned away in fury to confront a bunker wall of no particular interest. Gloria's face lit up the TV terminal.

'As a special tribute to the Dalai Lama, who cast away his Earthly form this very morning, we are going to screen a selection of humorous out-takes and bloopers from the last series of *Nemesis*. These show the more muddled, human side of our beloved Dan and it was his express wish that we show them, should an eventuality such as this occur.'

'You'll get yours, Gloria,' spat the floor-bound Dan from between seriously gritted teeth. 'You see if you don't.'

'We shall, of course interrupt this comic relief with any up-to-the-minute newsflashes of the war currently waging between the Jesuits and the Fundamentalists. *Om-mani-padme-hum.*'

Dan took to screaming and thrashing. It was most unbecoming.

28

. . . yeah, certainly, I work for the department. And all I'm saying is; if it came through here, it came through me. Nothing comes in or goes out except if it's through me. It gets checked in. It gets evaluated. It gets authenticated, or not, as the case may be. It gets indexed. It gets catalogued and it gets filed. All through me. Now, the date you are talking about is a date I'm hardly going to forget, am I? It being the date that the last object ever came through here. Although, as you can see, I'm sitting at my desk in case something else might come in. Which is unlikely as the digs have been closed for twenty years. But I'm still here. Boring? A pointless existence? Twenty years? Funny you should mention it. Do I get resentful? Do I get resentful? Sitting here looking at these four walls, while my life ticks away? What?

So regarding this object, this very last object that I ever recorded. And which by implication would indeed appear to be the very object you seek. And which you would like me to show you. Buddy, it would be more than my job's worth to pull a stunt like that. And I'm not messing.

The Suburban Book of the Dead

'There now,' said Mungo. 'Did I or did I not tell you not to panic?' The board members responded somewhat indifferently to Mungo's question. It was almost as if they needed a mite more convincing.

Jason put up his hand to speak. 'Sir, the fortuitous survival of Dan et al does, if I might dare voice the feelings of the entire board—' (the entire board made 'no such thing' rumblings) '—does take a fair bit of swallowing, credibility wise.'

'Let us not beat about the bush, Morgawr,' Mungo dusted pollen from his lapel, 'something specific on your mind?'

'Well . . . er . . .' Jason stared about at the surviving board members. Their faces said, 'Go on, fuck yourself up.' 'Ah, nothing. A lucky chance. Fortuitous is the word I shall stand by.'

'Good. Now regarding your technical staff. How long before they will be ready for the off?'

'An hour, sir. Two at the most.'

'And Morgawr, you are totally *au fait* with the situation, plotwise?'

'Oh yes, sir.' Jason's face bobbed up and down. 'Armageddon, that's what it's all about now, eh?'

Mungo made a thoughtful face. 'Yes, well it is and it isn't.'

'It is and it isn't.' Morgawr tried to look enlightened. 'It is Armageddon, but it's not Armageddon. Yes I see. I know it's not *the* Armageddon. Which is to say, that although it is our Armageddon, which will appear to be their Armageddon, it is not really *the* Armageddon. Which is what you are saying, is it not?'

'What I am saying is that whoever's Armageddon it turns out to be, it must have a happy ending. One which will satisfy the backers, the Holy Writ and the viewing public. Raise the ratings, not infuriate the advertisers, and allow me to sleep peacefully in my bed, should I ever wish so to do. This is the kind of scenario, in fact the exact scenario which you envisage, is it not?'

'Well . . .' said Jason Morgawr. 'Well . . .'

The doors of the Dalai's private lift opened into his equally private apartments. These occupied the entire floor toward the very apex of the Nemesis pyramid. The four glazed, sloping walls displayed the panorama of endless blue, beneath which, and in terrible contrast, the artificial cloud heaved like a poison sea.

Gloria took a step forward but checked herself. Dan's presence still hung in the air. An unsavoury psychic miasma. It said, 'Just you try it.' Gloria trembled, assailed by sudden doubt. She had done the unthinkable. She had murdered the World's foremost religious figure. The man which many regarded as God. That he was unquestionably a merciless tyrant hardly seemed to come into it. He was worshipped, adored. Gloria Mundi had murdered God.

And for what? For the common good? For the sake of mankind? The future of the race? Gloria shook her head. Out of revenge, out of a lust for power. And now she had it, what was she going to do with it? She realized for the first time that she really had no idea at all.

'Come on dear, I'll fix us both a drink.' Ms Vrillium placed a fleshy palm upon the small of Gloria's back.

'Be careful.'

'Careful?' Ms Vrillium marched from the lift, the martial clicks of her steel heels losing themselves in the rich pile of the carpet.

'Can't you feel him?' Gloria was suddenly afraid.

'I can smell that filthy musk he pomaded himself with. But nothing more. Come on dear, first night nerves is all.'

With faltering steps Gloria entered the apartment. She

277

had seen it all before. The fine hangings. The quilted sofas, their covers woven from the feathers of birds a century dead. The high-domed display cases, clustered with enigmatic antiques. The kilims and curios. Seen it all before. But somehow never really seen it. Never in depth, in clarity. Seen what it represented. What He represented.

'Permanence,' Dan had said. 'Safety, the status quo. I am part of all this, a metaphor, a symbol. A whatnot.'

Ms Vrillium rattled the neck of a Venetian decanter into a silvered goblet. 'We'll have that out of here for a kick off.' She addressed her words to a full-length portrait of the lad himself.

'His painting?' The voice was half gone in Gloria's throat.

'Painting nothing. That dear is what they call a patchwork quilt and it is patched from human skins.'

Gloria felt very sick indeed.

The ongoing situation currently ongoing between the Fundamentalists and the Jesuits was stepping up apace. Although the weaponry involved was somewhat cobwebby and of dubious serviceability, the protagonists went about their respective businesses with a will. For when both parties have God on their side, both can be equally assured of winning.

There had already been several unfortunate incidents involving certain 'Smart' weapons systems. Having had five decades to meditate upon their own smartness, these appeared to have reached states of enlightenment which put them above the whim of mortal man. Thus, few, if any, ever found their allotted targets.

Then, there was the matter of the anti-missile missiles, the anti-missile-missile missiles, the holographically-

278

projected decoy missiles, the holographically-projected decoy confusion missiles, the jamming systems, the anti-jamming rejamming systems and the systems which did nothing in particular but were still exciting for all of that. Adding to all this were the systems which failed immediately, those which reserved their malfunctionings until the vital moment and those, which included most of the foregoing, which required the skilled hand of the highly-trained expert. A breed now long gone to dust.

One further point is worthy of note. Both the edifices now currently under bombardment had withstood the now legendary Nuclear Holocaust Event, a time when men really knew how to chuck the sophisticated widow-making hardware about. The bumps and grinds now currently on the go appeared to pose but little threat in the 'laying waste to' department.

L. Ron Hubbard the twenty-third, sensing that Dan's tragic demise might well afford the opportunity for him to elevate himself from the role of two-dimensional character with hardly a sub-plot to call his own to that of major protagonist, paced the war-room floor unaided. The Hubbards never got wherever they got by thinking small.

'Ma many great times granpappy would have known how to kick ass with these no-count low-lifes,' he drawled southernly. 'All fair game to great times grampah.' The sharp young men with the far-away stares bent low over their instrument panels and said nothing. One didn't take liberties with the mighty L. Ron. Not any liberties. Not nohow.

'All this bin a long time coming,' quoth the great man, as his personal stenographers keyed up their shorthand computers, eager to take down his each and every holy word. 'In a world gone all to hell with avarice and greed and never a hint of a takeaway tandoori or a Colonel Sanders ^{TM} Chicken Nugget ^{TM}, a world of heartache and gloom, where few other than me ever glimpse the higher truths, such a world as this, my friends, and such a time as this, and did I ever tell you about the time my great times granpapa once sailed a ship halfway around the world and stopped off at this little island where the natives prepare a special brand of lobster which they take in a sauce of . . .' And it went on much in the same fashion, as it always did and no doubt always would, which gives the reader a fair idea why L. Ron really didn't merit a more prominent part. And why his forthcoming assassination at the hands of a jealous drug-crazed continuity girl over a love-triangle incident, which had nothing whatever to do with the controlling theme of this book, would go for the most part unrecorded, but, that is, for a brief mention of the sickening squelch made by his lifeless body as it struck the floor.

Pope Joan had always envisaged her role in the film version being played by Meryl Streep. Or if Meryl wasn't available, then at the very least by that fine character actor Mr Michael O'Hagan. Now she knelt in silent prayer. Joan hadn't had much to say as yet, and sadly for her she wouldn't have much more, as it happened. But, as she had always believed, it was in the way that lines were spoken that turned the words into an artform. In the connotation rather than the denotation. She considered language a means to convey, rather than an end in itself. And though the song is ended, the melody lingers on. And so forth.

'Although I have the body of a weak and frail woman,' she began.

Back in Aunty Norma's bunker imponderables were being pondered. Four men were huddled in the furthest corner from the bomb-bunged door. They comprised possibly the most unlikely quartet in literary history. Being: a risen-from-the-ranks bunker-boy, whose promotional prospects had never looked grimmer; a visitor from another star, who really wished he wasn't; his divine unholiness the Dalai Lama, now unemployed; and a time-travelling Elvis Presley with a sprout in his head.

And they say nothing is new. Bah, humbug!

'The way I see it, Barry,' said Elvis, addressing the Time Sprout. 'This could be a very dynamite show.' Inside the King's cerebellum Barry the sprout (he had chosen the name himself) nodded thoughtfully.

'This is, I think, chief, where Rex really comes into his own.'

'Oh yes?' Rex, who had been silently fulminating upon life in general, and his own in particular, turned sulkily at the mention of his name. 'And how might that be?'

'Deductive reasoning,' said friend sprout. 'You surely don't think that sheer chance led us here?'

'Cruel fate, more like.'

'Lighten up, chief. There is a purpose behind everything. Once one has divined the purpose, crystallized one's ideas, weighed up the pros and cons, taken the bull by the horns, surmounted the seemingly insurmountable, maximized one's options . . .'

Rex shook his head so violently that it made his eyes pop. 'My role so far in this has been one of exemplary stoicism. I'm now resigned to the conclusion that life makes no sense whatsoever. I shall now, I think, go it alone.'

'And which way might you go, chief?'

Rex glanced over at the Sneaky Reekie, which was now making determined tick tock noises. 'I am cogitating,' he replied.

'Rex is probably cogitating upon the secret trapdoor,' said Fergus Shaman, casually. Three pairs of eyes turned simultaneously upon him.

'Trapdoor,' Fergus reiterated, pre-empting the obvious joint response. 'It's definitely on file, I recall it from when we first set up the Rex scenari . . . oh.' His glance met that of Rex.

'Rex scenario,' said that man, very slowly.

'A star must always have options, as long as they are logical of course. A star . . .' But unfortunately the word star was already suffering from the law of diminishing returns. Rex Mundi punched Fergus Shaman on the nose.

'Easy there, big fella,' Elvis stepped forward to restrain Rex from further demonstrations of displeasure. 'If the alien dude says there's a trapdoor, let's not punch his lights out for it.'

Rex shook him off. Fergus nursed his beak whilst Dan sniggered silently. Bloodied noses seemed to have become something of a vogue lately, thought he.

'It's just possible,' said Rex in a tone which implied supreme unlikelihood, 'that I might even become more furious than I am now. I have been callously manipulated, at the very least, by everyone in this bunker and possibly, for all I know, others beyond number. I will have no more of it. I shall stay here and die like a man. Better it is to die on one's feet than live on one's knees.'

282

'Ah,' said the Sneaky Reekie, 'I think I have ironed out the problem. A bit of oil in the carburettor. That's better, now where was I? Oh yes, ten, nine, eight . . .'

'To the trapdoor,' cried Rex.

29

. . . the underground, yes, it was very much that. Amongst the network of metro-links, service tunnels, ventilation shafts, disused military installations, cellars, basements and vaults, the inner councils met. Plotted and planned. Started off, I guess, with NHE survivors trapped down there. They managed to tap into the synthafood pipes leading from the plants far below and the power lines. So once you have food and power you are up and running. The word of the Book gave hope. From the few remaining town planners' blueprints we burrowed up to what bunkers we could. Came across a lot of dead folk back then. But we had our successes. Just kept passing the word along.

The Suburban Book of the Dead

'So you see, Rex.' Fergus Shaman edged along in the near darkness, beyond the punishing range of Rex's fist. 'Your uncle was something of a revolutionary himself.'

'But what exactly did he want?'

'Same as all revolutionaries want. The genuine ones anyway. Create Utopia, destroy tyranny, win freedom, that kind of thing.'

'So you are telling me that there is an entire revolutionary army down here awaiting mobilization?' Rex found a sudden spring creeping into his step.

'Well, actually no.' Fergus lightened his own footsteps. 'Regretfully no.'

'Go on then, tell me the worst.'

'Someone got to them. We don't know who, perhaps it was a what. But something wiped them all out.'

'I don't like the sound of no what.' Elvis cuffed Dan in the ear to place an accent upon his words. 'I'll settle for a who. Some stooly sold them out to the Feds.' Cuff, cuff.

'Possibly so,' Fergus shrugged. 'We could never get a foothold down here, so we may never know for certain.'

'So they could all still be here.' Rex's optimism surprised even himself.

'They're not,' said Fergus.

You're damned right they're not, thought Dan, 'You'll get yours pal,' he told Elvis.

Back in Aunty Norma's bunker, the Sneaky Reekie appeared to have become a graduate of the Deathblade Eric School of Discorporate Numerics. 'Seven . . . six . . . eight, no, seven . . . eight . . . nine, no, nine seven, oh buggeration,' swore the frustrated killing machine.

'Zero and . . .'

A violent shock rocked the passage and sent the odd quartet reeling. Something big and bad had just gone boom somewhere above them. But on this occasion as upon the last, it wasn't the Sneaky Reekie.

Rex struggled to his feet. 'Things are becoming very dangerous indeed,' he complained. 'The unrecycled excrement seems to have made contact with the rotating segment of the atmospheric circulator, to coin a phrase.'

'Something like.' Elvis agreed. 'Anyone know where we are, for Chrissakes?'

'You're in deep shit,' said Dan. His outspokenness was rewarded in summary fashion. 'Ouch,' he added.

'I still find it hard to believe that my uncle was a revolutionary.' Rex made as to dust himself down, but the futility of the action was not slow in the dawning. He could no longer see the point. Nor could he see very much else as he felt his way along in the gloom. And what he could see, he knew to be illuminated by the generations of active fallout which had soaked down into the passages. It wasn't all that encouraging no matter how you viewed it. 'He was certainly an idealist, Uncle, for whatever that got him.'

'He taught you the trick with the eyes, though.'

'Trick with the eyes?' Dan voiced a sudden interest.

'Taught Rex how to sleep with his eyes open. Fool the EYESPI, clock up credits without having to suffer the rubbish on-screen..'

'Did he now?' Dan sensed rather than saw the swing Elvis took at his ear, and nimbly sidestepped it. 'Smart trick.'

Rex turned suddenly upon Dan. 'That why you killed him?'

Dan stared him eye to eye. 'You'd best keep your options open, Rex. You never know when you might need them.' Rex heard that, but no-one else did. Not even the telepathic sprout.

Mungo Madoc inhabited his boardroom chair. The boardroom board watched him and shared feelings of unease. Like the Magi of old, they were awaiting a sign. A star in the heavens, perhaps? Or perhaps not. A simple nod of the head or twitch of the forefinger might well have alleviated the tension somewhat. But Mungo did nothing. He sat and he stared and he stared. Mungo was communing with the backers. The switchboard girls had pulled the plugs and made their strategic withdrawal to the staff canteen, secure in the knowledge that unruly mobs were unlikely to besiege the building, seeking heads. Nothing was going to drag the population away from their television sets. For the first time ever these were now actually showing *The Earthers* in its full, unedited glory. Dan, Rex and Elvis might be lacking, but the violent spectacle of two of Earth's largest religious organizations blasting seven bells of unrecycled excrement out of each other was far too good to miss. And with Dan gone, and Gloria still an unknown quantity, allegiances were already starting to shift.

Mungo lurched suddenly forward, loosening the weaker bladders.

'Right,' said he. 'I have been in lengthy communication with the backers and you will be pleased to hear that they are willing to sanction Morgawr's Armageddon scenario. With one or two minor changes which need not concern any of you here. Now let us be one hundred per cent clear on the situation as it now stands. The series as we know it, is shortly to be brought to an end.' He put up his hands against the outcry. 'A great deal of thought has gone into this, I can assure you. But this series, like any other, had only a limited budget and the backers are not prepared to extend it any longer. No backing, no budget, no series. Morgawr, stop that man . . . '

'Too late.' Morgawr gazed down from the open window, the falling body diminished and was gone.

Mungo shook his head and snuffled at a lapel flower, savouring the heavily narcotized scent. 'Now, before any more of you make such an ill-considered move, I suggest that you just hear me out.' The board members settled themselves down, loosening ties and gulping water. 'We have all tried to keep this series going as long as possible.

288

And the Nose alone knows how many radical proposals and outrageous interventions there have been. But the big boys upstairs will have no more of it. They are adamant. The series must go out on a high note. Well, at least on a spectacular one. And cheap. Which will leave the way clear for something entirely new.'

'*Earth Two, The Sequel?*' Morgawr suggested.

'Sadly, no. We must play by the rules this time, I'm afraid. There will be no more tampering with scripts, no more improvisations. This is something altogether different and on a much larger scale. I can't tell you about it now, but if I say the words "substantial salary increases", then I hope they will be sufficient to put your minds at rest.'

The board rose as a single Phnaarg, cast metaphorical hats toward the sky and engulfed Mungo in a sea of hearty handclaps.

An entire aeon of human history was drawing to a close. A planet was about to be wiped from the heavens. All memories, thoughts and dreams, all hopes. Mankind was to be blotted out as if it had never needed to exist. But these lads were getting a pay rise!

30

Doubt everything and find your own light.
Buddha

'I really can't see the point in dragging him along. Why don't we simply kill him and have done?'

Elvis appeared to be stuck for a reply to this, but not so Fergus Shaman. 'You cannot kill the Dalai Lama, Rex. It simply isn't done.'

'But the man is a mass murderer. Only about two at a time, mind, but it adds up. He deserves execution, at the very least.'

'That may well be. But not by you. You've never actually killed anyone, have you?'

Rex made a thinking face. 'No,' said he. 'I'm sure that I haven't.'

'Nor have you.' Fergus peered toward the man in the white sequined number.

'Two or three.' Elvis did shoulder swaggers. 'In self defence, of course.'

'No, you haven't.' Fergus grinned. 'You're the good guys. You escape death by the skin of your teeth and fight for justice. Even, if like Rex, you don't even know why you do it most of the time. But you don't actually ever kill anyone.'

'*Om*,' said Dan. 'This being the case I will now take my leave.'

Elvis kicked him in the ankle. 'Never trust an alien,' he told the hopping holyman.

With Dan now muttering in muted tones that collectively, or one at a time, his persecutors would 'get theirs', the four continued along no particular passage, bound it seemed, for no particular destination. Or so it seemed.

'Holy shit,' cried Elvis Presley. 'Would you look at that?'

Now there have been rooms and there have been rooms. And this one was a bedroom as it happened. Of its furnishings and decor, it could be fairly stated that they were of the eclectic persuasion. A kidney-shaped dressing table with a crazed Formica top hob-nobbed with a gilded torchère which had once shed light upon Count Cagliostro. A faux-bamboo wall-case displayed the spines of rare and priceless books. The works of Crispin, Scott's *Phallic Worship*, the *Brentford Octology*, St Michael's *Book of Microwave Cooking*, Rushdie's *The Satanic Verses*. Kaffe Fassett cushions bulged upon a settee designed by Salvador Dali. And at the room's heart rose a Gothic four-poster covered with a candlewick bedspread. Upon this, and creating the room's immediate centre of interest, lay a voluptuous blonde woman wearing nought but a welcoming smile.

'Goddamn,' swore Elvis. 'I mean, well, pardon our intrusion, mam.'

The blonde rose upon her elbows and thrust out her bosom, in the manner once favoured by the Page Three Stunnas of old. She tossed back her hair and yawned silently.

'We're lost,' said Rex, rather foolishly.

'Yeah,' Elvis agreed. 'That's right.'

Fergus Shaman nodded his head. 'What amazing nipples,' he observed.

Dan said nothing. But then this kind of sight was hardly new to him.

'Sorry to invade your privacy.' Rex was trying not to look, but failing for the most part. 'If you could just offer some directions, we will be straight on our way.'

'I'm in no particular hurry,' Elvis produced a monogrammed comb and teased it through his quiff, 'if you guys want to go on ahead.'

'I think we should all stick together.'

Fergus shook pungent aromatics of an aphrodisiac nature on to his palm and began to pat them about his chin. Dan said nothing for the second time. The blonde on the bed rolled on to her side and fluttered her eyelids at Elvis.

'Sorry guys,' said the King, preparing for action. 'But it was really no contest, was it? Here, Rex, you take scumbag out for a walk. Say for a couple of hours.'

'I don't think so,' Rex pushed past the Dalai. Or at least he would have. As it was Rex pushed through the Dalai. The image faded into the air, a broad Cheshire Cat grin hovering for a moment before doing a likewise vanishing trick.

'Trickery dickery,' cried Fergus, very much impressed. There was a kind of loud pop and the entire room, blonde bombshell and all folded in upon itself and was gone. The three men now stood knee deep in raw sewerage. They began to sink. Dalai Dan was nowhere to be seen.

'Aw, shit!'

31

*. . . we knew where it was for sure and it was remarkable
how simple it actually was to discover what it was
pretending to be. Back in the nineties, the term for what
we did was 'super hacking'. Computer gate-crashing on an
international scale. Subversives hacked their ways into the
mainframes of all the major institutions: the military,
banking houses, religious, even the Big Three. Back doors
were created whereby the hacker could override pass-codes,
slip in and out at will, draw off programs, make subtle
adjustments, alter records. And introduce viruses which
self-replicated and spread, crashing the systems. At that
time the biggest of these hacking circuses was called CHAOS.
I swear to God it's true. Now the Buddhavision mainframe,
MOTHER, so called, had security blocks on it from the first.
Punch in the wrong passcode and it fed back. You were
fried meat at your terminal. Real mean. They took hacking
very seriously. But there was a backdoor all the same. Who
got it in there, I can't say. But it was there and we took it.
Called up the Department of Antiquities stock records and
skimmed through to the last recorded entry. And there it
was. Entry **%78:555:2323;*

All we had to do now was break right in and get it.
The Suburban Book of the Dead

*In the world there are two kinds of tragedies. One is not
getting what one wants. The other is getting it.*
Oscar Wilde

The surviving members of the Earthers Inc. executive board lined themselves against the wall, uncertain of what exactly was about to occur. Mungo faced them from his chair. 'This,' he displayed between thumb and forefinger a small sphere which glowed, as if lit from within, 'is a key. *The* key, in fact. It has lain in a secret place for over 1,000 Earther years. From the time, in fact, when it was supposed to be used the first time. But now I am informed by the backers that its moment has come for certain.'

'What does it do?' Jason asked.

'In short it ties up a lot of loose ends.'

'A McGuffin,' Jason suggested.

Mungo Madoc shook his head. 'You are a moron,' he said. 'Now just stay where you are and watch this carefully.'

Mungo took up the glowing sphere, popped it into his mouth and swallowed. The board members looked on in wonder. The possibilities were endless. There was a long and ponderous moment, during which nothing happened. Then, with a suddenness of trouser-filling intensity, everything did. Mungo's head bulged hideously. His fingers extended. Like so many pink serpents they darted through the air to attach themselves to the walls and ceiling. Then they began to pulsate. The Goldenwood table sank into the floor and the tufted carpeting swept in from all sides to cover its departure. A great cone of light sprang up and an impossible pressure popped ears and gritted teeth. The room quivered and shook as the living thing it was.

And then it was done. The room became still. The pressure ceased. Mungo's fingers returned to their natural proportions, his head shrank. The cone of light remained, glittering about the edges. Mungo whistled, shook his head and flexed his fingers. 'Yes indeedy,' he said.

No-one dared to ask.

Two menials in station fatigues carried the Dalai's portrait from the room. At Gloria's elbow, one of a dozen telephones purred. She picked it up. The voice on the other end of the line was unknown to her. It was shouting. Gloria held the receiver at arm's length and regarded it with distaste.

'Shall I, dear?' asked Ms Vrillium.

'Please do.' Ms Vrillium placed the thing to her head and listened for a moment. She then shouted, 'Fuck off,' before slamming it down.

'Who was that?'

'Artemis Scargill dear, chief convenor for the food and medico workers' union. He says that unless the long-running dispute between management and the shop floor is settled at once, his members will be forced to place a vote of No Confidence in you. And that just to be on the safe side, they are preparing for an all-out strike.'

'They didn't waste a lot of time, did they?'

The telephone purred again. Ms Vrillium tore the plug from the socket and hurled the wicked messenger into a far corner. The lights momentarily dimmed.

'That would no doubt be the electrical union letting you know that they are preparing to offer their support.'

Gloria made a pensive face. 'What about the technicians and the production teams?'

'Different unions again, dear. Although Dan never did get around to sorting out all their separate grievances. So I suppose it's just possible . . .'

Gloria slumped on to Dan's settee and tinkered distractedly with the holophon headset. 'This is something of a pain in the butt.'

The fat woman's eyes lit up. 'Would you like me to . . .'

'Not at present, thank you. What am I going to do?'

'Hardly for me to say,' Ms Vrillium replied tartly. 'Dan always kept them under control. It's down to you now.'

Gloria made sulks. 'How's the war going?' she asked, brightening.

'The Fundamentalists currently have the upper hand. Several of Joanie's transmitters are already in purgatory.'

'Jolly good. Then once both stations go off the air . . .'

'The victory would appear to be ours, yes.'

'Yes.' For Gloria it was all really starting to sink in. When the victory was hers, what then? What was she going to do with it? She discarded the headset and rose from the settee. Crossing the floor she paused to regard the sky through one of the great sloping walls of glass. Gazing down from it, she viewed the turmoil of foul brown cloud. Beneath this were thousands of people, huddled in bunkers and now relying on her for their survival. Gloria was capable of being dispassionate along with the best of them, but on such a scale? Dan had talked about his new tomorrow. Wafting away the clouds, opening up the land. A madman's dream of Utopia? Gloria made inward groans. Perhaps the cloud cover couldn't be lifted. Perhaps all of it was lies. All in all it was a bit of a mess. And all in all she was very much to blame.

Gloria Mundi suddenly began to miss Dalai Dan very much indeed.

There was a fair amount of slurping and slopping going on down in the bowels of the Earth. Elvis dragged Rex clear of the quagmire and hastened to the aid of Fergus

Shaman. 'These magic boots were one hell of a smart move, green buddy.'

Fergus slumped upon dry land. 'Thanks,' he gasped.

'No sweat. Rex, give me back my electronic doodad.' Rex delved into his sodden suit and fished it out. Elvis tinkered with it but got no response. 'Doesn't work down here. Look at my trouser cuffs. Good guy or not, I shall do for the father-raper as soon as we catch him up.'

Rex shook himself, but it did no good. The Dalai had really been saving himself for that one. From a detached point of view, it really was a remarkably clever trick, although it was hard to be detached when you smelt the way Rex did. But it was a bit of a mystery. Why had Dan chosen to dump them there, rather than over some precipice, where they might have plunged to oblivion? Perhaps he had just been strapped for time, or maybe it simply hadn't occurred to him. Mercy certainly would not have numbered amongst his reasons.

Fergus plucked gingerly at his knees. He had three things on his mind. Well, one, if you discarded the two amazing nipples, which he was somewhat loath to do. This one was that with him down here and out of the picture, what terrible wheels of chaos would Mungo Madoc be setting into motion? Without Fergus to guide him, Mungo's incompetence would be given its full head. 'Oh dear, oh dear, oh dear,' mumbled the unhappy Phnaarg.

32

. . . and so it has come to this. A hundred men went down there. They knew which ducts to enter. How to penetrate the building. Where to find the carbon. But none returned. And now he will come looking for me. He must have known they were coming. Someone must have talked. Been made to talk. When they have you in there you talk and you talk. So now I pass the Book on to Rex. He must continue the search. I will sit it out and wait. It won't be long.

The Suburban Book of the Dead

They come from a far country, from the end of Heaven. Even the Lord and the weapons of his indignation to destroy the whole land.

Isaiah 13:5

'You are probably wondering what all that palaver was all about.' Mungo adjusted his cuffs and snorted upon a lapel blossom. Heads bobbed in the affirmative manner. 'Something of a point of no return. The sphere contained the final programme. It's now interfaced with the corporate entity which is this building. All systems are now on stand-by and all channels feed directly through me. A little failsafe device employed by the backers to insure that no . . .'

'Improvisation should occur?' Jason Morgawr found

his voice. 'So whose programme is it running, ours or theirs?'

'As the visual scenario stands, ours. In terms of theological over-structure, theirs. Do I make myself clear?'

'No,' replied Jason. 'In all candour you don't.'

'The success of any show depends to a large part upon giving the public what they want. But not necessarily in the way they expect it. The Armageddon scenario – your version, Morgawr – will, as sanctioned, run visually. The fulfilling of certain contractual obligations, videlicet the original script, will be handled separately by the backers. Ours not to reason why.'

'And all this will run directly through you?'

'I'm now biologically linked to the station. My duty is to filter out whatever is deemed unsuitable for transmission.'

'Such as evidence of tampering.'

'You have no quarrel with that, surely?'

Jason scratched at his head. 'And what about our people on Earth? They will be brought out safely, I trust.'

'Regretfully, no.'

'But they are our people, that is murder.'

'No, Morgawr,' said Mungo, grandiloquently. 'That's showbiz.'

The umpteenth passage came to a boring conclusion. Fergus sat down and began to grizzle. Rex kicked hopelessly at the nearest wall. The sound hardly echoed.

'Aw, shit,' snarled Elvis, joining Rex in the futile wall-kicking. 'How many does that make it? We'll never get out of here.' They were rapidly losing all track of time. Rex squinted at his watch. Two-thirty. 'How long have we been down here?'

302

'Less than ten minutes, chief. Time sure do fly when you're having fun.'

'There wouldn't be any chance of you beaming us up?' Elvis asked. 'Sure getting sick of it down here.'

'No can do, I'm afraid, chief.'

'Hey,' said Elvis. 'Surely I can smell . . .'

'Violets,' said Rex. 'You can smell violets.'

'I would have thought you had sufficient ability to find your own way out,' said Christeen softly. 'But as you haven't, you'd better follow me.'

'Baby,' howled Elvis, spinning around to view the splendid woman. 'Baybee!'

'Don't even think about it.' Rex pushed past the boy wonder and took Christeen by the hand.

'We had best make haste,' said she.

'Battle wages on all fronts.' The newscaster loosened his tie and mopped his brow. 'Fundamentalist forces hammer at Vatican City. Air cars equipped with the very latest in air-to-air laser cannons cut a bloody swathe across the sky in a major strike offensive. Phew, and I'll bet those guys and gals giving their all up there are just crying out for a long cool glass of Buddhabeer. Buddhabeer, for when the going gets really hot . . .'

Gloria switched off the news terminal. The lights dimmed once more as if to say 'it's make your mind up time'. Three further terminals gabbled greenly upon the black marble desk-top. They displayed alarming production figures, budget over-runs, high wastage quotients, and the like. Bit-mapped graphics ran viewing statistics and projected forecasts to the effect that Buddhavision's slice of the market was growing by the hour. At first glance this might have appeared to be good news, but with the fall in food and medico production it was nothing short of disastrous. Buddhavision was hard pressed to supply its own followers; any increase could mean that all would starve. Gloria bit upon a black lacquered thumbnail. Cordless telephones began to ring out discordant fanfares.

'Nice to see you again.'

Christeen gave Rex a loving peck on the cheek. 'You're sweet. Although you smell as bad as ever.'

'We ran into a spot of bother. Dan got away.'

'Yes, I saw it. But I was in no position to help. I'm sorry.'

'Why is it,' Rex asked, 'that I can only remember you when I'm with you?'

'That's my little secret. But see, we're nearly here.' They had entered one of the sub-basements of the Nemesis Bunker.

'Here,' groaned Rex. 'Not here. Why here?'

'Because this is where all of it is going to happen. And I do mean happen. Come on.' Christeen led the way to the lift.

'Some honey, huh?' Elvis whispered to Fergus Shaman.

The other nodded enthusiastically. 'Massive bosoms.'

Mungo Madoc slid an intricate system of controls, all bulging bits and pulsating other bits and bits that glowed funny colours, out in front of him. He rattled a brisk finger tattoo upon it and a cross-mesh of laser light spun out toward the shining cone. The image of a mud-brown planet appeared, grim and forbidding, and relieved of its monotone only by two pale grey areas at its polar regions. The image enlarged and became solid. Mungo's gaze fell upon Jason Morgawr. 'All keyed in and ready for the off.

304

We shall now run your programme, Jason. Places everyone and action.'

The lights went out at Nemesis. Gloria swore fiercely and
sought objects to throw. Beyond the sloping windows the
sun was going down. Between the first and second floor,
the lift was going nowhere.

'Aw . . .'

'No, let me say it for you. Shit.'

'Thanks, Rex.'

In the darkness Fergus felt about for a switch. His
wandering hands made contact with something extremely nice. 'Urgh,' went Fergus Shaman as Christeen's
fist made contact with his nose.

High above in the darkness Ms Vrillium's voice
quavered strangely. 'Gloria dear, there is someone to see
you.'

Gloria Mundi turned in fury. 'Who?' But then words
rightly failed her.

'Come at a bad time, have I?' asked Dalai Dan.

33

Behold He cometh with clouds and every eye shall see Him.
Revelation 1:7

Gloria might have tried, 'Thank God you're alive,' for in fact that was exactly what she thought and exactly what Dan heard her think. But as it was her mouth opened and closed but nothing whatever came out.

'On your knees.' The tone in Dan's voice contained such exquisite menace and such unquestionable authority that Gloria hastened to obey. Ms Vrillium was already on all fours and cowering into the bargain. The High Lama strode across the darkling room and seated himself behind his great desk. He flipped the open channels on the terminals and punched codes into the row of telephones. And then he spoke. But it wasn't a single voice, it was a cacophony of voices, all his, yet all issuing separate instructions at exactly the same moment. Gloria pressed her hands about her ears. She sensed and felt the power of pure evil.

But to the terminal operators and those poised, telephone in hand, these heard but a single voice, directed personally to them. A voice which offered encouragement, assuaged doubts, made praise, made promises. When the terrible multiple tirade was done, Dan sat back in his chair and pressed the palms of his hands together. Small sparklets of energy crackled about his fingertips. After a moment or two the lights came back on.

'Did you really think you could run all this without me? Did you?' Gloria hid her face, she was shivering fearfully.

'You wretched creature. None of it ever got through to you, did it? All this! All this!' Dan rose from his seat. And he did it with style. He rose into the air and hovered above his desk. 'All this is *mine*. I made all this. I hold it together. Without me there is only chaos. I am the Living God King. Last of my line. You are nothing. Do you hear? Nothing.'

'I am nothing,' whispered Gloria. 'Nothing.'

'There, I've fixed it,' said Rex, as the lift rose again from the dead. Christeen gave him an old-fashioned look. Rex winked back.

'Nice one, Rex.' Elvis was cocking a selection of brutal-looking hardware. He thrust what appeared to be a ray gun into Fergus's fist.

'You've got a bogey hanging out of your nose,' he observed.

'It's blood.' Fergus made an unhappy face at Christeen and wiped a sleeve collar across his begored nostrils. The lift passed the eighteenth floor and continued upwards.

Upon the eighteenth-floor landing two young gentlemen, now beautifully turned out in Barbour jackets and tweed caps, were enjoying an early supper. This came in the form of a Nemesis continuity person.

'Pass the salt, old boy,' said Rambo Bloodaxe.

'Oh,' said Deathblade Eric. 'It's us, I thought we were dead.'

'Not a bit of it. We simply went to ground when Rex's

air car went off without us. We've been hiding out here ever since.'

'Oh,' said Eric again. 'It wasn't made clear, but I suppose it's remotely possible.' He felt at his head. 'Half my brain is still missing, I regret.'

'Keep your pecker up, me old cocksparrow. If we are back in the plot there is sure to be a reason for it. Now do tuck your napkin in. You're getting giblets all down your front.'

> After this I looked and beheld a door
> was opened in Heaven and the first
> voice which I heard was as it were a
> trumpet talking with me.
>
> Revelation 4:1

'And cue the trumpet,' pronounced Mungo. Above the planet, hovering in the cone of light, a trapdoor creaked open and the bell of a battered bugle poked out. 'Taraa Taraa,' it went, somewhat discordantly. 'Now hear this, now hear this . . .'

Jason Morgawr chewed upon his knuckles. 'It comes across a lot better on the small screen,' he ventured.

'The balance of equipoise—' Dan was once more standing upon the floor, but he looked no less impressive for it '—fragile, precise. The perfect balance between love and hate, peace and war, sanity and insanity, life and death. And so forth. Tip the scales but a fraction to either end and the balance is lost. The harmony is gone, and then . . .' Dan searched for an example. Far off there was a sickening squelch as the lifeless body of L. Ron Hubbard the twenty-third hit the floor.

'Like that,' said Dan. 'Squelch.'

'Squelch?' queried Ms Vrillium, still cowering.

'Squelch. Crash bang wallop, whatever you please. Chaos, disorder. But harmony and peace has existed between the Big Three for fifty years and why? Because I wanted it so, that's why. Those ants in their bunkers, propped up before their terminals, we need them as much as they need us. Singularly they are just rubbish, expendable. But en masse they represent a nation, an empire. But we could never have hoped to feed them all. You've seen that for yourself. The balance between the Three had to be maintained. Until I chose it otherwise. I could have destroyed Hubbard and that papal harpy when ever I wanted. MOTHER hacked into their networks years ago. She could have closed them down whenever I ordered it. I'm in control here. Do you understand that? I run this planet.'

'I would like to bear your children,' said Gloria, which was unexpected, if nothing else.

The lift doors opened to announce the arrival of Rex and his fellow revolutionaries.

'Wotcher Gloria,' said Rex Mundi. 'How's your luck?'

Dan closed his eyes to them. 'What is done cannot be undone. You die now.'

'Rex,' said Gloria, 'oh, Rex, I'm so sorry.'

Mungo, totally disenchanted with the naff trumpet, keyed in the next bit.

> And I saw the horses in the vision
> and those that sat upon them.
> Revelation 9:17

The four housemen sprang out upon the clouds of Earth. Mungo's face fell. 'Those are pantomime horses!' he screamed. 'Morgawr, you idiot!'

'They'll be all right. Patch this through to the Earth networks, the folk in the bunkers should watch all this.'

'Yes,' Mungo actually agreed. 'They should.' He punched out sequences amongst the bulging bits and bobs. Vision blurred upon Earth terminal screens. The interior of the Dalai's apartments suddenly appeared.

'And what's all this then?' asked the bunker-bound, popping cans of Buddhabeer and leaning forward in their seats.

'Ant-eye-Christ!' cried Elvis, levelling his gun at Dan and shooting off a charge. The gun spat a line of crimson energy. But inches from the Dalai's head it crumpled, dissolved and was gone.

Rex came up from the cover he had instantly taken as the gun went bang. 'He's not the Antichrist, I've told you.'

'Oh yes he is . . .'

'Oh no he's not . . .'

'Oh yes he is,' said Christeen.

'Oh yes I am,' Dan agreed. 'You never got it, either, did you Rex? No-one ever does. That's the way it goes.' The third eye opened in Dan's forehead. All three eyes glowed a bloody red. 'The end time approaches. But this time I prevail. All this is mine and I'm keeping it.'

'Cor, look at them.' Ms Vrillium was pointing furiously. 'Dirty big . . . what are those things called?'

'Horses,' Gloria told her. 'They are horses.'

'Horses, what?' Dan turned to view the unlikely spectacle. 'No, not yet.'

The cameras panned over and those in the bunkers were offered a good look too. 'Crikey,' they said and things similar.

'Your time is up.' Christeen advanced upon the Dalai Lama. 'The reckoning is at hand.'

'You.' Dan's red eyes widened. All three. It wasn't a pretty sight. His tall spare frame trembled and shook. Veins stood out upon his naked shaven head. They formed the triple tadpole station logo. Six Six Six. The number of the Beast. His long fingers were cruel inhuman claws. Dan turned slowly away and vanished.

'Where'd he go?' Elvis plunged forward, to stand a brave heroic figure, two guns raised like the Duke of old.

'Fergus, close the lift.' Rex ordered. 'It's the only way out.' Fergus did so and stood with his back to the doors, brandishing his gun with forced conviction. That Gloria looks even better in the flesh, he thought.

'Come out, come out, wherever you are,' called Rex. 'Come and get your medici . . . urgh.' He doubled up, holding his groin. Elvis fired, blindly destroying priceless artefacts.

'Hold on.' Rex climbed unsteadily to his feet. He took a deep breath and gazed about the room. As with Gloria he had seen it all before. But never really seen it. Each and every item seemed threatening. Cloaked by a sinister gloom. The word 'eldritch' sprang into his mind. The four central columns with their frantically erotic frescoes appeared top heavy, ready to fall. The carved furniture was too large, oppressive. The great desk was now the tomb slab of some titanic sarcophagus. The woven faces upon the carpets yawned, open mouthed, waiting to swallow him up.

And then Rex knew. He had come here to die. The thought was strong in his head. Stronger than anything else. He had been shoved about, tricked, lied to and manipulated for long enough. It had all led him to this. And now there was nowhere left to run to. Nowhere left to hide. Here he must die. To fight further was out of the question. He must give the whole thing up. Submit to the Dalai and his fate. To power far greater than his own. Tell Elvis to lay down his weapon . . .

'Tell him yourself!' Rex struck out with his fist. It pounded something in the empty air before him.

Dan materialized upon the floor clutching his face. 'My nose again,' he wailed. 'But how?'

'If you are going to do my thoughts for me,' replied Rex, examining his skinned knuckle. 'Then you might at least have the courtesy to do them in my own voice. And your breath smells.'

'It doesn't.' Dan blew into his palms and sniffed through his unbloodied nostril. 'A mite sulphurous perhaps.'

'Bravo Rex.' Christeen was once more at his side. 'I had to let you do it for yourself.'

Dan raised himself upon an elbow. 'Who are you? You murder my sleep. Who are you? I've got to know.'

Christeen rose above him. Clothed as with the sun. Upon her head was a crown of twelve stars. Beneath her feet, a crescent moon. Rex stepped back, taking in the wonder.

'I am Christeen,' said Christeen. 'Twin sister of Jesus Christ.'

'You are what?' the Dalai's question was heartily enjoined by Elvis, Fergus, Rex, Gloria and the fat woman who had quite lost all interest in horses, flying or otherwise.

This was one major revelation by any account.

'I am as I say, and this is my time.'

Dan curled his lip and glared her a prial of daggers. 'You wish,' said he.

Elvis stepped forward. 'Let me blow this sucker away.'

'No,' Christeen raised her hand. 'He must hear this. Everyone must hear this. The truth must now be told.'

The bunker-bound popped further ringpulls. 'It's good this,' they agreed.

Mungo shifted uneasily at the controls. 'It's not good this,' he said.

'In the beginning God created the Heaven and the Earth . . .' Dan groaned. Stooping, Christeen clouted him one in the ear. Dan kept further groans to himself.

'Pardon that,' Christeen dusted her hands together. 'A touch of PMT.'

'PMT?' Rex asked.

'Pre monotheistic tension. Now where was I?'

'Your daddy created the Heaven and the Earth.' Elvis tried to make his tone convincing.

'Thank you. And it's all here.' A large black Bible had appeared miraculously (well, how else?) in her hands. 'Nearly all. There is an essential point about this book which mankind has never come to realize. This isn't a record of events which occurred. This is a record of events which were scheduled to occur. In short this a script. The Big Script. Isn't it, Fergus?'

Fergus Shaman hung his head. 'Some say. The backers . . .'

'Backer. There is only one. On Earth here, Dad sold the thing originally to the Jews, through Moses. One of your first "script advisers", Fergus. The Jews were well chuffed. They were to be the Chosen People, blessed of God. Nice work if you can get it. And so they went along whole-heartedly. But of course what they didn't know at the time was that it was a two-book deal. And that the sequel had already been written. Bible Two. The New Testament. Dead peeved were the Jews when they discovered the consequences of killing my brother. They've been getting it in the neck ever since. Simply victims of circumstance. Just like me.'

'Just like you?' Dan flinched in advance. 'You're not in the New Testament. Never were.'

'Oh, yes I was. When mother Mary gave birth it was to twins. But the small print in my brother's contract gave him overall artistic control. He only got his part through nepotism. The New Testament was nothing more than a vehicle for his stardom.'

'Scandalous,' said Rex.

'So I got written out,' Christeen continued. 'A victim of male chauvinistic editing.'

Dan was climbing warily to his feet, the muzzles of deadly weapons upon him. 'So then,' said he. 'If any of this is true, how come you are here now? You're not in *Revelation*.'

'Am too. Chapter twelve, verse one.'

'Bah humbug. You can read anything you want into *Revelation*. John was stoned out of his mind when he wrote it.'

'Well, you would say that, wouldn't you.'

Dan made a grumpy face. 'And so where does he—' the gesture was aimed at Fergus '—and his backer come into all this?'

'Father's little helpers,' said Christeen scornfully. 'Dad, as my brother might tell you, has a very large ego and an extremely perverse sense of humour. He thrives on flattery, worship and applause. He created man in his own image. So he's only human after all. Dad created another planet called Phnaargos and a race, the Phnaargs, whose job it was to stage-manage the whole show. They were to see that the controlling idea of the plot remained intact. And so they did, for a while, until it was time to

315

close the show down. Armageddon was scheduled to take place in the year 1000 AD. You see it is Dad's policy never to get personally involved in anything. He just starts the ball rolling, sits back and watches. But back in 999 someone tipped the Phnaargs off that this was the case. Didn't they, Dan?'

Dan made a ferocious face. 'And what if they did? You admit that you've got nothing out of it, and you are his only daughter. I have a major role, and I don't intend to be written out.'

'Hubba hubba,' said Elvis, 'he's going to spill the beans.'

'Oh yes?' said Rex.

'Yeah,' snarled Dan. He was standing and he was mean. 'Major role. I was there back in the Garden of Eden tempting that silly woman without the navel. I had all the best parts back then, Tower of Babel, Sodom and Gomorrah. I was really rolling. Then along comes her brother with volume two and it's get thee behind me Satan and sorry Mr Beelzebub, you get the chop in the last chapter. Do I shit, says I. Because there ain't going to be no final chapter. This series is going to run and run, because your dad ain't going to step in and stop it.'

'Does this mean the wedding's off?' Gloria asked.

'Sure I tipped off the Phnaargs,' Dan went on, ignoring his opportunity of the honeymoon of a lifetime. 'Slipped them a few home truths. They weren't too keen to kill off their golden goose. Especially when they'd seen my new script. Give 'em what they want, I said, plenty of sex and violence. And for the last thousand years this world had been running on my script. Anyone with any intelligence at all could see that. And I got all the best parts, Attila the Hun, this king, that emperor, the other dictator, wherever the power was, I was it. Century after century and nobody knew. Why, only fifty years ago I was . . .'

'President Wormwood,' said Christeen.

Dan stroked his chin. 'Yeah,' said he. 'The Nuclear Holocaust Event seemed like a good idea at the time.'

Rex was speechless. There are disclosures and there are disclosures, but this . . .

Elvis wasn't speechless. 'Let me put a bullet through this motherfu . . .'

'Don't even think about it.' Dan was once more behind his desk.

'How does he do that?' Fergus asked.

'Don't anybody move,' crowed Dan. 'Or I press this button.'

'Oh dear,' sighed Christeen. 'Or I press this button. What a cliché.'

'Be that as it may, once pressed not even you can halt the consequence.'

'I'm trying to guess this one,' said Rex. 'But I can't.'

'It controls the artificial cloud-cover. I need but to press the button to increase the density and bring the whole lot down. It will suffocate everyone on Earth. No-one will survive.'

'No shit?' Elvis was impressed.

'You fiend,' cried Ms Vrillium. And quite rightly so.

'And then what?' Christeen stepped before him. 'Lord of a barren planet? No-one to rule? No-one to worship you?'

'It's a demonic stratagem,' Dan argued. 'I never said it was perfect.'

'Holy cow,' whistled Elvis. 'Look at these dudes.'

Fergus Shaman had been nothing if not correct regarding Mungo's incompetence. For Mungo, who had been

317

fuming away that between them Dan and Christeen had now given the whole game away, had quite forgotten that whatever he was watching the entire viewing populations of two worlds were also watching. So when the terrible realization finally dawned, minutes before, he had given the all-systems-go to the final Armageddon wipe-out.

Down from the skies of Earth came Michael and all the saints. Flaming swords, wild-eyed war-horses, thunder and lightning and the whole damn shooting gallery.

'Boo boo,' went the bunker-bound, kicking their terminals. Their one-time messiah was up in the Nemesis building planning to snuff them all out. They didn't want to see all this rubbish. 'Boo boo,' they went. 'Bring back Christeen.'

Jam, jam, jam, went the newly-staffed switchboard at Earthers Inc.

'The show must go on.' Mungo rammed buttons willy nilly. Stock footage jumped through the system. Michael and all the saints were met head on by the Charge of the Light Brigade (the 1930s black and white version). General Custer aimed his six-shooter at the wildly circling indians. Zulus bore down upon Rorke's Drift and chariots raced about the Circus Maximus.

'Morgawr!' screamed the apoplectic Mungo. 'Stop him someone. Don't let him jump.'

Down through the chaos of holographic projection, through the Zulus and the seventh cavalry and the Great White shark, which was circling a sinking lilo, shone a beam of golden light. The Heavens opened, and upon high angelic hosts made with the harp strumming and the songs of praise.

And I heard the voice of harpers harping
with their harps.

Revelation 14:2

(look it up if you don't believe me)

Upon a throne of beryl surrounded by beasts of mythical origin, but undoubted authenticity, a shining figure descended. Mungo smiled approvingly. 'There,' said he. 'That is a lot better. That really looks the business, Morgawr.'

Jason Morgawr, now under heavy restraint, gazed into the hologram. A foolish titter of laughter escaped through his lips. 'That's not me,' he whimpered. 'Not me.'

'Enough of this nonsense,' cried Dan. 'Everybody gets theirs. Everybody.' He thrust his fist down upon the blood-red button. Amidst the swirling confusion there was a terrible hush. Pope Joan and the minions of the late L. Ron looked on. They had long ago run out of weaponry and had given it all up, anyway, to watch the show. In the Dalai's apartment the players became a frozen tableau: Dan, grinning like the very Devil he was; Christeen, her hands locked in prayer; Fergus comforting Gloria somewhat more than was necessary; Ms Vrillium cowering once more; Elvis standing noble and defiant; Rex doing likewise, perhaps a little more so.

Suddenly a telephone rang. Dan snatched it up. A recorded voice said, 'We regret that the Doomsday button has been disconnected due to a maintenance dispute. It's hoped that meaningful negotiations between management and shop floor will shortly return it to full operational capability. We hope that this temporary suspension of service has not inconvenienced you too much. Have another day.'

'What?' Dan began to foam at the mouth. 'What???'

Rex looked toward Christeen. She shrugged. 'Not me, I didn't . . . oh no . . .'

The room was suddenly swallowed up by a blinding golden light which poured through the windows from all sides. Rex screwed up his eyes and squinted into the glare. A dazzling throne hovered beyond the west-facing window and even now a shining figure was stepping down from it. The light dulled slightly in intensity as Christeen knotted her fists and kicked furniture. 'Him. I should have known. It had to be him.'

'Him who?' Dan turned to view the radiant figure who was now waving away the throne as one might a taxi.

The figure smoothed out the creases in his immaculate white suit and waved gaily toward the gaping group within. 'Hi, sis',' he called.

'Oh bugger,' said Dan.

Christeen buried her face in her hands. 'Not fair,' she protested, stamping her feet. 'Not fair.' The windows parted of their own accord and the shining figure entered the room.

'God save all here,' said Jesus Christ, for it was none other. He beamed around the room. All, with the exception of Dan and Christeen, were now kneeling. 'Oh let's not be formal.' Such perfect diction. 'We're all friends here. Well, nearly all.'

'My button,' said the disgruntled Dan. 'You broke my button.'

'Yes, sorry about that. But we couldn't really have you killing everyone off just out of bad grace, could we?'

Dan sniffed. 'You can't pull a stroke like that. No-one

is going to swallow a *Deus ex machina* ending in this day and age.'

'A *Deus* what?' Elvis asked. Such shoulder pads, he thought, who is this man's tailor?

'*Deus ex machina,*' Jesus said. 'I think, all things considered, that it's truly justified. And if I think so, I can't see who's going to argue. So you'll just have to lump it, won't you?'

'Well, really.' Dan folded his arms and got a huff on.

'He's such a tiresome little tick, isn't he?' As the question appeared to have been directed toward Rex, he nodded in ready response.

'Yes sir,' he said, as the warmth of Jesus's smile dried out his acne.

'Enough of that "sir" stuff, Rex. You're almost one of the family.'

'I am?' Rex gazed up at the fantastic figure. Even with the close-clipped beard and the designer sunglasses his resemblance to Christeen was undeniable. God, what a handsome bloke, thought Gloria, I wonder if he's married yet.

'Christeen,' said Jesus kindly. 'Aren't you going to say hello to your brother?'

Christeen shook her beautiful head. 'It's not fair,' said she. Jesus gazed about him, taking it all in. Ms Vrillium watched him at it. What a lovely mover, she thought.

'Why, thank you.' Jesus flashed her a smile which took twelve inches off her waistline. 'Now I see that the gang is almost all here.'

'Almost all?' gasped Mungo Madoc. 'There's more?'

'Almost all, Mungo.' Jesus replied. 'Does anybody know who's missing?' Faces were universally vacant. 'Oh come on,' Jesus urged. 'Surely you've been following the

321

sub-plot? No?' He looked imploringly out from the book. 'Shall we tell them, readers?'

PLEASE ENTER YOUR REPLY HERE. YES . . . NO . . . SEARCH ME . . .

'Well, I'm going to tell them anyway.' Jesus took out a remote control from the waistcoat pocket of his Heavenly three-piece, aimed it at the ceiling, mid point of the erotic columns (which had now, unaccountably, toned down their dirty doings and were all hearts and flowers), pressed a button and stood back.

'And tonight's star guest. Mr Mystery himself. Come on down.'

An ethereal Hammond organ, of a generation now mercifully gone to dust, made with the showtime fanfares. Lights flashed. The special star buzzer buzzed and a section of ceiling drifted down. Bearing upon it the famous Mastermind chair. Perched upon this and making with the Royal hand waves sat . . .

'Jspht,' said Fergus Shaman. 'Jovil Jspht.'

'Fergus,' said Jovil. 'This is a surprise.'

'Mr Shaman to you. But how? What? You can't be here. You're back in 1958. How can you? Oh dear, oh dear, oh dear . . .'

Jovil held up his waving hand. 'All in good time,' he checked his watch. 'Now I think I'm right in supposing that . . .'

A station menial of deathly aspect burst into the boardroom of Earthers Inc. 'Mr Madoc,' he wailed. 'Mr Madoc, the virus, the virus. It has caught us up . . .' He might have had more to say, but he didn't get the chance. He was trampled to oblivion beneath the mad lemming dash for the window.

'And so it's good night to all our viewers on Phnaargos,' said Jovil. 'You won't forget to turn off your sets now, will you?'

'You haven't,' gasped Fergus.

'Have too. *The Earthers* just went off the air.'

'God's nose.' Fergus slumped into the nearest seat.

'Get off,' Gloria protested.

'I'm sorry to show my ignorance,' said Rex. 'But should I know this person?'

'That's the alien who jumped me back in fifty-eight.' Elvis gestured with his weapons. 'I nearly cashed in my chips at the Bates Motel because of him. Luckily Barry threw in his lot with me and hauled me out in the nick of time.'

'Then how can he?'

'Honestly, Rex.' Jesus smiled again. Rex felt new hair sprouting on his head. 'You really should have reasoned it out by now.'

'I should?'

'It's all right there in your pocket.'

'It is?' Rex patted at his multiple pocketry. One bulged. He unzipped it. 'The *Book*,' he said, recalling, as will the reader, that he had left it behind, hidden in his apartment. '*The Suburban Book of the Dead*.'

'I've been here all along in the sub-plot, just like the Good Lord told you,' Jovil said. 'I got marooned back in fifty-eight. But I could hardly die there, could I? I hadn't even been born yet, back then.' Heads nodded thoughtfully. Thoughts nodded doubtfully. 'So with my advanced knowledge I built an empire. And with more than a little Divine guidance pieced a certain thing together. And I was in on the genesis of this place. My money built it. I designed the MOTHER computer, the lot. I went completely underground when the big bang came in 1999. The Phnaargs never knew it but I was the virus in their system. By sending me back in time they had poisoned their own storage beds. I never killed that operative, the system did it. As I moved forward in time, changing the past, the cells mutated. Now I am here, and so their whole system has collapsed, bio-feedback.'

'So where have you been for the last fifty years?' Rex asked.

'Up there, sitting in cryogenic suspension. We Phnaargs are of vegetable origin, you know. I've been in cold storage. Just waiting for the big day to thaw out.'

'Big day?' Rex gazed down at his battered book.

'Sure, when the big secret would be disclosed. You've read the book, what do you think it is?'

'I've tried to read it. But from what I can gather it all seems to be some kind of quest. A search for something which was never found.'

'He found it.' Jovil pointed towards Dan, who was seeking invisibility with no apparent success.

'Oh, I'm in this again, am I?' croaked the stinker. 'And what did I find, pray tell me, do?'

'It's all in Rex's book. The book you killed his uncle to get your hands on. The location of the K^2 carbon containing the Ultimate Secret of the Universe.' (What else? Rex thought.) 'It was the last item checked in by the Department Of Antiquities. After you had it you closed down the commission. So why didn't you use it?'

'Sorry to disappoint you, but I closed the commission down because they were all on the fiddle. Of Universal Secrets my cupboard is bare.'

All faces now turned back to Jovil Jspht.

'I think not.' Jovil sprang from his chair like the legendary sleuth of old, plunged across the room and drew the SUN recording from the holophon.

'Hey, shit,' said Elvis, as the thing passed him by at close quarters, 'that looks like one of mine.'

'And a load of old brain damage it is too. Remember my eyeballs, Gloria?'

'I'm not speaking to you,' that lady replied. 'You're not nice.'

'Well, whacky stuff it may be. But Secret of the Universe it ain't.'

'Oh no? Well that's where you're wrong, schmucko.' Jovil turned the plasticized disc betwen his fingers. 'Because you have been playing the wrong side.' Great roars of applause from the bunker-bound.

'Foiled again.' Dan struck his fist into his palm and made with the melodrama. 'Do leave me out. Secret of the Universe, if you please.' The only person looking in his direction was Ms Vrillium. 'I ask you,' said Dan.

'Shitbag,' the woman with the perfect waistline replied.

Jovil held the record's flip-side towards Rex. 'You know old English, Rex, what does it say?'

Rex perused it. Faintly etched upon the ancient vinyl was a pentacle enclosed within two circles and between these a single word: TETRAGRAMMATON.

Rex spelt it out. Those who were in the know went Blimey, Cor, and things of that nature. Those who weren't, and this included Rex, asked, 'What's a Tetragrammaton, when he she or it is at home?'

'Tetragrammaton,' sighed Christeen, who could feel another 2000 years of obscurity coming on. 'The four syllables which compose the unknowable name of God. A name so sacred that none may know it. To speak the name is to unlock the ultimate power in the universe.'

'Some big number,' said Elvis.

'Got the edge on killer maggots, eh Fergus?' Fergus nodded. It was all well beyond him.

'But you couldn't know this,' Christeen stared at Jovil Jspht, who wilted visibly beneath her gaze. 'No-one can know this. That is the point.'

Dan was searching for an exit. None was readily at hand.

'Ask your brother,' said Jovil. 'He put me up to it. He was the brains behind the whole operation.'

Jesus shrugged modestly, he knew no other way. 'What did I preach?' he asked. 'Love and peace. And I tried really hard in the 1960s to get it across. It was all there in the music, Jovil and I saw to that. You only had to listen. And perhaps turn on a little, but that is neither here nor there. Some did, of course, but not enough. So I had Jovil programme a tiny piece of the jigsaw into all of it. Into the music. And it got pieced back together by a chosen few. It's all in there. All you have to do is play it.'

'The name of God,' said Rex. Impressed was hardly the word.

'The Name. The Sound. The Universal Note. It was always there in all the world's music. You only had to listen. All the universe is composed of a single note. All atoms and all molecules are but vibrations of a single note. The big note. The Buddha sussed it out. Which makes the present incarnation of this blighter' – Dan flinched – 'all the more perverse.'

'And where, exactly, does this leave me?' asked Christeen sulkily. 'Out of the picture again I suppose.'

Jesus shook his head. You should have seen it, a picture, I kid you not. 'It's here.' A small black book appeared in his hand. He offered it to Christeen. 'Even now a baby moves within you. Rex's child. You are to be the mother of Mankind.'

'Another TV series?' Christeen took the book. It was

entitled *The Third Testament*. She opened it. The pages were blank.

'No more series,' said Jesus. 'Dad may have a sense of humour but he also has a sense of justice. You can write it yourself. Put the record on, Rex. Play us a tune.'

Rex's fingers trembled. He was going to become the father to a child whose grandfather was . . . 'Yes,' said Rex Mundi, who still hadn't figured out what his name really meant. 'Put the record on, indeed.' He placed it reverently upon the turntable. 'What are the settings?' he asked.

'Play Loud,' Jesus replied. 'That's the way we did it back in the sixties.' Nice fellow, the future brother-in-law, thought Rex.

> And I saw a new Heaven and a new Earth;
>   for the old
> Heaven and the old Earth were passed away.
> Revelation 21:1

And the word of the Tetragrammaton played upon the turntable. And God said, Let there be light and there was light. And was it a sound? Was it a note? Was it a something? It was Hendrix at Woodstock as the sun was rising. The Stones in Hyde Park. Pink Floyd at The Roundhouse. The Grateful Dead at Winterland, San Francisco. It was Beefheart at his best. And it was all those marvellous moments you ever had all rolled into a great big one.

It was hard to describe really. You know that amazing bit at the end of 'Day in the Life'? It was a bit like that, only much more so.

The Universal Note. I mean, like, Wow man.

*

At Earthers Inc. the cone of light faded and died. The circuits fused and the network closed down. The great spiral tower sagged and fell.

'And that's all the thanks I get,' mumbled Mungo, as he of the Nose Divine, a not inconsiderable deity in his own right but hardly on a par with the Big Figure, squeezed his pimple and saturated the Phnaargian universe with you know what.

On Earth a great wind tore across the sky. The clouds flew before it. They rolled back, drew themselves into a swirling vortex and spun into the heavens. The sun shown down upon the tortured landscape. And a cry went up. Bunker doors opened upon the new day. Pale faces gazed toward the sky. Blinking and wondering, the denizens of the sub-world crept forth to view the new world. For already the world was turning. The irradiated wastes were vanishing. Lush fields spread to every side, rivers flowed, trees rose and blossomed. That which had been done was undone. The gates of the city were open to the fingers of the sun.

It was now or never for the ex-High Lama. Dan made a break for it. He grabbed Gloria about the throat and dragged her towards the lift door. Elvis spun around and let fly. Beams of fire ripped across the room, wreaking havoc. Dan thrust Gloria into Elvis. 'You haven't heard the last of me,' he cried in the traditional manner. Fergus Shaman shot him in the backside. The lift doors opened and Dan staggered through them into the waiting knives and forks of Rambo and Eric.

'The main course.' Rambo raised his filleting knife and did something quite unprintable. The lift doors closed mercifully upon it.

'That isn't exactly in the script,' said Jesus. 'But it does have a certain charm. I think we'll leave it in.'

'Shall I be mother?' came the muffled voice of Death-blade Eric.

Jesus turned to Christeen. 'It's all up to you now. You and Rex. Make it right this time.' And without even waiting for a thank you, he vanished. Which was just like him, wouldn't you say?

'Well,' said Rex, the way that formerly only the great Jack Benny had been able to say it, 'what a day this has been.'

'Started poorly but finished well,' Fergus added. 'Although I'm not exactly sure where it leaves me.'

'Redundant,' said Jovil Jspht. 'I think you will find that we are no longer required.'

'I haven't a spaceship any more,' Fergus complained. 'And even if I had . . .'

'I have,' said Jovil. 'The top of this pyramid. Designed it myself. Works on a principle which even I conclude is scarcely credible. But who cares, eh? Shall we away, new worlds to conquer and that kind of thing?'

'Sounds good to me.' Fergus waved his farewells, but as everyone seemed to be gazing out of the windows, oohing and aahing, they were largely ignored. 'Do you think we will find a planet where all the ladies have big . . .' His words were lost as the Mastermind chair carried him and Jovil aloft.

Rex took Christeen in his arms. Violins welled in the background. No doubt a wedding present from the brother. Christeen smiled up at Rex and kissed him. An old couple in a bunker who had only just switched on said, 'Ah, bless 'em.'

Christeen turned her face toward Elvis who was

scuffing his advanced footware upon the carpet. 'What of you?' she asked. The King shrugged.

'Back to 1958, I guess.' His voice lacked any enthusiasm.

'You going to take the draft, then?' Rex posed the question.

'Can't see that I have a lot of choice. This was all preordained, wasn't it?' Christeen nodded.

"Fraid so chief,' the Time Sprout agreed.

'The thing that really peeves me,' said Elvis, 'is that I come across real two-dimensional in all this. No depth of character, d'you know what I mean?'

'But you never had any real depth of character, chief. You're one shallow son of a gun.'

'Guess so,' Elvis shrugged. 'Rich and pretty, though.'

'So it can't all be bad, can it, chief? And anyway, sprouts can't really travel through time. I'm just a figment of your imagination. All this is just an illusion for you. You won't remember any of it, once you're back in fifty-eight.'

'What a bummer. I gotta do all that bad stuff again and no-one ever gets to know what a hero I really was.'

'We know,' said Christeen.

'Yeah, I guess you do. Uh, and just a couple of things before I go.' The look of enlightenment was once more upon the King's face.

'Oh yes?' said Rex, who had seen it before.

'Right,' said Elvis. 'Now, if that cat Jovil has spent the last fifty years in cold storage, how could he also have been on Phnaargos when they sent him back in time to get me? And if the Dalai had been all those other people through history, how come he never knew who I was? All that SUN baloney. And I'll have you know that Heartbreak Hotel was recorded on RCA. So that SUN disc is a phoney, which probably means that all this is a . . .'

'Come on, chief,' chirruped the sprout. 'We really must be going . . .' And in a flash they were.

Rex and Christeen were left alone. Above them the pyramid's pinnacle broke away and roared off into the sky. 'Big boobies,' said Fergus. 'I'm sorry to keep on, but it's something of a fixation.'

'To boldly go,' Jovil told him, 'where no Phnaarg has ever gone before.'

'If the disc is a fake and Jovil couldn't be in two places at once,' said Rex. 'Doesn't this mean that all this . . .' Christeen smiled up at him. She was the most beautiful woman who had ever lived. 'Oh, nothing,' said Rex.

'Kiss me, you fool,' said God's only daughter.

Planet Earth rolled on in ever decreasing circles about the sun. But everything was really going to be all right this time, wasn't it?

'I can't eat this,' came the voice of Deathblade Eric. 'This fellow's got green blood and he smells like stale cabbage.'

'So he does,' Rambo agreed. 'Now there's a thing.'

'And what about me?' Gloria asked.

'Buggered if I know dear.' Ms Vrillium admired herself in the mirror. 'I expect we'll find out in the sequel. All this is really far too good to be true.'

And it was.

THE END

SPROUT⟨P⟩LŌRE

The Now Official
RŌBERT
RANKIN
Fan Club

Members Will Receive:

Four Fabulous Issues of the *Brentford Mercury*, featuring previously unpublished stories by Robert Rankin. Also containing News, Reviews, Fiction and Fun.

A coveted Sproutlore Badge.

Special rates on exclusive T-shirts and merchandise.

'Amazing Stuff!' – Robert Rankin.

Annual Membership Costs £5 (Ireland), £7 (UK) or £11 (Rest of the World). Send a Cheque/PO to: **Sproutlore, 211 Blackhorse Avenue, Dublin 7, Ireland.**

Email: sproutlore@lostcarpark.com WWW: http://www.lostcarpark.com/sproutlore

Sproutlore exists thanks to the permission of Robert Rankin and his publishers.

THEY CAME AND ATE US
ARMAGEDDON II: THE B-MOVIE
by Robert Rankin

'Mr Rankin levitates even more amazingly than in his first novel, and is a flotation not to be missed . . . *Hellzapoppin* with hallucinatory knobs on and a talent to bemuse which is hugely welcome in this grey-suited time'
The Times

QUIVER AT! horrible demonic stuff oozing out of computer screens!

SHOCK HORROR! Elvis Presley pulling his face off!

GASP AT! a talking brussels sprout!

SEE! Cannibal on the rampage!

HEAR! Fido the Dog do Frankie Howerd impressions!

SEE! Rex Mundi, Rambo Bloodaxe, Deathblade Eric, Hugo Rune and a cast of millions caught up in Events Beyond Their Control!

THRILL TO! all the loose ends from *Armageddon The Musical* magically tied up!

WATCH! A comic genius doing the business!

SEE?

0 552 13832 0

THE SUBURBAN BOOK OF THE DEAD
ARMAGEDDON III: THE REMAKE
by Robert Rankin

AT LAST!
The final and much-longed-for part of the stupendous ARMAGEDDON trilogy.

And so it came to pass that on 27 July 2061 in the land of Eden, the money-free Utopia, Rex Mundi did toil mightily in his back garden. And he did excavate a cesspit like unto the one which his wife Christeen – the daughter of God and twin sister of Christ – had been giving him GBH of the earholes regarding the need for therewith.

And verily in the midst of his labours did Rex's spade strike a buried object of not inconsiderable size.

And lo. It were a marble statue of Elvis Presley.

Oh yes siree!

For Elvis looms large here, much to Rex's discomfort, which is further increased when he discovers that the walls of Jericho fell to the strains of 'It's Now or Never' and that David slew the dwarf Goliath wearing blue suede shoes. When Rex is confronted with The Singular Case of the Purloined Presliana, and the Luminous Order of the Sacred Sprout, he realises things are getting out of control . . .

'Rankin is, without a doubt, one of the finest living comic writers . . . a sort of drinking man's H.G. Wells'
Midweek

0 552 13923 8

THE ANTIPOPE
by Robert Rankin

'Wonderful . . . A ready mix of Flann O'Brien, Douglas Adams, Tom Sharpe, and Ken Campbell, but with an inbuilt irreverence and indelicacy that is unique – and makes it the long awaited, heavy smoker's answer to *The Lord of the Rings*'
Time Out

'*Outside the sun shines. Buses rumble towards Ealing Broadway and I'm expected to do battle with the powers of darkness. It all seems a little unfair . . .*'

You could say it all started with the red-eyed tramp with the slimy fingers who put the wind up Neville the part-time barman something rotten. Or when Archroy's wife swapped his trusty Morris Minor for five magic beans while he was out at the rubber factory.

On the other hand, you could say it all started a lot earlier. Like 450 years ago, when Borgias walked the earth.

Pooley and Omally, stars of the Brentford Labour Exchange and the Flying Swan, want nothing to do with it, especially if there's a Yankee and a pint of lager in the offing. Pope Alexander VI, last of the Borgias, has other ideas . . .

'Wonderfully entertaining . . . reads like a Flann O'Brien rewrite of *Close Encounters*'
City Limits

The first book in the now legendary *Brentford Trilogy*

0 552 13841 X

A SELECTED LIST OF FANTASY TITLES
AVAILABLE FROM CORGI AND BLACK SWAN

THE PRICES SHOWN BELOW WERE CORRECT AT THE TIME OF GOING TO PRESS. HOWEVER TRANSWORLD PUBLISHERS RESERVE THE RIGHT TO SHOW NEW RETAIL PRICES ON COVERS WHICH MAY DIFFER FROM THOSE PREVIOUSLY ADVERTISED IN THE TEXT OR ELSEWHERE.

All Transworld titles are available by post from:

Bookpost, P.O. Box 29, Douglas, Isle of Man IM99 1BQ

Credit cards accepted. Please telephone 01624 836000, fax 01624 837033, Internet http://www.bookpost.co.uk or e-mail: bookshop@enterprise.net for details.

Free postage and packing in the UK. Overseas customers allow £1 per book (paperbacks) and £3 per book (hardbacks).